Other Selves

Chris Bridge

Other Selves is the sequel to *Girl Without a Voice* but was written to be read in its own right.

Praise for *Back Behind Enemy Lines* by Chris Bridge

'This contemporary story which pits generation against generation ... suspenseful, poignant and funny ... This was a world I didn't want to leave when I came to the end of the book.'

Helen Cadbury: Author of To Catch a Rabbit

'Back Behind Enemy Lines is beautifully written. This is an author who excels at hinting at the unsaid, allowing the reader to fill in the blanks, whose contained and precise prose marches across the pages ... at times bursting apart to reveal the oceans of unhealed pain that lie deep within Anna.'

Historical Novel Society Review

'I could not put this book down. The tension of the wartime love story behind enemy lines draws you into the novel and doesn't let you leave. It is beautifully and clearly written. The characterisation is skilfully done, there is a terrific sense of place throughout and it is clear that the author has researched the background carefully. The ending is satisfying and redemptive. I loved the book and recommend it wholeheartedly.'

Carole Bromley: Author of The Stonegate Devil and A Guided Tour of the Ice House

'Sometimes I come across a novel, that grabs hold of me and will not let go until I have completed the book and sometimes that book would do well set on the small screen as a TV drama. 'Back Behind Enemy Lines' by Chris Bridge has it on both accounts. This is an exceptional debut novel.'

John Fish: The Last Word review

'Compulsive and from my own knowledge a very accurate interpretation of "what it was really like" during the war for some of our unsung heroes and heroines. Excellent seems too short a word for this entrancing read.'

Mr C: Amazon

Dedication

This novel is dedicated to the two bored policemen who caught me speeding in the Highlands, then allowed me to pester them with all sorts of questions about those who disappear, including how easy it is to buy a new driving licence in Glasgow and the thousand unidentified bodies the police are dealing with at any one time. Every novelist feeds off other people's stories.

If you don't like who you are ...
... can you become someone else?

'Becoming someone else is the best hope I've got.'

Kurt Cobain

'A lie can travel half-way around the world while the truth is putting on its shoes.'

Attributed to Mark Twain

September 1986

It wasn't to be. He knew that now.

Sometimes he thought it had come within a whisker. There'd been that week in Crete, eating together in the harbour at Chania opposite the mosque, looking across the calm, warm sea whose tiny consistent waves reflected the lights from restaurants and patinated the image of the ancient lighthouse. She had responded to him, hadn't she? She had stretched out a hand and gently stroked the back of his. It had been that close.

The sea in front of him was very different: the North Sea, not the Mediterranean. Even in the darkness he could make out the white insistence of its breakers, their grasping nature. He could hear the way they tore at the beach, rasping the pebbles. He was cold and he was still dressed. When he stripped he would be colder still. He'd keep his pants on.

There was no one around so no one would know when he entered the water. It must look as if he went for a swim, as if, in this September heatwave, he'd simply wanted to cool off and had got into difficulties. He knew about guilt and he didn't want her feeling guilty. The point was to give her permission to be who she was, to free her from whatever pact she thought bound them together.

Was it always like this in a relationship? Is there always a more and a less loving one?

He slipped his trousers down his legs and kicked them off his feet. But he mustn't leave them there to be washed out to sea. For her sake he folded them, then placed them above the tideline on a wide rock. When he removed his socks he placed them neatly inside his shoes. Then he pulled off his shirt.

It wasn't much of a body, was it? He was so thin at school they had called him the Oxfam advert. Because his mother insisted on buying him shirts he could grow into, they used to ask him, 'Where's your other neck?' Even then he had liked to think there was a certain wiriness about his body, like a shepherd or a long-distance runner. She hadn't complained. She'd looked at him naked and smiled. Was it then she had decided against him?

In every relationship he'd ever had he was always the more loving one.

When he'd seen her that first time – such an open face, mousy blonde hair parted just off centre, and that way she had of holding her head on one side. No make-up, he'd noticed, an evenness of features. Brown eyes when he got closer, brown eyes and a smile that ...

When he first saw her that lovely head had tilted for someone else, someone he thought too old for her, someone who seemed grizzled against her loveliness.

Cold sea air bit into his flesh. He must act quickly. There could be no going back.

He'd won her over, and for a time her head tilted towards him. It was a period of ecstasy sharpened by several absences as work forced her to travel. Then, so imperceptibly at first that he wondered if she was merely tired or feeling unwell, everything changed. She began to hold her head upright, there was occasionally a compression about her lips, sometimes even a shake of the head. Those had been the dreadful days when every time they met felt like an act of kindness on her part.

And he had compensated, bought her gifts, tried by the power of his own love to rekindle hers. He loved her so much he couldn't bear it.

He added his glasses and his watch to the pile on the rock. In the darkness he noticed, as he folded his glasses and placed them pointing upwards on top of his shirt, that each lens reflected the same single star.

Now.

He ran towards the waves. He didn't want her constrained. He wanted her free. This was an unselfish act, an act of great love and he knew, to his detriment, that he had enough love inside him to light up even this dark and dangerous beach.

Stop thinking. That's what all this is about: to stop thinking, to stop the repetition of doubts, to act decisively.

I commit this body to the deep in the sure and certain hope of the resurrection ...

If you want it to be quick you have to open your mouth when you are deep underwater and deliberately breathe in the salt fluidity of the sea.

But first he must be far enough out, must reach the point where the rip tides meet.

1

It's April 1st, one of those rare days when it seems as if spring and summer have arrived together. Overnight the jet stream has shifted north, pulling hot air in from Africa. London, the forecast boasts, will have a mini heatwave. Glasgow is set to break records. Snow is melting high above the Corrie Cas in Aviemore, threatening to bring an abrupt end to the skiing season. In Yorkshire, daffodils lift their heads and tulips stiffen. In the kitchen of Leah's North Yorkshire home, sunlight is splitting the room in two. It illuminates the kitchen table and her family but intensifies the shadows where Leah is standing.

She's back in the shadows. Most of Leah's life has been lived there. When she was nine years old she was so badly traumatised that she stopped speaking. She was mute for more than twenty years. Only recently has she begun to talk again. Only recently has she left the margins and stepped into the limelight. To be the centre of events, even to be noticed, still takes an effort of will, so it is easier simply to stand in the darkest corner of the kitchen watching her family eat breakfast.

Leah is small, scarcely five feet tall. She has long, indifferently coloured hair. She's wearing jeans and a rather gaudy roll-neck pullover she bought from the local charity shop. She pulls at her clothes as she watches her family. The clothes may be second-hand, but they are still too new to her and she feels uncomfortable in them. When she got up this morning she reached for her baggy chinos and long cardigan with its sagging pockets, but to put them on would have been to slip backwards into her old self. She knows she mustn't do that, so she picked out this pullover with its floppy neck. She slipped it over her head even though she remembers precisely what happened the last time she wore it. There can be no going back, she reminds herself. She's thirty-four years old and she needs to start over: new haircut, new clothes.

Talking is as new to her as the pullover and still requires an effort. In those twenty-five silent years she developed special talents. From the margins of every social situation she developed a special sensitivity to moods and atmosphere. She can read people because she learnt to look at them, to focus completely on the person without part of her mind thinking about what she might say next. She can read buildings too. Her father, Gary Goulden, was rich, and Leah lives in a large house that dates from the Arts and Crafts Movement. There is an art nouveau copper jardinière in the hallway with a pattern of oak leaves. When she is alone in the house she likes to ping the jardinière and listen to the echoes. Sometimes they come back as clear as water and she knows everything is alright. Recently the house was troubled and all the echoes were shrill. When the rest of her family leave she will check the echoes again.

The Goulden family have been together for a week now and the strain is beginning to tell. Leah knows she needs to come out of the shadows and join the others.

She has a place at the table. Her coffee is waiting for her. She's had one piece of toast already but she's still hungry. Julia, her statuesque older sister, has put herself in charge of breakfast and is ensuring a constant supply of hot toast. Julia's even been to the cupboard and found a fresh jar of marmalade. Leah tells herself to sit down and eat some more but she doesn't. She stays where she is and watches the others.

Izzy, Leah's mother, isn't eating. Izzy is sixty-seven years old. It's four months since Gary, her husband, died. As soon as his company, Gouldens, can be sold she will be a very rich widow, still young enough to enjoy her new status. For the first time in her adult life she can be independent and move out from Gary's control. Leah studies her mother's face. It's becoming deeply lined, pulled in at the edge of the eyes, set in a frown. Izzy always had an inward look but that has worsened. Now she appears abandoned. Leah watches her mother pick up a piece of toast and attempt to eat it. But then she returns it, unbitten, to the plate. Izzy looks up and notices Leah watching. She attempts a smile, but it withers before it can be accomplished. Then she leans back in her chair, baffled. No wonder. Leah looks away. She can't bear her mother's misery, she who might have prevented it if only Izzy had let her.

As Leah turns away her eyes reach Martin. Martin is ... but that is the problem. She doesn't know exactly what he is to her. He was her silent lover. Recently he has been her friend and co-conspirator. Last night they slept in the same bed for the very first time. They met because Martin runs the local second-hand bookshop.

She saw him as another marginal, an unsuccessful man who was somehow like her. He isn't beautiful. He has a round, somewhat babyish face and his hair rises in tufts from a receding forehead. His body lacks definition, but he is also a surprising and very clever man when he needs to be. Suddenly he looks up at her and smiles.

She can't, she mustn't, stay where she is. It's time to re-join the others. She makes herself cross the room and sit down. As soon as she does, Martin reaches under the table and touches her knee. It's a light touch hidden from the others. She moves to cover his hand with her own but is too late. The touch was fleeting. His hand has moved away and Julia is offering her more toast. As she accepts it she turns to face Martin. He's sitting with his back to the sun and the tufts of hair are lit up, leaving his face in shadow.

They exchange smiles, but then Julia is ringing her empty coffee cup with her spoon, calling for silence quite unnecessarily because no one is talking, announcing herself as the head of the family.

'Before we go our separate ways,' she begins, 'we need to decide exactly what we are, and more importantly, what we are not going to say if we are asked about ...' she hesitates, glances at her mother, choosing her words carefully '... about what happened the other day, what we all witnessed.'

Julia is tall and accentuates her height. She stands incredibly straight, she wears heels and she has a quiff on the top of her forehead as if she means to be formidable.

'Unnecessary,' James says, 'quite unnecessary.'

James is stout with a head of hair that tells you everything you need to know about him. It is a look-at-me hairstyle. It hangs in ringlets down each side of his face. It can act like a curtain or be flung backwards as it is now while he takes his sister on. James is Izzy's second child. He combines cleverness with indolence but hates to be outranked by Julia. James is sitting next to his girlfriend, Roz. He gives her a knowing look and continues.

'There is no body. That is the important point. No body means there will be no questions, and if there are no questions then it stands to reason that we won't have to give any answers.' He doesn't add Q.E.D. but it is understood. He often speaks as if his audience is less intelligent than he is. When he has finished he looks round at his family as if there is nothing else to be said.

Julia decides there is. 'We witnessed a death,' she states, as if they need reminding. 'A man died. Nobody killed him but he died all the same.'

'A man who didn't exist,' James interrupts, 'a man who we know was on no formal data base, a man whose birth was probably never registered as a child and who certainly never went to a registered school. He both lived and he died under the official radar and there is no body.'

'He was known.' Leah finds herself speaking even though she didn't intend to. Her part in the recent events has been a strain and she'd hoped to step backwards. 'Within his circle some people admired and even loved him. These people know about his link with us. One of them may come searching.' Leah looks round the table. 'Julia is right. We need to know what we are going to say if that were to happen.'

'In that most unlikely scenario we refer them to Katherine, fiancée of the deceased.' James sees his role as providing answers to other people's problems. 'After all, she knew him better than anyone else. I thought we'd already agreed that we'd leave it to Katherine if anything had to be reported. Only she can tell the full story of what happened that day.'

'She won't.'

They turn and look at Martin. It's clear to Leah that, like her, he hadn't meant to say anything. In spite of recent events he isn't family.

Only Leah knows how hard Martin finds this being exposed to such an audience. But she also knows he won't flinch. She remembers how he killed the injured deer, the way he quietly stands up for what he knows to be true. Even before he speaks she's urging him on.

'I mean,' Martin explains, 'she's complicit. If she goes to the police and tells the full story she can be charged with kidnapping, assisting an offender, perhaps even with conspiracy to murder. Think what secrets might be hidden in that place. She'll do everything she can to keep the police away. My guess is that she'll report nothing.'

His voice is persistent rather than confident. He has none of Julia's brashness or James's arrogant certainty.

No one has challenged Martin so he continues. 'I know it's not my call to make, but we must go to the police ourselves. Do it today. It's already suspicious that we've let four days go by and said nothing.'

No one challenges this either. It's as if they know Martin's right. Then Izzy suddenly pushes her chair back and stands up. 'For God's sake, use his name. You all talk about him as if he was a stranger. He was Patrick. He was my son. Whatever he did he was my flesh and my blood. Yours too because he was your half-brother. Everything you say might be true but he wasn't a thing, he wasn't nameless.' She sways for a moment before stepping backwards. Her chair falls over as she swivels and walks away. They hear her feet climbing the stairs. A moment later her bedroom door slams shut.

* * *

An hour later Danny is the first to leave. From the moment Izzy left the room Leah's sixth sense has made her aware of the change in her younger brother. There's something about his shoulders. They are no longer ramrod straight. His handsome face is down. He's stopped eating but is sitting still. When did he ever do that?

Not you too, Leah thinks. I have enough on my hands with Izzy.

Danny is Leah's younger brother and her favourite, usually so wrapped up in himself that, even during her silent years, he occasionally treated her decently. He's thirty, clean shaven and smartly dressed. He was alright last night sitting close to his mother, drinking whisky, talking to James. He has always been the best looking and most athletic member of the family. He rarely takes part in family discussions so his silence at the breakfast table hadn't been a surprise.

Since Patrick died Danny's role has been to look

after his mother, but when she went up to sleep yesterday afternoon Danny chose to go running. Leah watched him set off, head upright facing into the wind. There was something machine-like about the way he ran. He didn't slow down for the hill that rises from the back of the house, nor did he increase his speed when, two hours later, he came back down, scarcely out of breath. Yesterday he was alright. Yesterday he was Danny.

Now he has a lost look about the eyes. It's a look Leah recognises because she has seen it in her own mirror.

As she watches him he pushes his chair back. He stands up swiftly and moves with deliberation. But at the same time he appears crestfallen so that his natural good looks and the strut that goes with them are absent.

Leah hears him go up the stairs two at a time. Clearly he's packed his bag already because he is soon down again.

He goes through the handshake or peck on the cheek ritual with everyone else but ignores Martin who follows him outside.

When Leah reaches the door she sees that Danny is talking earnestly, has hold of Martin's hand and isn't letting it go.

'I owe you a lot,' she hears Danny say. 'I was so angry about Mum.'

Martin looks uncomfortable. He isn't used to his hand being gripped. 'I don't know what came over me,' he says. 'I'm not brave. Normally I run a mile from trouble.'

'You saved me from myself.' Danny fiercely shakes the hand he holds, then lets it go.

'But surely the knife was only a threat?' Martin insists. 'You'd never have used it?' Martin's brows are pulled tightly together as he seeks reassurance. Leah knows that look.

Danny picks up his holdall and hoists it onto his right shoulder. 'I don't know. I don't know very much at all.' And he's gone.

'Do you want a lift to the station?' Martin calls after him.

Danny doesn't answer, simply strides away.

Martin stares after him, then turns and sees Leah in the doorway. He smiles and spreads his arms in a what-was-all-that-about gesture.

She walks up to him. They kiss passionately to the surprise of both.

'I've a house clearance to do today,' he says when the clinch breaks up. 'Do you want me to cancel it?'

She does, but she shakes her head. This is her new life and she'd better get used to it.

* * *

As Leah and Martin turn and go into the house Danny strides away, back to his old life. He knows if he catches the 1.35pm train from York he can be in his London gym by 5pm. A thorough work-out should fix his mood. He walks quickly. The important thing is to get away. His weight will be up after last night. He can solve that by having nothing to eat on the train and a punishing two hours of exercise. Then ...

By concentrating on his feet, on the rhythm of walking, he drives away this small stumble in his thinking. The path takes him downhill. It's dry. There's a blue sky above his head. He's a fit, handsome young man, striding along with a holdall on his shoulder. That's what people will think when they see him. Tonight in the gym, among his own, there will be envious looks at how he trains. Nothing will be said but he will know, and then ...

He reaches the old railway line. Now he can really stride out. The trees on either side give him a satisfying sense of speed. He loves the way his limbs flow. He loves it in the same way that people love the effortless acceleration of a fast car or the way their voice can launch a pure note, absolutely on pitch. This is him.

But four days ago he saw Patrick square up to James and knock him flying with a single punch. It had been laughable, almost brilliant, to see the clever James stumbling backwards, his ringlets flying, arms windmilling. James who always despised him, James who said that Danny was only in love with himself. If it hadn't been for what Patrick had done to his mother, Danny might have shaken his hand.

But Danny had just met Mum as she stumbled along the path towards them. He'd seen her hands were cruelly tied and freed her using the knife he always carried. He was angry. When Leah came to look after Mum he was still holding the knife as he walked straight at Patrick.

It had been a funny moment, an odd feeling. His family standing round, defeated. He, Danny, totally

2

As Danny reaches the main road Wendy Welbeck walks towards her office. She walks with determination but not with pleasure. She's in her forties, and the one important thing she has learnt about life in those forty years is you have to brace yourself and just get on with it. As she approaches the building she is alert for damage. People scrawl things on constituency office doors. They throw bricks at the windows. A quick glance tells her nothing has changed. There'll be no clearing up necessary. In the window a full-size portrait of their constituency MP smiles across the road. She peers at the bottom of the picture. His strap line is intact: **Jud Mindsett works for you**. Just occasionally someone thinks it funny to cover over the word **you** and replace it with **himself**, or to cover over both the **for** and the **you** and substitute a large question mark. Once someone changed the **or** of **works** to **an**. They'd used a permanent marker, and even today a faint shadow remains on the glass after almost five months of rubbing. Now that Wendy allows herself to despise her employer it makes her smile.

She opens the door and her heart sinks as it does every morning. A constituency office is not a happy place. Once every four or five years, at election time, it becomes a hive of activity. Then it's too small. Usually it's too large, badly heated in winter, and has an echo. As she sits down Wendy switches on the fan heater and makes sure it's aimed at her.

When he was a candidate Jud Mindsett had haunted the office. There was a sense of urgency and passion about the place. Her desk was a rash of post-its covered with names, phone numbers and brief messages. Then her job had seemed important.

And when they won the seat together Jud publicly thanked her, acclaimed her organisational brilliance. Her parents heard her name on television (it was an early result and his acceptance speech was shown live). You could just make her out in the corner of the shot. It was the night of her life. When she saw the numbers she thrilled that, working together, they had turned a marginal into a safe seat.

She remembers with shame her presumption that he'd take her to London with him, that she'd be his parliamentary secretary. But he didn't take her and he appointed someone else.

Newly elected Jud still had time for her. He'd held surgeries every Friday when Parliament was sitting and twice a week when it wasn't. In those days he never cancelled. Surgeries, he used to preach at her, were vital occasions. The great thing about the British system is that every individual knows who their Member of Parliament is and everyone should have access to their MP. In those early days he'd met constituents and listened to their concerns. He'd written letters on their behalf. He even made proper notes of meetings and asked her to file them.

In no time at all her amazement had turned into something else. Invitations to preside over constituency affairs which had once been fished for were now declined, even at weekends. The man who'd once haunted this office rarely came near it. Promotion made matters worse. After he became Junior Minister in the Transport Department she was lucky if he turned up once a month. At least he used to be apologetic. Now he just tells her he won't be there. He's even given up making excuses.

She puts the kettle on. These days she doesn't have to label her coffee and milk or lock the six teaspoons in her drawer. She spends her days alone and misses the squabbling.

Junior Minister for Transport. She still can't believe it. He must have smooched them as much as he'd once smooched her. His respect for her, she realises with some bitterness, had only ever been majority deep. She should never have worked for him. She now thinks she always guessed that his feelings for his constituents and for her were minor flirtations; that his abiding, passionate, eternal love was reserved for himself.

Nevertheless he should have taken her with him. She's heard he's already messing up on a big scale. If he'd taken her to London she could have prevented the howlers. Even if he didn't respect her he might have learnt to rely on her.

Today is Friday. Friday is surgery day. Parliament doesn't sit on a Friday. Jud hasn't been near his constituency for over a month. Cases are piling up. She's nagged him and he's promised to be here today. 'That's a definite,' he said. Certain people are coming back for a third attempt to meet him. She's fed up with having to lie.

The office feels particularly silent. She turns on the

24hour news channel. The Southern Rail strike is entering its third month. The company is under no pressure to resolve it. Unbelievably they have a contract with the government which means the taxpayer compensates the company when the workers go on strike. That way the company can lay up their shiny new trains for days on end and not lose out. Who wrote that contract, she wonders. Who signed it? Which idiot didn't see that it was bound to lead to an endless series of unresolved strikes? She knows the answer, just as she knows who gave the billion pound contract to a firm that had already issued several profit warnings. A few months later they went bust. Jud as a backbench MP had been barely adequate. As a Minister he was a disaster.

The news rolls on. Journalists interview other journalists. Back then, she thinks, it was important to have facts. Now you only need locations. The really important thing for a rolling news reporter is to be in the right place. Wendy stops herself mid-thought. She's getting bitter. She's getting bitter and she's getting fat. She's never met Jud Mindsett's new secretary but her voice always sounds disconcertingly slim.

Wendy deals with the correspondence. She puts the board outside advertising this afternoon's surgery. She sets out chairs. She washes the cups. She cleans Jud's office, scattering papers on his desk so it looks as if he sometimes works there. This is politics and appearances matter.

When she gets back to the news channel in the main room she realises something has happened whilst she was out. Speculation has gone into overdrive. The

Prime Minister has called an unscheduled press conference. No one knows what he is going to say. Journalists waffle and exchange confused smiles.

* * *

Martin is the last to leave. Leah watches him drive off in his old van, remembers their journey back from Ullapool and the deer they killed. She hesitates before going back into the house. The sun is warm on her face.

She should feel relieved. Their long struggle against Patrick and his cult is finally over. She's back.

Her mute self would have gone for a walk. She'd like to do that now. She needs to think about everything that's happened, to think about Martin and what she wants from the relationship. Her old, silent self would have been free to do just that. Nothing was expected of Leah the mute, Leah the marginal.

Patrick has changed all that.

She knows she should stay where she is and look after Izzy but the sharpness of April sunshine calls to her. Izzy is a grown up. Izzy can look after herself. She isn't yet old, not yet seventy. She's lived thirty years without Patrick. She can do so again.

A thrush calls from a high branch, pouring its song into the still air. Each note clambers over the one before.

Is Martin coming back tonight? She didn't ask and he didn't suggest. Typical of him not to presume. At one time they had a pattern to their meetings, but that was before. He's her friend. He's been her lover and last night he was again. What does she want from him? It's the old question.

Another thrush answers. The first bird listens. Recently there's been so much noise in her life. She needs to be silent for a while. She needs to think.

Leah turns back towards the house. If Izzy is alright to be left she'll go for a walk and start to work it all out.

* * *

In any decent society Jud Mindsett would have been sacked and forgotten. But he's a celebrity whose status is entirely unconnected to any actual achievement. He's appeared on quiz shows. Why train for a decade to win a gold medal when that may or may not result in you being famous? Why spend a lifetime making documentaries about exotic species when you can bypass the whole effort thing and simply become an exotic species by the way you act, by something as simple as never combing your hair? Why attempt to manage the National Health Service at the mercy of bad winters and sudden crises when you can cause a crisis with a few choice words and snatch the resulting fame with such little effort? Fame is self-replicating. In Britain, in this still young century, you can be famous just for being famous.

Mindsett is the product of an expensive private education. That education began by stripping him of his dignity with its regime of communal baths and cold showers. It then stripped him of parental ties and substituted the school as his new family. Almost surgically it scraped away at whatever religion he had imbibed so far and any morality that went with it. Why worship other gods, his public school taught him, when, like a Roman Emperor, you can be your own god? By the time he sat GCEs Jud had learnt that he was a superior being, that these exams were really beneath him but he'd better sit them anyway.

He did. He passed.

In the sixth form his education became more intense. Make an argument, the masters taught him. Any argument. It doesn't matter if you believe what you are saying or not. At first Jud found this difficult. He tried to be logical. He tried to be consistent. The school shook its head. 'No one cares about that stuff except Private Eye,' they told him. 'Leave truth for the small print. Winning is about headlines. Contradict yourself as much as you like. No one remembers. Develop a personality, a way of dressing, and whatever you do don't show in your face what you are really feeling. We have made you into a god but you need to do the believing.'

Then suddenly school was over and so was university. He was on his own and in the world.

When you went to private school you paid for the teaching and the bad food but you were really buying contacts. Jud tried the City, bought the right suit, frequented the right bars, but hated the hours and the numbers. He ditched that suit, bought another with more style and, through another school contact, went to work for a PR firm. There was an actual entry test for this company, mercifully short and so well within Jud's concentration span:

Imagine you were hired by the Gestapo to write a PR

statement for Dachau concentration camp.

Jud thought for a minute and wrote:

> *The AMFI (Arbeit Macht Frei Institution) is fully committed to the welfare of all those in our care. We are passionate about equal opportunities. Working within our allocated resources we ensure that work and food are equally shared. We maintain an ordered environment that is second to none. This is essential given the sheer number of our clients. Innovative methods are enabling us to dramatically increase our throughput. Our waste-disposal record is excellent.*

When he had finished Jud handed it in to the interview panel and was hired immediately.

But it didn't work out. The problem with PR was the clients. You had to be nice to them. You had to let them judge your work. A flippant comment and they wanted the firm to send someone else next time. Worse than that, you never got any personal fame. What you produced was always the product of the company. Adverts and puff pieces are by-line free.

When Jud joined the Party he was determined to become an MP. Another school contact steered him towards a marginal seat with potential. He knuckled down and worked for his victory. Walking into the Commons, Jud knew he was home and dry. This was where he belonged. Several of his school friends were already there. One was dressed like a remnant of a previous century. Another borrowed his language from PG Woodhouse. A third pulled the strings behind the scenes, running a data scam. Jud bowed to the speaker and found his seat. In all that schoolboy uproar he felt in the heart of things.

* * *

It's Friday morning. Ministry civil servants love Friday. MPs leave London, abandon the Westminster bubble, and catch trains back to their constituencies. Even Ministers intent on climbing the greasy pole and dreaming of being Prime Minister abandon their pretence of running ministries and head back to partners and families. Civil servants can breathe again, can meet without fear of interruption and quietly arrange how to win back any ground lost during the week.

Jud Mindsett knows this. He also knows he has a surgery at 2pm, 180 miles north of Westminster. He knows he must leave the office in the next thirty minutes if he is to catch his train, but this self-styled People's Champion hates people. He tells friends that no one remotely competent ever comes to an MP's surgery. Many who come will be old or ill. Some will be both. There will be at least two with incipient dementia and one who smells. Off camera Mindsett refers to his constituents as chlamydia: an occasional irritating consequence of the promiscuous pursuit of power and fame. He is a Minister in what is now a safe seat. Sometimes he feels sorry for colleagues nursing marginals. They have to involve themselves in the minutiae of their constituents' lives. They have to grub for votes. He doesn't, so he lingers in his Whitehall office enjoying the sense of frustration that his presence creates there.

A discreet cough. 'Your train, Sir.'

Jud Mindsett ignores this. There are other trains. He has an open ticket. Mrs Mindsett won't expect him home for hours. He'll phone her from the station, and by the time he gets home she'll be waiting with his favourite cut glass tumbler containing a double whisky and soda with two piglet-shaped ice cubes.

That will all come later. For now, Mindsett tells himself, there is work to be done. On Monday he must give a speech. It's in his diary. He makes a point of never working at weekends so he must go through the final draft before he leaves.

'Well, if you won't be needing me I'll ...'

The Underling makes for the door. Jud watches him without seeming to, sees that he has reached the door and pulled it open, waits until he is about to step through, then calls him back.

'Do I really have to say all this?'

'I thought we agreed. We have re-drafted.'

Jud jams his pen into the document as if trying to skewer it. 'Dull, dull, dull. No soundbites. It's a technocrat's speech.'

'A speech to bankers about the importance of maintaining healthy balance sheets is bound to be technical, Sir. The Prime Minister asked you to make it because you once worked in the City.'

Mindsett sighs. 'You don't have a reputation. I do. Why do the press turn up to a Jud Mindsett speech?

Because they know I'll go off script, because they know I'll be different. News isn't about facts, it's a branch of entertainment. Don't you understand that? Show me a single entertaining sentence in this shit and I might let you go to your weekly conspiracy.'

'Sir, the Prime Minister intimated ...'

'Intimated! What sort of a word is that? He told me I had to stick to the script from now on. I can do that, of course I can, but only if you put the stuff I want to say into the script in the first place. Simple.'

'What is it you particularly want to say?' The Underling asks the question as if it is a new thought that has just come to him. He knows he must never let his impatience show. Ministers are there to be ground down. In a nutshell, that is his job description. To be an underling you have to be willing to have the same conversation over and over, and each time you have to speak as if what you say is fresh and new. If he ever gets fed up here, he's told his wife, he'll go and work in a care home.

'I want to blame the bankers for the crash,' Jud tells him. 'I want to remind them they fucked up so badly they should have been sacked. I want to rub their noses so deep in the fact that if they had been one of their own small businesses they'd have foreclosed on themselves. I want to suggest that bank CEOs should have a banking background and – dare I say this – even a banking qualification.'

The Underling shakes his head. He is meant to stay out of politics but that isn't always possible. 'But they fund your party ...'

'As part of their civic duty, without fear or favour, I

hope. Well, I'm not afraid of them and I won't do them any favours.'

'We can add something about there must be no going back to past errors.'

Jud snorts. 'Past errors! That would probably satisfy the blessed Stella but it isn't good enough for me.'

His phone pings. He opens the message, stares at the screen in disbelief.

He shakes his phone, taps it, and reads the message again. Then he looks up.

'And why, Underling, is Number 10 holding an unannounced press conference in 15 minutes' time?'

So it's true, the Underling thinks. He'd heard the rumour but discounted it. 'I really have no idea. Such matters are well above my pay grade …'

Now Jud is out of his chair and staring down on the wretched man. 'Tell me,' he yells.

The Underling wilts. 'The rumour, if we give any credence to rumours, is that the Prime Minister has been diagnosed with a serious illness.'

'So he's resigning and picking his moment when everyone's out of the way.'

The Underling stays silent and retreats into philosophical speculation. Staying silent is actually fraught with danger because Ministers take silence to mean consent, but to deny what is most likely true is a greater danger to an underling's future prospects. He should distract the Minister with a joke but he isn't good at jokes.

Jud ignores him completely and begins to career around the room. A slow-motion film of his perambulations as he passes the door would show that the first part of his bulk to reach and cross that vertical line is his stomach, closely followed by his flapping jacket and then his knees. He walks with his head flung back and with almost regimentally exact shoulders. Slow the film down further and you notice that bringing up the rear of the Mindsett persona is his hair. Jet black and luxurious, it streams out in a triangle before bouncing on his collar. The effect is to give the whole performance an expression of speed. Suddenly Jud stops. His stomach quivers and his hair goes back to being vertical.

'Except Stella,' he pronounces. 'I bet Stella has been pre-warned. I bet Stella is all ready to start her campaign.'

The Underling begins to panic. Party politics is dangerous, but in-party rivalries are deadly to a civil service career. He must distract. 'The speech, Sir. Shall I add a mention of past errors to the speech?'

'Sod the speech. This changes everything. I'll call you when I need you.'

The Underling leaves his office.

The moment Jud is quite sure he is alone he speed dials his long suffering agent. He remembers he promised.

'Wendy, love, something's come up ... No, something huge ... I suggest you watch 24 hour news ... Oh, you were ... Well, I'm sorry but you'll have to cope. The big time beckons.' He rings off quickly before she can nag him. This is his chance, the chance to leave behind his past mistakes and be someone else. He needs to organise.

In Yorkshire Wendy slams down the phone. *Something huge.* For a moment she hopes it's about the Southern Rail contract. Is Jud about to be exposed at last?

Later, when she listens to the Prime Minister's resignation speech, she feels for the man. His dignity is as enormous as his disappointment. When the cameras go in close she can see that the terminal illness is already etched on his face. She watches his wife watching the man she loves close the curtain on his life's work and senses their joint despair.

The commentators all agree. It's Stella's to lose. Stella will become Prime Minister and she'll do a re-shuffle. Wendy hopes she'll bring in genuine talent, get rid of the yes-men. Then Jud will be out on his ear. His political career will be over before it's even begun. With a bit of luck he'll resign as an MP and she will have someone decent to work for.

3

The moment Leah turns to get ready for her walk she sees that Izzy is in the doorway watching her. Even to Leah Izzy looks smaller than she was, as if she's shrunk into herself since her son died. Before a word has been spoken Leah postpones her walk. What does she really feel about being needed?

'You were thinking of going for a walk, weren't you?' Izzy says.

Leah realises it's a yes or no question, the kind Izzy used to ask.

'Yes,' Leah says. 'I need to think. But it's April. The days are longer. I can walk later. Shall we start tidying up?'

'I'm not sure I'm up to that just now.'

Her mother is developing a whine which Leah ignores. 'We can at least strip the beds. It's a good drying day.'

'If we must.'

'Activity, activity,' Leah says, and realises she's already taking charge. Will this be the new order of things?

She knows she should hug her mother to comfort her, but instead she walks past her and into the house. The phrase 'cruel to be kind' comes into her head.

'Leah.'

Her mother has turned but she hasn't moved. 'I'm in a terrible place,' Izzy says. 'I'm out of the cult but I'm nowhere I want to be.'

There's no answer to her mother's cry. 'Look, Mum, it's a lovely morning. Let's leave the clearing up and go for a walk together.'

The offer is calculated. She thinks Izzy will say no, but she doesn't.

'Will it be wet underfoot?' Izzy asks.

It takes ages for Izzy to get ready. There is a new fussiness about her, and when they set off she walks slowly. However much Leah slows down she finds she has to continually stop and wait for Izzy to catch up.

They reach the old railway line. Here it's easier to walk side by side. Everywhere, little birds move urgently between the trees. Will it help if she encourages Izzy to talk?

'We need to talk about Patrick,' Leah says. 'I think it might help. You've never told me what happened to you the morning he died.'

The moment she's said this she becomes painfully conscious of another thing that spoken words do. They define status. When she was silent everyone saw her as a non-player. She listened to her siblings as they used words to clamber all over each other, in much the same way as they had done physically when they were smaller. Taking on Patrick had been an urgent matter that had thrust her to the top of the pile. Now that's done she has to decide what she wants from life, but even before she can do so her words are already defining her. Think before you speak, she remembers from somewhere, but no one does because there isn't time. Already her words are speaking themselves. She's taking charge of Izzy and her words are taking charge of her.

Izzy is silent.

'Then let me tell you what the others know and you don't,' Leah says.

She remembers Martin quoting a sentence from Buddhism: *The truth will set you free, but first it may make you miserable.*

Leah knows she mustn't tell the whole story. She skips over the way she disguised herself to observe her mother's first meeting with Patrick, the child she gave up for adoption. Instead she starts with the rape. She tells in graphic detail how Patrick, her half-brother, raped her. She realises as she describes it that the story has shifted in her own head, that the way she once blamed herself has disappeared. She emphasises Patrick's slickness, proof that she wasn't the first. She tells of the journey to Scotland with Martin and fills in details about Uncle Joshua and Mrs Evans.

They are slowing down as they walk but Izzy is listening.

Leah tells her mother about being groped in the cult church, how she broke her attacker's finger and ran into Patrick's arms and how everything changed after that. Before she talks about her meeting with God's Man she warns Izzy that this will be painful and says that she'll stop now if Izzy wants her to.

Izzy says nothing but continues to walk along the old railway line, placing one foot in front of the other like an automaton.

So Leah carries on. She tells Izzy about meeting the dying God's Man, about the conversation between Katherine and Patrick, and finishes with Patrick smothering the leader of his own cult with a pillow.

She spares her mother none of the detail. She describes the way the old man's legs kicked and the old arms tried to push Patrick away, how it seemed to go on for ever. As she reaches the end of her story they stop walking and stand still.

'Katherine and Patrick were always in it together,' she explains. 'We were both their victims. Patrick had been told he could be God's Man if he brought you and me, our house and the money back into the cult.'

Izzy is silent. She's staring at the ground.

'I can prove all this,' Leah gently tells her. 'I even have some of it on film.'

Izzy says nothing for a while, then, 'I think I've walked far enough. Shall we go back now?'

They are nearly at the end of the railway track when Izzy suddenly blurts out, 'I don't like to think of Patrick just lying there.'

'He fell into the sinkhole. He's buried,' Leah responds. 'He's lying buried in the North York Moors at one of what used to be your favourite places.'

'No words have been said over him. There's no marker.' Izzy's tone is petulant.

They climb out of the cutting and set off across the fields. 'I miss your dad. I didn't used to but I do now,' Izzy says.

As they turn into the drive she adds, after a long silence, 'What have I got to look forward to?'

After lunch Izzy goes up to rest. It's clouded over outside and a thin rain is falling. Leah lights a fire and stares into the flames. She could have answered her mother's question. She could have said, 'You are alive. You are healthy. You are rich. You have a wonderful house. Patrick would have locked you away in one of his safe houses. Instead of that you are free. For God's sake, Izzy, count your blessings.'

She couldn't because each of these things also applies to her, with the addition that she has a kind man who loves and makes love to her. If all that isn't enough for her, why should life after Patrick satisfy Izzy?

The coal glows. The flames dance against the black of the chimney. I can't go back to not talking, she thinks. I've gone into the world and the only way is onward. I'm thirty-four. I've never worked. I have no qualifications at all. There's a lot of catching up I need to do. I suppose I should become a job seeker.

I need to talk to someone about finding work.

* * *

Danny's train is 50 miles north of King's Cross. It's on time. His holdall is above him on the rack. Outside his window the flat fields of England segue into fishing lakes and small villages, then fill with cattle or sheep. He doesn't see any of this detail, doesn't notice the car at the level-crossing or three swans in a flooded field because his thoughts are turned inward. For the first time in his life he is aware of time itself, of its incessant passing. In this new and confusing world time isn't just a thing. It becomes a person. It asks him a question.

'What do you have to show for all your time?'

Questions suggest their own answers. The fact of the question worries Danny. It means the answer he might have given is no longer totally satisfactory. It's the lack of an answer that has prompted the question.

Myself, he would once have said. My body. Bench press against me. You go on that running machine and I'll go on this one. Shall we say 12k? Strip off and stand next to me in front of this mirror. You're probably holding your stomach in; mine is always like this. Walk down this street with me and count the heads that turn. I have real pride in what I am.

A whooshing noise disturbs his thoughts. The train that Jud Mindsett should have been on pulses past him, heading north. For a few seconds Danny's sense of urgency doubles then settles.

Next month he'll be thirty and close to his physical peak. How long can he stay there? By thirty a gymnast has already retired. A footballer dreams of a last few years of raking the money in by playing for Shandong Luneng in the Chinese Super League. Being his age and Danny Goulden is alright, but being thirty-five and still being the same Danny Goulden might be something quite different. Much later, when he's ninety, there might be another chance of physical fame if he's still running marathons. He winces at the thought.

York to King's Cross. Thirty to thirty-five. Thirty-five to ninety. It's what intervenes, what separates them, that is beginning to worry him. How much longer can he beat off the challenge of younger versions of himself?

Occasionally he hears of someone at the gym who's moved in with a partner, settled down, even married. He knows what will happen next. They won't attend as often. They'll fall off the pace. In two years' time they won't even renew their membership. He'll catch a glimpse of them in the street and they'll have put on weight.

Disturbed at these thoughts, at the way his doubts are spreading, he pulls his eyes away from the window. Opposite him a woman sits in front of her laptop. She's probably around his age, perhaps a little younger. Nice face. Regular nose. Chin just a fraction long. Hair black. Eyebrows brownish, mousey. She dyes her hair. Danny doesn't, but he's thought of it. What will he do when his hair turns grey?

The girl is absorbed in her computer so Danny continues his appraisal. She has calf muscles. He can see her legs under the table and the way they stretch the fabric of her trousers. Is she a runner? Nice small breasts. He likes that about her. Just enough to give shape. She's quite tall, not as tall as he is but tall enough.

Danny is absorbed in his scrutiny when she suddenly looks across at him. Was she aware that he was examining her? She catches his eye. He sees her hostile look quiver and turn into a lop-sided smile. Then she goes back to her computer.

It's enough encouragement. He knows what to do. Keep looking, show interest. He doesn't think she has a ring on her finger. Add her to the list?

No.

It's that computer and her obvious competence that put him off. She frightens him. Even if she fancies his looks she'll ask him what he does and walk away.

What does he do? Nothing. He lives off his allowance. Why work when you have a rich dad, he used to joke. Not working gives him the edge in the gym. He can train whenever he wants. He can be Danny Goulden.

But at this moment he feels trapped. Here on the train he feels caught between life passing by outside the window and a girl who he knows would want more from him than he can give. He's glad the train is heading for London. London is the city you can get lost in. He won't see the girl again. He'll settle back into his house and his street and his gym. He knows the girl is looking at him as women often do, but he keeps his eyes down, senses London closing round him, and welcomes its vital anonymity.

No. He'll stay as he is. He'll be content. But, having decided this, he recalls the feeling of having a knife welded to his hand.

4

The call comes through to all cars at 11.30am. PC Keith Loadstone is the first responder. Does he know where Black Rigg Beck joins Rutmoor Dike on the south side of Wheeldale Moor?

Not exactly, but he's at Rosedale and he can easily head up that way.

'What is it this time?' Loadstone asks.

'A walker has reported finding a body. It's just past the second footbridge. He says the site is partially roped off.'

'I'll go.'

Keith Loadstone sets off.

North Yorkshire isn't exactly North London. It doesn't have the pace of the Met or the sheer variety of cases. It's ten years since he's worn body armour and picked up a shield for riot control. He sees guns often, but they are full-barrelled shotguns. He hears shots, but if pointed upwards they are aimed only at grouse, partridge, pigeons or pheasants. If pointed downwards they kill rabbits, hares or foxes. Just occasionally they take the life of their owner when debt and a farmer's isolation rob living of its point. They are never aimed at him.

And his patch on a day like this is its own reward. No traffic lights, no choked streets. Just occasionally a slow vehicle you can't get past. But always the rise of the moors, the sense of a thin road leading you across a heather landscape where sheep stray slowly across the tarmac and you have to watch out for the lamb that might run out in front of you to join its ewe.

He parks, finds the footpath and begins to walk.

Another body. He pulls motorcyclists out of hedges on the Stokesley road. He fishes in the River Ouse for drunken students. He breaks down doors when old people haven't been seen for a few days. Death is one of his routines. But he's never been called to a body on the moors. You don't wander onto Wheeldale Moor by chance. It's a serious place even in summer. Walkers stick to the paths. Yes, in winter a blizzard could keep you out longer than you intended and freeze you. Yes, there are numerous old mine-workings it's possible to fall down. But if you break your ankle another walker will find you in time, provided you stick to the paths. The air ambulance will pick you up and whisk you to hospital. If you stick to the paths you're safe. He looks round him. It's actually difficult not to stick to the paths. If you wander off, the heather trips you up. It's difficult walking through heather. This person hasn't wandered. If the description's accurate, the body's lying close to a path.

Heart attack? Struck by lightning?

He reaches the spot: a triangle of grass like a small arena, the stream running past it. At the top of the triangle is some kind of sinkhole, and in the sinkhole he can see two legs.

He takes his radio out.

'Okay, I've located the so-called body.'

'So-called?'

'All I can see are two male legs still wearing shoes.'

'Just legs?

'I don't know. The rest of him, if there is a rest of him, is buried. What do you want me to do?'

He puts the radio down on the grass, knowing its crackle will alert him to his next instruction, and gingerly walks up to the edge of the sinkhole. It seems firm enough. To check this isn't some sort of hoax he reaches in and tentatively pulls at a shoe. He feels it move on the foot without the foot or the leg moving. He kneels down and touches the leg itself. It feels cold, like a leg of lamb straight from the butchers. The flesh is soft, so rigor must have already come and gone. Then he grasps the leg and pulls. At first he thinks nothing is moving, then he notices his knees are sinking. He looks round him, sees the rope and the caution sign lying in the heather. He lets go of the leg and steps back, hearing the squelch his foot makes as he pulls it away.

He examines the hillside above the victim. It looks unstable. Parts of it sag and there are what he can only describe as stretch marks in the grass and shale. He looks back at the stream in the valley bottom. It's twisted at the point directly below him. Is there some kind of underground cavern that occasionally subsides and pulls the hillside down towards it? If so the hole may shift, opening and closing. Near the legs there are signs of recent movement. The grass is ruffled like a rug, a large boulder has loosened exposing a patch of soil. The boulder itself has a ring of earth clearly visible on it. This makes it look like a recently extracted tooth. It's big, the size of a wheelie bin. Considerable forces must be at work here, Loadstone thinks.

The radio crackles. Was he still there? What had he found?

'I've made a preliminary investigation. Yes, there is a body attached to the legs. I'd say it's recent but not fresh. The area is very wet and unstable. It looks as if it's once been roped off. I've found a warning sign. Can you check on that, see if Ryedale has a record of a roped-off area? I can't pull the body out by myself. What do you want me to do?'

He knows what the answer will be but he has to ask. In the Met initiative was banned; you followed the rule book. Here they like to pretend they have both rules and a command structure. He is already thinking Bill is close by. Bill Goff owes him a favour. Bill has a tractor and a winch. Can he get the body out that way? Wet ground hangs onto its secrets or lets go only with reluctance and a great sucking noise. Of course, he could wait until forensics get here but the ground is unstable. Is the body already being pulled down into the mud? If they leave it a day, might the body have disappeared by then?

He pauses. No body, no investigation, no paperwork. Too late for that now. All radio calls are recorded and monitored for training purposes.

The radio crackles and a red grouse answers from nearby. That's a first, but it's spring. Everything except himself is geared to mating.

The static voice tells him to use his initiative. He hears the grouse again. It sounds like 'Come to me, come to me.'

The thing with grouse is you can talk to them and they will answer. To amuse himself he begins the conversation. The grouse answers once, then gives up.

* * *

Jud Mindsett is still in his office when he watches the broadcast. Now he's cancelled his surgery he has the whole day to himself. The Prime Minister is exactly on time, so Jud doesn't have to listen to journalists inanely filling in. The Prime Minister's wife is with him. She looks unhappy and stands just behind him. Jud notices that he approaches the lectern a little more slowly than usual, and that when he reaches it he grips it with both hands. The Prime Minister always talks from notes but this time is different.

'First, can I thank you all for coming here at short notice.' He pauses, then something of the man he once was comes back to him. His voice strengthens. 'In the past I have warned the country about listening to rumours. Rumours are dangerous. They unsettle. They destabilise. As you well know, I have always preferred to govern from the facts. Recently you may have heard rumours about my health. I have to inform you this morning that those rumours are true, and I must face the facts as they have been explained to me by my consultant. Put bluntly, I have a terminal illness and will soon lose the ability to govern. I care too much about our country to wish to cling on into a period of incapacity. Therefore I will, as soon as my successor can be elected, be tendering my resignation as your Prime Minister.'

He stops. His voice weakens. He's said all he meant to say but seems reluctant to leave the stage. He pauses. 'That's it. I have nothing to add.' He nods at the journalists, turns and holds out his hand. His wife clutches it and together they walk away.

Jud doesn't react to the Prime Minister's obvious sadness. He fails to notice the way his illness is already written on his face. The quiet dignity of the man quite escapes him. What he sees is an opportunity, his opportunity. Even as the Prime Minister walks back through the door of Number 10 Jud sees himself going through the same door. Before the tributes start he switches off the television and rocks backwards in his ministerial chair.

He was right not to go to his surgery. His constituents can wait. If he plays his cards right he will be free from the need to meet the great unwashed ever again. Chlamydia will be a thing of the past. It will be set speeches and grand interviews from now on. No public transport. Instead, a chauffeur-driven car and police escorts, all blue lights and sirens.

He closes his eyes. He hears far-off music playing. A series of lecterns appears in front of him. Some are serenely empty. Others are festooned with microphones. He sees a large audience standing and clapping. A smile creeps over his face. In his daydream the audience begin singing, 'Hail to the Chief.' That's when he realises he's on the wrong continent and he opens his eyes.

Why not? he asks the four walls of his office.

And the walls answer. 'Stella,' they shout at him. 'Stella Stelling.'

* * *

By the time Bill and his tractor arrive Keith Loadstone has smoked two cigarettes and inspected the ground. People walk here all the time. The path by the stream has many sets of footprints. Few people climb up the small slope to where the body's buried. He makes out only one set of prints leading up there. These are recent, probably made by the man who reported it. A woman or a child has also stood there recently but has left only the vaguest impression. He thinks he can make out where the footmarks turned and walked away but he can't be sure. He finds several pieces of blue plastic-type string. These are looped together and have been cut. There's a curve to them as if they have been used to bind something. It's the sort of discarded string you find in every farmyard. He also finds a knife. The knife interests him. It's nowhere near the string, but the string's been cut and the knife is sharp enough to do it. It's a common enough knife to find in London but out of place here on the moor.

Walkers occasionally carry and leave behind penknives or picnic knives. Farmers and gamekeepers favour chunky clasp knives. This knife is long and thin, cumbersome for a walker to carry and not robust enough for a farmer. It's a kind PC Loadstone recognises, borderline between practical knife and offensive weapon. Not a flick knife but capable of killing. Does the body have a knife wound?

'Watch the ground, Bill,' Keith shouts. 'I don't think it's a mineshaft. It could be a sinkhole.'

The two men stand together looking down at three sets of feet.

'Have you done anything like this before?'

'Often. Sheep, cows.'

'What do you do?'

'Tie the feet together to give the rope a firm grip, then pull.'

'Can you pull him out straight?'

Bill looks at the angle of the legs. 'I think so. He must be lying on his back. It depends if the knees are straight.'

'What's the worst that can happen?'

'The legs snap.'

'Well, take it gently. None of your sheep and cows needs an autopsy. This one might.'

Keith Loadstone removes the victim's shoes and socks. He can see Bill is squeamish about a human body, so he offers to do the tying under instruction. The ground is definitely squelchy. He can feel it moving as he works. They are perhaps only just in time.

Distracted by the task, they never notice they have an audience. Now, with the knot tied and the winch ready, they see a girl standing on the path watching them. How long has she been there? What has she seen?

'Pull him out, Bill. I'll see to her.'

Keith turns to see who it is. He's in uniform. A bystander might walk away or stay their ground. This girl walks towards him. Then he recognises her.

'Hello Marie. Council send you?'

She's standing at his side, looking into the hole, staring at the feet and then watching the tractor.

She nods and looks up at his face sideways. He keeps his eyes on the tractor.

'We tried your phone but there was no signal.'

'So you thought you'd come. Ever seen a body before?'

'My grandad.'

The way she says it, as if the fact of his death still hurts, makes him turn and look at her. 'Well, you're about to see another. Are you sure you're up to this?'

She nods.

Bill gives the winch a last check, tugs at the ropes, then climbs into his cab.

'And what did they send you to tell me, Marie?'

'It was roped off because it was a sinkhole. It opened up years ago. Walkers reported it. Apparently it moves a little every now and then, has a habit of opening and closing depending on the rainfall and landslides.'

The winch cable straightens. They hear a leathery noise as the two parts of the rope tighten against each other.

'You know he could snap in half,' Keith says.

She holds her ground, gives him no reaction until the two legs seem to shake themselves. It's as if the rest of the body is waking up.

'Hold it there,' Keith shouts.

A lever slaps, the cable quivers and the legs stop moving.

Keith walks to the very edge. 'Okay, slowly. I need to watch. There may be clues.'

He doesn't want Marie watching this. He tells her to move away but she doesn't. Where was backup when you needed it? In the Met there'd have been a rope and tent and PCs on crowd control. Here there are sheep and Marie. She's come up slowly to stand at his side on the very lip.

The lever slaps again and this time the legs behave, just slither slowly out of the mud. Then there's a small hiatus. 'It'll be the arms,' Keith explains. 'They've nowhere to go. They'll stick down there and only follow the body out when the shoulders have gone past them.'

The mud on the body has a clay look like the slick of a pottery class. It's a yellow colour. The body comes to a halt, seems to shake itself. There's a sucking noise and then everything starts moving again.

'Slow down.'

He doesn't want the body popping out of the hole in an undignified manner.

The body is facing them as it emerges. Did he tumble backwards? If so, that's odd. Keith can just about imagine someone walking to the edge, getting too close and falling in face forwards. But to topple backwards? Was the victim alone at the time? Was he a victim?

The head follows the body and then come the shoulders and strangely twisted arms. Soon the whole of him is out in the open air.

The winch stops.

'A bit farther,' Keith instructs. 'We need to examine him on firmer ground.'

While the body is being pulled farther down the hill Keith leans into the hole. What a place to die. If the victim was living when he went in, then he'd drown in mud, buried alive, conscious but unable to move. If he was already dead, then a sinkhole might seem a good place to bury a body. But, unless he was killed on the spot, it was a long way to carry someone who was already dead, and only walkers would know this area.

There are no more clues. He turns and walks towards the body.

'Hey, you mustn't do that.'

'It's the first thing his mother would do.'

Marie is leaning over the body, wiping the face with a tissue. She doesn't stop when he approaches. He leans over her. The victim's middle-aged. He'd guess at forty. The face that's emerging under Marie's cloth is still unlined.

'Handsome devil,' Marie says.

Keith looks at the body. The victim must be more than six feet tall. Who was he?

He touches Marie on the shoulder. 'Leave the rest to forensics, eh?'

He fishes in his own pockets and finds a pair of gloves. Then he delves into the mud-encrusted pockets of the corpse. He finds a handkerchief and nothing else. No wallet, no coins, no receipt and no mobile phone.

Everyone carries a mobile phone these days, and on that phone you find all the data you need to identify a corpse.

Bill has come out of his tractor and joined them. 'How the hell does a relatively young man fall into a sinkhole? It was never very big. I can imagine him hurdling it.'

Keith nods. 'There's something not right about this.'

5

Wendy Welbeck passes on Jud Mindsett's apologies for not turning up to his constituency surgery. The phrases drip off her tongue all day: 'unavoidably delayed'; 'now he's a Minister'; 'the demands of his job are considerable'; 'he does know of your case'; 'I'll get him to write to you'. The words he and him are hateful to her. She wants to say *the bastard* instead, as in *the bastard's unavoidably delayed* and *I'll get the bastard to write to you*.

All afternoon she watches the faces fall, the disappointment cloud hopeful eyes. 'What do I do now?' an old man asks. 'I live two bus rides away and it's the third week I've tried to see him. I'm exhausted by the time I get home.' It's the flatness of the way he speaks that upsets Wendy. His voice betrays a lack of belief that anyone could ever help him.

'I'm sorry,' she says. 'I'm sure he'll be here next week.' Except she knows the bastard won't.

The old man picks up his stick and begins the clearly painful walk out of the room. He is too well-mannered to remind her that she said those same words to him each of the previous Fridays. At the door he pauses and turns. 'I know it's not your fault,' he says.

She can deal with anger. It brings out the toughness in her. Fair-minded reasonableness gets to her every time.

She watches the old man walk away. He heads for the bus stop. As she turns, Wendy looks at the poster.

Jud Mindsett works for you. She wants to pick up the phone and blast him. She wants to give him a piece of her mind. Twenty minutes later she notices that the old man is still waiting at the bus stop. It's started raining and he doesn't have a hat.

She wonders how long she can stomach this.

The foreigner is the last to turn up and the last to leave. He doesn't upset her. He simply shrugs when she tells him the MP isn't coming. He holds documents in his right hand and taps them on his left. Then he walks away. Because of the documents Wendy presumes he's an asylum seeker and that he wants the MP's support for his application for full British citizenship. She nearly tells him he's wasting his time. One day she'll tell the truth to these people but not yet, not today.

'I'm so sorry, but the Minister has been unable to leave the Ministry,' Wendy says.

This is one of the days she hates herself.

* * *

The tall man with the papers is called Ivor and he isn't surprised. He's developed the patience of the refugee. Tall and painfully thin with thick black hair, he shrugs and walks away. From the back he looks like a busy junior doctor. But there's something both knowing and determined about his face. As he turns to leave he thrusts the documents back in the inner pocket of his North Face gilet. Because he's so tall it only just overlaps the top of his jeans. Both these items of clothing are relatively new. He wants to look his best when he finally comes face to face with Jud Mindsett, the man he can blackmail into giving him citizenship.

Born in Minsk, Ivor is one of Gorbachev's children. He was baptised in hope, raised in a democracy, taught to speak his mind because speech was newly free. One of his teachers he particularly remembers. This history teacher told his class that the age of the Czars, Communist or Romanoff, was finally over, that long winters of dictatorship would never happen again. The secret services would finally lose their hold over the country and all Russians would be free.

Then Russia woke up from the long hangover of Yeltsin to find they had become a mafia state with a bareback-riding KGB man in charge who acted as if he was a mafia godfather. Ivor was too young to vote at the 2000 rigged election, but in 2014, fired up by events in Ukraine, he'd shown himself to be a believer in democracy. Like other young Russians he felt the time was right and demonstrated outside the Kremlin. Pushing himself to the front of the crowd he had hurled abuse at the police and demanded Putin's resignation. For his pains he was locked up for a month without trial and badly beaten. After his release he told his parents that he intended to flee the country.

'Stay,' his parents had urged him. 'Freedom will return.'

'1917,' he told them, 'freedom followed by Stalin. 1985 freedom followed by Putin. This freedom thing happens every seventy years in Russia and it never lasts. I might just live long enough to see the next one, but only if I leave Russia.'

By this time his history teacher had disappeared and

two of his friends had been given long jail sentences, so he caught a flight to Britain and registered as an asylum seeker.

If living in Russia has already taught him not to trust in hope, his reception in the land of the free has taught him to trust no one but himself.

There were no welcoming arms for him when he arrived. He found Britain to be a sour country, full of contradictory beliefs. After nearly a year of living here Ivor still doesn't understand the people. To have the privilege of voting free and fair but not to bother. To have clever people from other countries want to come to live here and to denigrate them and turn them away. To have the benefit of the rule of law and to attack judges. He reads the headlines and watches the faces in disbelief. The British, he decides, are turned in on themselves. No one wants to hear his story. Britain is not so different from Russia. The bureaucracy is instantly recognisable. Processing his application for citizenship has been endlessly delayed. He's escaped from the land of the oligarchs into the land of the plutocrats. They control the press and the press rails against all foreigners, even though newspaper owners often live abroad themselves. Hedge funds dominate political parties through donations. Short the pound at the same time as you back the government. Okay, Ivor decides, if the world is always like this then he must fight for himself at every turn. He can't go back. He needs to make this work.

The papers and photographs in his jacket are copies. The originals, that can sink Jud Mindsett, are hidden. Even though the British secret services are not as efficient as the FSB, he takes Russian precautions.

As he walks away from the constituency office he pats the papers in his pocket. They are valuable. They will work for him and ease him through the bureaucracy of this mad country. They will unlock all the doors that are for the moment closed to him. Jud Mindsett will be his sponsor. Once he's shown Jud what he knows about him he will get citizenship.

Meanwhile he is improving his English. The phrase *can't work* in the sentence *asylum seekers can't work* in reality translates as *can work almost anywhere. Alright, they won't get paid even the minimum wage but they'll never have to pay taxes*.

Ivor has found work in IT. He's always been good with computers. He works for a small firm in a shabby office. That too is much like Minsk. But inside the office the computers are shiny and powerful. The company develops software to guard against the Russian threat. It's a modern, up-to-date company. That means it operates in Britain but has headquarters in the British Virgin Islands for tax purposes. Its workers are all illegals. It exists in spite of the law and thrives in spite of political rhetoric (another similarity to his homeland). The boss is an Iraqi. He had the idea and the start-up capital. He pays the wages and sells the product. He is already a rich man and intends to be richer still. He pretends to supervise his workers but is handicapped by not speaking Russian. This gives his workers time to get on with their own projects.

Ivor walks down the high street. What he loves about sour Britain is its colour, its variety of shops and particularly its cafés. He has enough money for a coffee and a piece of cake. The cafés are always warm and full of women in pairs and groups. They talk quietly and, Ivor notices, actually listen to what each other says.

His way to the café takes him past the local war memorial. He stops in front of it. Its simplicity attracts him: just a white stone with a carved straight sword and names in alphabetical order. No heroic statue, no nationalistic fervour. He thinks of this as the pre-sour Britain. This Britain calls out to him. He knows it exists only in black and white movies but he has retained a streak of Russian sentimentality. He knows this Britain lost merchant vessels and sailors on the Russian convoys, even though this fact has been written out of Great Patriotic War myth taught to all Russian children. This Britain can list the names of its war dead without embarrassment. This Britain spends millions investigating the past, even for football fans. When Russia puts up memorials to all those who died in Stalin's purges, then and only then will he risk returning.

He finds a café called Spring. It's nearly full. It's hot so he takes his gilet off and uses it to reserve a table. He orders an Americano with cold milk on the side and a piece of lemon slice. The waitress is pretty and of mixed race. Her eyes are black. He smiles at her and knows she's noticed him, probably clocked his whiteness and his height. Russians are naturally pallid and prison did nothing for his skin tones. He knows he spends too long looking at screens.

As he sits down an image of the Steppes slips into his head. He sees sky and space whereas England is enclosed. Like every Russian he needs to know there are vast flat lands somewhere within national boundaries, and dark forests you can walk through for weeks and never reach the end.

His coffee comes and is excellent. He still cannot get used to the range and variety of coffees you can buy here. As he sips he closes his eyes and keeps them closed for a long time. When he opens them the waitress is frowning at him.

'Everything alright?'

'Superb,' he says, first in Russian so she can hear him relish its five syllables, then in English.

Was he trying to interest her? If so it hasn't worked. She walks back to the hiss of the coffee machine, bangs out a scoop of used coffee, sets up another. He watches her but she doesn't turn round. Anyway, where could he take her? He has to be back in London tomorrow.

The door opens. An older couple come into the café and look for a seat. There is only one at the window where the stools are too high so Ivor gets to his feet, sweeps up his gilet, coffee and cake, and offers them his table.

'Thank you,' the woman says, 'so kind.'

'You're welcome,' he tells them. Has the waitress noticed his gesture?

He makes his way to the single seat which is a stool with a view out of the window. He settles himself again.

Across the road is an old cinema building. It has an arch resting on pillars and in the middle of the curve is a large face. To either side a frieze of fruit and vines falls away. The plaster is incomplete. Plants are growing out of the roof. The furniture store it became has closed. He notices it's been sold. A young man is sleeping in the doorway. His bearded face peers out of an old sleeping bag. He's wearing a woolly hat pulled down over his ears. As Ivor watches he wakes and sits up. He does this suddenly, as if he's surprised to find himself where he is. There is a look of disgust on his face. He must be hungry because he stares across at the steamed-up windows of the café. He catches Ivor's eye and ducks his head as if he's ashamed.

Ivor remembers his parents saying no one slept rough in Russia until Glasnost. 'Let capitalism in and this is what you get.' Fairy tales, he thinks. Children grow too old for fairy tales but the old fall back into them.

The homeless man has his head down again. He's found a plastic cup and put it on the pavement in front of him. He keeps his head down now and his hands clasped in front of him as if he is praying.

Intrigued, Ivor watches. Who is the man? What's his story? Not a professional beggar, Ivor thinks. The way he slept and woke up tells you that. Not a refugee either. He's not used to this way of life. Drug addict? Alcoholic? Perhaps.

Some people look away as they pass him. Others look straight through him. Women avoid him. Men give something hurriedly. Of course, Ivor thinks. If no one gave, no one would beg.

A woman comes along the road. She's about thirty. He notices she holds her head up as she walks and looks around her the whole time as if she doesn't know where she is. She's wearing a rather gaudy roll-neck jumper and jeans. She doesn't carry a handbag. When she sees the young man she digs into her pockets and several coins fall into his cup. The beggar says something but doesn't look up. The woman carries on, walking slowly, then her pace quickens and she disappears down the narrow alley that leads into the Job Centre.

6

With Martin out of the way and Izzy sleeping, Leah takes another step into being normal. She's never been inside a Job Centre. She's surprised to see security staff wandering round. There are four of them. They are tall, weighty and male. They wear black trousers and white shirts with G4S on the shirt sleeves. Badges are hung round their necks and their faces have an unkempt look, not unlike some of the clients.

Being here under the low ceiling reminds her of the cult and of her special school. She shivers inside as she looks round. A middle-aged woman wearing a blue dress and badged like the security men steps forward. She wears reading glasses on a chain round her neck. Her face is set with that earnest, encouraging, sympathetic look that Leah remembers from social workers. Her earlier self always refused their help and refused to do their assessments. Her earlier self is still there, telling her this is for other people, urging her to turn and go.

But she stays where she is, lets the woman come up to her.

'Can I help?' the woman says.

It takes Leah several attempts to get the words out. She's talked to Martin, to the dying God's Man, to Katherine and to members of her family. This is the first stranger she's ever spoken to. She knows if she had her pad of paper with her she would write the words but she hasn't and there is no going back.

'I'd like a job,' she says.

'Have you an appointment?' the woman asks.

Leah shakes her head, the way she has always dealt with yes / no questions. This won't do, she tells herself.

'No,' she makes herself say and then adds, 'Do I need an appointment?' She's trying to present herself as competent but she stammers over 'appointment'.

'Yes,' the woman says, 'as you can see, we are very busy.'

Now's the time to walk away. But the thought of days at home with Izzy makes her stay where she is. Patrick has shaken the family, turned them upside down. He's made Izzy into a dependent, needy person. He's killed off the mute Leah, forced her to speak and to be responsible. She takes a deep breath.

'Can I make an appointment now?' she asks.

The woman slips her glasses on and consults her sheet. '4.30,' she says, 'with Mr Huyton, desk 6. Will that do?'

Leah stops herself nodding. 'Fine,' she says, 'th-thanks.'

She turns to go, wondering how she will fill her time until then, but the woman says, 'If this is your first visit, why don't you register on-line? It'll speed things up.'

Leah goes to one of the grey tables and stares at the screen. She reads the terms and conditions, clicks on accept.

The world doesn't welcome you slowly, bit by bit, drip-feeding you with what you need to know, she thinks. It demands you enter at once and completely.

You can't immerse yourself slowly, you have to dive in. She fills in her email, adds her name, gender and age, then her address. She doesn't know what kind of job she is looking for so she scrolls the list. She notices how the job title always sounds more impressive than the job actually is. A local taxi firm wants a *Call Advisor*. When she looks at the job description it's simply someone to answer the phone and make bookings.

When the time comes she closes down the pages and makes her way to desk 6. Mr Huyton is waiting.

'Hello Leah,' he says. 'Take a seat.'

He has a thin face, she notices, with a long nose. He frowns a lot. It's as if his face is pinched and he has the same grey pallor as the security men.

'Is this your first time here?' he asks.

'Yes.'

'Qualifications?'

Leah had hoped he'd take longer to get to this point. 'None,' she says.

He tuts. He actually tuts at her, then types.

'Okay. Levels? Scores?'

She shakes her head.

'You did go to school?'

'Yes.'

Should she explain about the series of special schools, the taxi that took her backwards and forwards? She knows she's sinking in his estimation and she doesn't want that.

'I've only just started talking,' she tells him.

He stares at her.

'I stopped talking when I was nine,' she explains.

'After that I never spoke a word the whole time I was at school. They thought I was stupid and I didn't like to disappoint them.'

He is still staring at her.

'It was just easier to go along with what they thought,' she adds. 'I kept my head down.'

'So you have no qualifications at all, no certificates for anything?'

'I'm afraid not.'

He types. Leah waits.

'Skills?' Mr Huyton asks. 'What skills do you have?'

'I'm not sure what you mean.'

Now he's exasperated. 'What can you do? Can you cook? Can you drive a car?'

'No to both of those,' she tells him.

He just looks at her.

'I can clean. I can garden. I can walk.'

He adds none of these things to her dossier and continues to stare at her.

Leah hesitates. She won't tell him that she knows how to break a man's little finger, that's she's good at finding her way along dark corridors, that she knows how to hurl a suitcase. She shakes her head.

Mr Huyton doesn't give up. He's still waiting. 'There must be something else.'

So, because she hates him looking at her, she says, 'I'm quite good with people.'

He types that in. 'Can you elaborate?'

'I've watched people all my life,' she explains. 'Sometimes it's as if I can see inside their heads.'

It's the only way she can put it but he clearly isn't satisfied. He has added nothing to what he has already typed so she takes a deep breath and forces herself to go on. 'For instance, I suspect you came into this job to help people. You probably thought you could change lives but it hasn't worked out that way, has it? I mean, the whole purpose of your job is to launch people into worthwhile, meaningful work. That's your skill. But you've allowed yourself to get trapped in a career that feels neither worthwhile nor meaningful. So you're serving out your time because there's nothing else you can do. And ...' Should she add this bit? 'And I think you really hate it.'

Mr Huyton's mouth falls open. He pushes his keyboard away and his eyes bore into hers. She sees him quiver and shake his head. Then he pulls himself together.

'English and maths,' he says, typing quickly. 'You need to get English and maths GCSE. I'll enrol you on the relevant training courses. You may not get a place for a few months. We can start you on Job Seekers Allowance now, but it's conditional on you turning up to each and every training session without fail.'

'And what if I don't want training?' she asks.

'Then I can only offer you cleaning work or farm work.'

'Farm work?' Leah thinks of animals and being outside.

'Cutting cabbages,' he explains.

She shakes her head.

He smiles for the first time. 'I didn't think so.'

He types some more. Then she hears the printer start up. He hands her two pages with dates and times and places. She takes them and gets up to go. Because she feels sorry for him she says, 'I don't always get people right. I once made a serious mistake.'

Mr Huyton continues to stare at her. Then he nods and smiles. 'Good luck, and I'll try to forgive you,' he says.

She glances at her papers, sees the first training session is in a week's time.

'Next,' Mr Huyton says, already looking past her.

Suddenly there are raised voices. 'You can't do that,' a young man is shouting. 'What am I going to live on for fuck's sake?' The security guards come to life and move closer but Leah doesn't turn to look. She walks past the grey Meccano tables and the red and blue settees out into the open air.

Six youths are smoking at the end of the alley. They force her to step round them and then she is walking down the path towards the bus station.

English will be fine. She can pass English, she reckons. But maths? Maths could be much harder. She wonders if Martin has maths GCSE. Could he help her? She's feeling pleased with herself. It's as if something has clicked inside her. She needs to join the world, be part of it. She needs to catch up for the mute years. She needs to become what she can be.

7

The post of Prime Minister is officially vacant. If Stella stands, Jud knows he hasn't a chance. If Stella stands, no MP will nominate him. It won't be a contest, it'll be a coronation. Stella will walk into Number 10 and he will be a laughing-stock for even trying to stand against her, his career finished.

He explores that scenario. She won't sack him, of course not. She'll leave him in his present job. He'll spend the rest of his life in charge of railway strikes, forced to hear the thunderous noise of his own chickens coming home to roost. Those contracts he blithely signed without bothering to read them will haunt him for ever. It would be better to lose the general election than be trapped as Junior Minister for Transport.

There has to be a way.

Jud Mindsett swings in his chair. With eyes wide open he stares out of the window but he sees nothing, not the sky nor the clouds nor the planes stacking up ready to land at Heathrow. He doesn't even notice the peregrine stooping for a pigeon. His eyes bore through all vestiges of the real world. He goes into a visionary state.

He knows that somewhere he has a brain. At school they thought he was clever. That was before puberty. His brain has long since grown obese with laziness. He needs to find it, exercise it, force it to work. There is always a way. There has to be a way. He thinks of

Hannibal at the battle of Cannae, Wellington outnumbered by Napoleon at Waterloo, Bobby Fischer inventing Fischerandom to defeat Boris Spassky.

What was it Oscar Wilde had said? Jud dredges it out of his student memory. 'One should always play fairly when one has the winning cards.'

The trouble is that he doesn't have a single winning card in his hand. Stella holds all the aces. Invert Oscar Wilde. That's it. That has to be it. Unfairly suits him.

Jud reaches for the phone, dials a number. 'Darling,' he says. 'Have you heard the news?'

She hasn't, so he explains. Then he adds, 'So I'm sorry, darling. There are things I need to do. It's a bore, but I need to stay in London this weekend. I'm sure you understand.'

He listens, then adds softly, 'And you.'

He puts the phone down. He should phone his wife at once but he'll stick by his self-imposed rule: always leave half an hour's gap between his mistress and his wife.

He goes back to staring out of the window.

The Underling is back. 'The speech,' he says. 'I don't think we quite finished that particular conversation.'

Jud tries to tear his mind back from its blue-sky thinking. The speech is somewhere on his desk. The Underling finds it, hands it to him.

It's all or nothing, Jud thinks, as he reaches for the speech. In one flowing, unchoreographed moment he takes the papers, folds them and flings them straight into the wastepaper basket. The speech lodges for a moment on the rim, then slips inside.

'Bullseye,' Jud exclaims. It's a good omen, he thinks.

'What do you want me to do, Sir?' The Underling is unfazed by these theatricals. He's seen them before. They have to have a speech for Monday.

'Nothing, thank you. I'll write my own speech.'

Go along with that, the Underling thinks. The Minister is far too lazy to write his own speech, so when Monday comes he can simply use the one they already have. Just to make sure he ramps up the pressure. 'Well in that case, Minister, we'll need to have it by Sunday at 1.30pm. That will give us time to check it over and send copies to the press.'

'There will be no advance copies,' Jud snorts. 'I know that trick. You think you can just send out the speech I've binned and that will force me to deliver it. The Prime Minister's thrown in the towel, so I don't have to follow his rules anymore.'

The Underling's face remains inscrutable. 'Sir ...'

Mindsett finishes his sentence for him. 'Sir is a way of putting a polite gloss on insubordination. Can I remind you that I am an elected representative of the people with a substantial majority? I will write my own speech. I will deliver my own speech and there will be no advance copies.'

The Underling rallies. 'But journalists need copies if they are to report you accurately, Sir, so these will have to be available as soon as you've finished speaking, Sir. If we are to print them and collate them in time, the speech will need to be here in the Department by 3.30pm on Sunday, Sir, at the very latest. That does give you an extra two hours I suppose.'

'Nice try. No way.'

'Your boss, the Transport Minister, will have to be informed.'

It sounds like a threat.

'He won't thank you for that. He will already be at his constituency surgery. His lack of a large majority like mine makes that a weekly necessity, poor man.'

The Underling tries again. 'The Permanent Secretary will, I'm sure, have something to say about this, Sir.'

It's time to draw this meeting to a close. Jud has things to do, people to see.

'Tell him I'm about to leave for Portcullis House. If he wants to see me he'll have to go there. It won't be worth his while. The clue about our relative seniority,' he tells the young man, 'is in our respective job titles. I am a Minister. He is a Secretary.'

The Underling shrugs. Jud determines that when he reaches Number 10 he will turn shrugging by civil servants into a sackable, perhaps even a capital offence.

8

'And there are these,' Vikki says. 'Take them if you want them. It'll save me chucking them in the skip.'

Martin's old van has got him to his house clearance without mechanical mishap. House clearances are hard work. Books weigh a lot. Martin knows he needs a break from all the carrying but he's also nearly done.

Vikki is about Martin's own age and he's noticed how pretty she is. She has faintly red natural-looking hair and a scattering of freckles on what is a round and open face. She has a way of standing that is very relaxed.

She points to another two boxes. Martin glances at them, notices the cardboard is an odd yellow colour and has a sheen to it.

Has he room in the van? The rest of the old man's books are already piled up in the back and he's worried about the weight on the axles. He picks up the first of the other two boxes.

It's surprisingly light. For a moment he even wonders if it's empty, but he won't ask.

'I'm sure I can find room.'

Martin carries the box out of the house. Perhaps because it's light and he isn't straining under the dead weight of yet another pile of books he finds himself responding to the house in the way Leah would. He feels its sadness, its sense of loss. Dismissing the thought, he walks quickly down the drive, puts the box on the front seat and goes back for the other one.

But as he turns to face the dull squat house he sees what it once was before the paint peeled, before someone let ivy climb its walls, settle there and spread outwards. There's a pink vase in an upstairs window and he thinks of the person who lived there, of the act of buying the vase, bringing it home, unwrapping it and placing it on the sill. Did it look as they hoped? How long had it taken to become invisible?

Martin shakes his head.

He has only to fetch the second box and he can be away. House clearances follow a pattern. You get little chance to check what you are actually buying until you unload the van. The bookshelves in the houses are often full of gaps because relatives have already cherry-picked. Of course, you notice the odd title as you carry piles away, but Martin learnt long ago that if you take an unusual interest in a particular book, someone is bound to notice, sidle up to you and say, 'Oh, is that one still there? It shouldn't be ... sorry.' And it's deftly removed. You end up buying remnants by the ton and sometimes you don't make your initial outlay in subsequent sales.

This house clearance has been different. The bookshelves are intact, no gaps. There's been no supervision. Vikki is entirely business-like, unfussy and seemingly untroubled by the recent death of the man she called Dad. It's more like dealing with an estate agent than a daughter.

Martin picks up the final box. It too is light. Perhaps he'd better settle up first, then this can be the last trip. He'll take the load to Leah's house. There's more room there. Will she ask him to stay? They made no plans this morning, but then her siblings were all there.

He hears Vikki moving stuff in the lounge. He walks through.

'Two hundred?' he checks.

She nods and he holds out the notes. She takes them from him and, without counting, folds them over and shoves them into her back pocket.

He thinks that's it but, 'Coffee before you go?' she asks and smiles.

Is it the smile? Leah used to smile at him just like that when she walked into his shop. He wants to get back to her. Coffee will delay him. He isn't particularly thirsty. 'Great,' he says.

Martin has never been able to say no, not even when Leah, the first time she ever spoke to him, asked him to go to Ullapool with her and to pay for the hotel.

It's April and suddenly warm. They sit on the back step and look out over the garden. It's neglected, unpruned. The trees have expanded to shade the lawn, hence the patches. A climbing rose is taking over on one side. What lawn is left can't have been mowed since the autumn and perhaps before that. Martin can see where borders have been abandoned, probably several years ago. He makes out the pattern of the original garden. In some places honeysuckle has curled rampantly round the fence, not quite disguising it. Everywhere there are little green shoots.

He glances across at Vikki. Her head is tilted back and her eyes are closed as if she's sunbathing.

'Are you selling the house?' he asks.

'Yes, as soon as it's empty.' She doesn't open her eyes.

He thinks, to be with a stranger and so relaxed. With Leah there's always tension.

Conversation lapses. The first real warmth in spring always intoxicates. Should he just close his eyes and stay silent? But he can't do that.

'Is this where you grew up?'

This time she stirs, remembers her coffee. 'We moved here when I was thirteen ...'

The statement seems unfinished. Martin waits. Vikki shakes her head. Stands of fine hair swing and settle. Her eyebrows are redder than her hair.

Then, 'This used to be my uncle's house. We moved here after he died.' Vikki pauses. 'When he took his own life.'

He waits for her to continue. It seems there is a story to tell, an explanation for the house's sadness, but Vikki lapses into silence.

The coffee is scalding hot. Martin can't drink it fast, but just asking questions will make it feel like an interrogation. He takes another sip.

'You know, they never told me that,' Vikki continues. 'About the suicide, I mean. I only found it out later. But the house always gave me the creeps. It seemed unhappy when we moved in and I felt we were never going to cheer it up.'

She goes silent but she doesn't close her eyes. She has a fixed look and her face is suddenly tense.

If only he hadn't accepted the coffee. He could have been away by now, on the way home, driving carefully so as not to damage the suspension or break the axles.

'I felt the sadness,' he says, 'just now, walking to the van.'

Vikki looks at him and the look is piercing, almost invasive.

'I kept urging Dad to sell it,' she says. 'I mean, there are other places, other houses, but he wouldn't hear of it.'

'Did he give you a reason?'

'He said we were lucky to have it. We'd been living in rented accommodation before that. This was ours. By that time it was also the house where my mum had died. 'It's just a house,' I told him. We argued about that.' She smiles ruefully. 'I was seventeen, eighteen, so full of certainty you could have based a curriculum on me. He wouldn't leave so I did. I left the house and I abandoned him. I haven't ...' She pauses and corrects herself. '... I hadn't talked to him for twenty years.'

There's hurt in her voice but also resignation. Martin realises he's tapped into her need to talk. She's opening up to him and he doesn't want that. Things follow when women tell you stuff. He'd better make a move. He drinks some more coffee but it's still too hot and all the excuses are clichés.

'What will I find among the books?' he asks, to turn the conversation.

It doesn't shake her off. 'The remnants of a wasted life, I wouldn't be surprised.'

'Clearing houses always feels like that,' he tells her.

'I wouldn't know. This is my first.'

She's hunched forward now, more like a young girl than a business woman. 'I should have come to see him,' she says quietly. 'I should have made the effort but he was such an unhappy man. After Mum died you couldn't live with him.'

'Tell me,' Martin says, giving way to his better feelings. 'Tell me if it helps.'

She flashes him a smile that he's not sure he wants, then she sits and thinks.

Martin waits, sips at the coffee. At last it's cooling. He won't have to be here much longer.

'I'll give you an instance. It's about the boxes as a matter of fact, the one you've just put in your van and the other you're about to take. One day I was bored so I wandered into his study and poked about in his stuff. I found a pack of letters in one of those boxes. I was about to start reading them when he caught me there, saw what I was holding and snatched them from me. He was white-faced and he frightened me. I thought I was used to his moods but this was different. He was beside himself, told me those were my uncle's things and I was to leave them alone. I remember I started to cry and then he softened and said something I've never understood.'

Vikki pauses.

'What did he say?' Martin asks this in spite of himself.

'Knowledge is dangerous. Once you know something it's impossible to forget it.'

Her voice softens. 'I never knew what he meant. What does it matter now? It was so long ago but I've not touched them since. I never read them.' She laughs. 'I'd take them to the nearest tip if I were you, or burn them. That's what Dad should have done.'

She stands up and he holds out his mug. 'Thanks for the coffee. Hope you get the house cleared and sold.'

'Yes,' she says. 'The past is past, isn't it?'

She flashes him another smile.

'Goodbye,' she says.

When Martin picks up the second box he hears a slight scraping noise from inside as if whatever's in it has slid to the lowest point. Is it the pack of letters still unopened? It feels at that moment as if whatever is in the box is alive and settling down for the next stage of its journey.

* * *

Danny's journey is nearly over. Home, change, glass of water and a long session in the gym to work off the indolence and last night's whisky. He'll need to rehydrate afterwards and bottled water at the gym is expensive. He dives into a newsagents and buys three bottles of water. On impulse he also buys a lottery ticket. He doesn't know why.

When the train reached King's Cross the girl with the computer actually brushed against him. He was sure she contrived it. The carriage was hardly full. He'd been reaching for his holdall when she bent over her computer. Their bottoms had touched for a moment. He'd immediately apologised and she hadn't, only given him another of her lopsided smiles. And the thought had come into his head that if they got together he could take her to his mother's house on his next visit and impress the others.

James is still with Roz. That was a surprise. Now Leah has Martin, the most unsuitable unfit specimen to be sure, but they seem to be in a relationship. They slept in the same bed last night. Julia's been married.

At the time of Dad's funeral they were all single. Now suddenly he's the odd one out, the one who's always been alone.

After the funeral he'd stoutly asserted, 'I've been in love.'

'With yourself or someone else?' Julia had countered. And that comment, at the time, had bounced off him.

Not now. Not anymore.

Words are sharper than knives, he realises. They can hurt for years. He should have talked to the girl, walked with her to the barrier.

He reaches home, bounds up the front steps, key in hand. What do you do with a lottery ticket? He puts it on the kitchen table with the three bottles of water, changes quickly, picks up the waters and pushes them into his gym bag. The gym won't be full. It's Friday night. Only the die-hards will be there on Friday night.

9

By Friday evening Jud has had time to think and to phone his wife.

'I'm sorry, darling.' Stick with the safe word, he tells himself. You've never been much good with names. 'I'm going to have to stay in London all weekend.'

Jud remembers that he married her for many reasons. Youth and beauty were important, as was a certain physicality. But top of the list was her belief in him. She has a wonderful ability to stay on the surface of things. She trusts him. She takes his word as gospel.

'Does the Prime Minister need you?' she asks. 'I watched his resignation.'

'Something like that.'

He hears her sigh. 'You know it's your son's birthday tomorrow, don't you?'

Jud had forgotten.

'... and we are having a birthday party for him.'

When Jud is Prime Minister he will need someone to keep his diary, all his diaries.

'Tell him I'm sorry, will you?' That sounds feeble. 'Tell him I'm doing this for him ... for all of us,' he quickly adds.

He listens, says, 'and you,' then hangs up.

It's time to make that list. The list of his failings and inadequacies. It's what all great leaders do. If you are to win a battle you must first know every weakness that the enemy might exploit against you. Jud knows he has do this and he dreads it. He isn't one to dwell on his weaknesses, so it will be a deeply painful process, but it has to be done. He's no longer in his office but in his London flat. He takes a piece of paper, places it on the desk and unscrews his fountain pen. He stares at the blank page for a while and then he smirks. He imagines himself outside Number 10 as the new Prime Minister. He'll have this paper with him in the inside pocket of his expensive new suit. When he clasps his right hand to his left breast as he vows to serve his country he'll feel this piece of paper, know that it got him there. It'll be a private joke, one he saves for his memoirs.

Before he writes he folds the paper vertically in half, heads one half *Deficiencies* and the other *Assets*. He underlines both headings.

'Just do it,' he says aloud. 'Break the habit of a lifetime. Be honest with yourself.'

Deficiencies

I'm an incompetent Junior Minister.

Not a single member of my party wants me as their leader, so I won't be able to get enough MPs to sign my nomination papers.

I have a mistress as well as a wife. That would be okay in France but not here.

I don't understand economics.

I am not trusted.

I don't have a strong national profile.

Stand-up comedians use my name as a punchline.

Is that everything? He re-reads the list. It'll do for now.

<u>*Assets*</u>

I really want the glory and power so I'm prepared to do the job.

I'm newsworthy. I know how to grab and hold attention. I know that politics has become a branch of entertainment.

I was a journalist. I know it's alright to lie. I know if you get caught out you just move the story on with an even more outrageous lie. The public only ever follows the same story for three days.

I know that those who have gone to University will always be a minority and the majority can be made to hate them for being clever. I can exploit that.

Events derail politicians so you have to make your own events.

Once I'm Prime Minister I won't have to think. I can leave that to the elite, listen to lobbyists, do what they want and take their donations so that I can win the next election. It will be a virtuous circle.

I am a free agent. I am not in love with anybody. I don't really love my country. I have no moral scruples.

I have a speech to make on Monday. It's already in the diary. I can be out of the blocks fast.

Jud reads the list through. The page is full. It's a start.

He thinks for a bit, then turns the split page over and writes on the reverse a single point which he numbers.

1.   *Get on the ballot paper.*

Time to phone Joseph, Jud tells himself. Time to invite him out to dinner.

* * *

Danny is heading back home after the gym. He's in good shape. He's hit each target. His body is awash with dopamine. He's showered to clean out the sweat and the impact of four days spent with his family. He's too tired to think any more. Now for food, a film, then sleep.

He slings the bag over his shoulder and walks out into the London night. Friday. Even though he doesn't work he feels the Friday night effect, that sense of a week completed and a weekend ahead. The world is alright.

Only it isn't. The gym monitors were full of the Prime Minister's resignation, but what's that to Danny? Politics has never mattered. He's registered to vote but he never does. Politicians are all phonies.

Phonies. The word he shouted. It comes stinging back to him. 'You're a phoney. I meet phonies all the time.' What had he meant by that? He tries to shut the thought out, laugh it off. But who are the phonies he meets all the time? And in spite of his determination he's back in the moment, has a knife welded to his hand, and fleetingly he feels immense. Only he knows it's a borrowed feeling, like waking from a dream.

Julia, James and Leah were all fully involved in what happened. Their mother had joined the cult. They all knew but no one told him. Only when they needed some muscle right at the end did he get the phone call. Even Martin had been more involved than he was.

Leah. He can't get over it. Leah talking, Leah giving orders. Leah whispering to him, sending him to catch his mother who was crawling along the path. And everyone deferring to Leah's judgement. Last Christmas she'd been good for pouring a glass of wine, nothing more.

As he walks home it feels as if everyone is rushing past him. Julia was always high-powered and going places, but now James has Roz and is doing his

Master's, getting good grades, making something of his life. In the pecking order of four siblings Danny had always been first in fitness, third in brains. In retrospect it had been a comfort to know his sister Leah didn't do anything, didn't even talk. He, Danny, had always been bracketed with the others and superior to his silent sister. That was then.

He was always the youngest but now he is the least regarded. He could vanish and they'd never notice.

* * *

'But it can't be a coronation,' Jud argues, 'whatever the press says. Stella will only have a mandate if there is a contest.'

'So you are going to offer yourself as the sacrificial victim. How altruistic.'

Two bottles of a rather good Chablis are lodged in the ice bucket, upside down. Two glasses of brandy are swirling in two right hands.

Jud and Joseph are known in one of the upmarket dailies as the Brothers Grimm: cheerful fabricators; tellers of fairy stories. They are lumped together because of their backgrounds: the same public school; the same university; the same year's parliamentary intake. They are seen as inseparable and can be publicly mocked because they are considered as low grade and essentially harmless.

'That's how I can sell it,' Jud says. He pauses. 'Or rather, that's how you can sell it for me.'

Joseph stares at him.

Jud continues. 'Look at the facts, Joseph. The public

like to feel it is they who choose a Prime Minister, not us. They hate fixes. Stella is going to be Prime Minister, but what happens at the next general election which is only two years away? She must win that election. We must win that election. And she will have a much better chance of winning if she has faced a proper contest. That's my point.'

'But with you as candidate! Jud, you don't stand a chance.'

Jud smiles at his friend. 'Exactly. I don't stand a chance.'

He has to elaborate even if he hates what he must say about himself. 'I'm not a threat. I can't possibly win. I won't damage party unity. But I can give the country the appearance of a genuine contest. That's important.' He'll say the next bit too. 'I can make Stella look good, even better than she already does.'

Joseph is unconvinced.

'Anointed candidates usually lose the next election. Remember Alec Douglas-Home. Remember Jim Callaghan. Remember Gordon Brown.'

Joseph slurps his brandy. Some goes down the wrong way. He coughs. 'The party will have its own thoughts,' he says.

'The party is capable of making a real hash of things. The Chair will want a coronation done in a weekend. He's terminally lazy, wants the glory not the work. If he tries to fix this the public will hate us.'

'I concede the point.'

It's time to go for the kill.

'Something else. If we make this real, if we give the contest time and,' Jud swallows because this is the key point, 'if we find a way to involve the public, we can refresh ourselves as a government, guarantee that we win the next election and probably the one after that. A real contest will be all about us and the opposition will be nowhere. They won't get a look in.'

Find a way to involve the public? As a good democrat Joseph seems offended.

'Crucial for the party,' Jud says, 'and no danger to Stella provided I'm the other candidate.'

Joseph swirls his glass and takes a long swig of his brandy. 'It's a good plan, I've got to hand you that. I can't see what can possibly go wrong.'

'So you'll talk to Uncle George.'

'Are you referring to the terminally lazy man who wants the glory but not the work?'

'The best Chair we've ever had.'

'Yes, I'll talk to my Uncle George.'

'Another brandy?' Joseph's glass is empty.

'I don't mind if I do.'

Jud signals for the waiter, places the order and asks for the bill. He has a long weekend ahead of him. Joseph is only the start.

* * *

On Saturday night Danny walks a different way home from the gym. It's drizzling but he doesn't care. The rain on his head is doing something to his thinking. He finds he's relishing its coldness. When he crosses the road the wind scythes into his face and he likes that too. It hurts but he keeps his head up, walks against nature's cold shower. This way home takes him under a long railway arch. It's a dark place with no lighting. He's been to the cash machine and is carrying money but he knows what to do. Keep walking fast. He'll outrun anyone who dares tackle him.

He scans the pavement as he walks. The ribs of the bridge create sections of greater darkness and he notices that each one has its rough sleeper, wrapped in a sleeping bag, wearing a beanie. Some are surrounded by cardboard. Some have a mat. Do they hear his footsteps? Do they hear the traffic echoing under the arch? Drugs, he thinks. Drink. Are they all ratted before they go to sleep?

He's slowing down. A train passes overhead. Its noise trampolines between the bridge and the pavement. None of the sleepers stir. At the end of the bridge, where a streetlight reaches under the arches, he sees a green sleeping bag and a man sitting up with a white polystyrene cup in front of him. Danny focuses on the cup, the way a cheap cup of coffee turns into a begging bowl.

He walks forwards, slips a couple of pound coins into the polystyrene. The man is either asleep or too proud to say thanks. It's the first time Danny has given anything to a beggar and he doesn't understand his own gesture. He walks away. The rain hits his face again and he's glad.

He doesn't go straight home. He takes a left turn instead of going right. He paces through the city while the rain washes him and he wonders what it would be like to have no home to go to. In the darkness the terraced houses seem more than ever like boxes. He lives in a box. A box and a gym. What's happened to those people to make them rough sleepers? What's happening to him? He walks to tire himself, to stop this awful introspection. He walks fast as if sheer pace will dull his sense of failure. The rain no longer seems cold. He feels he could walk like this for ever. An image of walking through the night and into the first light of a spring morning comes into his head. Could he reach the outskirts of the city, find countryside?

A drunkard calls to him. He answers but keeps moving. What he's doing is different and he's happy.

An hour later he stops suddenly, no longer recognising where he is. He looks for a main road and a sign to get his bearings, turns for home.

It's a long way back but he gets there. On the kitchen table is the lottery ticket. Before he changes he'll do what everyone else does: check the numbers. He looks at the ticket, checks his phone, double checks. There is one lucky winner of two and a half million pounds. He's that winner. He shakes his head, tells himself to check it a third time.

He does.

He is.

Why isn't he elated? Why is he suddenly terribly afraid?

10

Danny stares at the lottery ticket. His phone is in his hand. He only has to make a phone call and he can be set for life. He can move out of the terraced house into a real pad, one with its own gym. The life of the millionaire beckons. £2.5 million even in London will give him a home to be proud of, and when his mother dies and he inherits his dad's millions he can buy another house, perhaps in Spain.

Danny's still wet and now he's feeling cold. The water on his skin that was exhilarating is beginning to make him shiver. He puts the phone down. There's no hurry. He leaves the lottery ticket on the table. He strips in the kitchen, hangs his wet clothes on the dryer and runs upstairs two at a time. After towelling himself down he looks in the mirror. He has a good body. He knows that. But even he can see that it is slipping to the far edges of being young. Staying so long in wet clothes has made his skin look grey. His hair is in tangles. He remembers the young man sleeping rough under the railway arches, same grey face, same tangled hair.

Who am I? he asks himself.

But that's not the question, is it? Who do I want to be?

He's cold so he dresses quickly. He's also hungry. Sausages, chips, ketchup. That will fill him up. The lottery ticket is still on the table. He does nothing with it. Oven on. Check timing. Meanwhile the sausage packaging rubs up against the lottery ticket. The black polystyrene tray now covers a corner. Is a marked ticket still valid? Danny doesn't immediately rescue it but busies himself setting the timer. Once everything's in the oven he pours himself a beer, sits down at his kitchen table and stares at the ticket.

A single enormous question is taking root. At first it's only a feeling, a sense of immense unease. But it gradually takes shape, sorts itself into words, then phrases. He snorts as he waits for his food, sounds like Julia does when she's angry. It's as if he can't credit what's happening to him. Cashing the lottery ticket will only work if he wants to stay as he is. It's like a gelling agent. It will fix him in his present way of life. Its numbers will become the links of a chain that imprisons him in the same way that his allowance, which once seemed such an enormous freedom, has always restricted him. He sees that now.

A knife welded to his hand.

'You're a phoney. I meet phoneys all the time.'

Did this voice that came from nowhere mean himself? Is he the phoney?

He puts the beer down.

That moment is alive to him still. Knife and shout. Stepping over the comatose James, carrying his family's sense of honour. Called up to do his duty. Doing it.

The thought is clearer and it's finding a persistent form.

Back then, with the knife in his hand, he felt as if he'd been taken over by an alien being. But what if that other being was a hidden part of him, another self?

He'd felt truly alive. He'd felt as if he was worth something. Can he become this other self? Can you really change and become someone else?

He looks around him. Table, kitchen, food in the oven, everything functional, nothing personal. What once was his own delightful London pad is now a cage. If he is to make a change he has to leave all this behind.

And that includes the lottery ticket.

The timer pings. He opens the oven door. His food already smells better.

* * *

On Sunday morning Leah wakes early. The room is full of light even though it's only 5.30am. Martin is still asleep. She had to phone him yesterday. She'd hoped he'd just appear on Friday afternoon. She wanted to tell him about going to the Job Centre and to ask him about the house clearance. But he didn't show up. They'd made no arrangements and he would never just presume, damn him. He always has to be invited.

So she spent Friday evening with her mother. Izzy was lousy company and Leah found herself thinking wistfully of the crowded hotel bar in Ullapool, even of listening to music in Martin's flat.

Izzy is sinking. There's no other word for it. When Leah got back from the Job Centre she found her mother just sitting in front of a fire that had nearly gone out. No lights were on. Leah knew at once that no beds had been made while she was away.

She poked and fed the fire, took Izzy a sherry, got a meal for them both which they ate in silence in the kitchen. She tried to talk to her mother but she had run out of questions to ask. At one point Izzy rudely interrupted Leah's efforts at conversation by saying, 'I think I preferred it when you were silent.'

Where was Martin when you needed him? No doubt eating a takeaway curry and listening to his music, free and easy.

So on Saturday she'd invited him over. 'I'm so pleased you phoned,' he'd said. 'I was wondering if I could store a few things at your house. I'm running out of space here. Would you mind?'

Was that the only reason Martin was pleased she'd phoned?

He came with flowers and a bottle of wine. He tried to talk to Izzy over dinner, really persisted but eventually gave up. What a date, Leah thought. It's the first meal I've ever cooked for him. We've now done the flowers and the wine thing but no candles, no holding hands, just Mum like a great sack of unhappiness chaperoning us. Is this what life is going to be like from now on? Izzy's not yet seventy. She has years ahead of her. She has to snap out of this. She has to cope.

It was a relief when Izzy went to bed.

Leah had seen her mum up the stairs, poured Martin and herself a whisky, then banked up the fire. She ordered him to come and sit next to her and put her arm round him.

And for a while they'd sat there, snogging like teenagers.

She had to lead him. But then she's always led him. Only when she took his hand and put it on her breast did he begin to make love to her properly. She'd wanted to complete the act in front of the fire, but she realised he wasn't ready for that and she didn't know if Izzy would come downstairs because she couldn't sleep. So they'd gathered up their clothes and crept upstairs quietly, then dived into bed.

It had been nice, quick and silent and nice. She'd no complaints.

But she's woken early on Sunday morning and Martin is still asleep. Well, it is Sunday. The bookshop is closed.

She tries going back to sleep but she is wide awake so she creeps out of bed, puts her dressing gown on and goes downstairs. She can make them both a coffee and carry it back. It'll give her an excuse to wake him.

She listens to the house in the way she always has. Sunlight gleams through the stained glass, splashing colour across the floor. She thinks the house has settled again, but before going into the kitchen she gently pings the bowl and waits. A clear note rings through the house, echoing off the walls and beams. Everything is okay. The iris are content in their glass world, stretching upwards. The chair is solid, gleaming in the low sun. No one knows about pinging the bowl and listening to the house. It has always been her secret. Should she tell Martin? Are they that intimate? Will he understand?

Sex, she's always known, isn't the greatest intimacy. Its nakedness is literal and messy. She suspects that knowing someone, really knowing them, is like a geological survey, one that goes down through the layers of hidden stuff that only we know about ourselves, then moves further down to metamorphic structures before reaching the core. That is true intimacy.

She fills the kettle, switches it on. In the silence of this Sunday morning its heating up seems too loud. She strains to listen above the noise for the sound of anyone moving round upstairs, is immensely relieved when the kettle switches off and silence floods back.

It isn't yet six, she thinks, as she quietly carries the coffees back upstairs. Will he mind my waking him at this time? He can always go to sleep again afterwards.

11

It's Monday morning. Jud's nomination is secure. He is on the ballot paper. After an exhausting weekend he has the votes, but only just. He's played the need-for-a-real-challenge card and the I-don't-stand-a-chance card until he begins to believe his own falsehoods. He is acutely aware that those who have nominated him also don't believe he has a chance. They all think Stella will walk it, that he really is there only to make it into a contest.

So now is the time to shake the tree.

As he walks towards the lectern Jud Mindsett takes a long look at his audience: bankers and hedge fund managers. Their suits are a thousand pounds a piece, shirts two hundred plus. Their shoes are handmade, hand stitched. Their PAs will have told them the speech is innocuous. They are there to listen, greet each other and get their faces on television. It's a swanky event, and Jud Mindsett can be good for a laugh when he goes off script. It's years since the banking crisis. They know they have been absolved. Nothing dangerous to them will happen in the next thirty minutes.

Looking at Jud as he waits to begin is like looking at an employee. To them he is a hired man. They bought him through party donations. They swamped his regulatory boards with their own people, so the regulations never bite and no banker ever goes to jail. They also know he is a fool. Everyone knew that construction company was going bust. Their hedge funds made millions by betting on just that eventuality. But government Ministers must believe they are in charge if they are to be useful, which is why the audience is here. If you keep a tame monkey, the least you can do is pay it some attention. Jud is ready to speak. They go silent.

'I love you people,' Jud begins, then pauses and looks around him. 'Or rather, I would love you if I were a hard-left politician. Then you'd be my raison d'être.' He looks at them long enough to make them uneasy. 'And the funny thing is, if I were on the alt-right and planning a coup I'd love you people even more. I'd love you to pieces, as they say. To a left winger, if I were one, you are the unacceptable face of capitalism and your untouchability can start a revolution anytime I call it. You are hated enough to bring people out onto the streets. To a right winger who wants to make Britain a dictatorship you are the ultimate excuse. If I were a member of the alt-right I would use your shameless buying of democracy through party donations to discredit the very system that gives you all your freedoms. Luckily for you I'm a centrist. I like democracy and I want to improve it. But that means I cannot be your friend, and it also means I don't love you at all.'

No stir yet. They haven't heard him. It's Monday morning and they aren't switched on. Everyone hears what they expect to hear. Very few people listen.

'But don't worry, you do have some real friends. Putin and other mafia chiefs love you. They use you to launder their money. Every dictator loves you for much the same reason. It is only worth their while to be corrupt and rake in the cash from foreign aid if there is a safe place to hide their funds abroad. You provide that. You service the needs of rotten swine worldwide. You do this brilliantly.'

Now they are listening.

'And to your credit I have to say that you are wonderfully eclectic in what you provide. You truly believe in equality. That's why you take money from anyone who has the stuff. You launder the proceeds from illegal drugs, from poaching rhinos, from trafficking human beings, from elephant slaughter, from the sex trade. You work with the mafia and with arms dealers and you assist the already wealthy when they no longer wish to pay taxes.'

Copies of the speech he was meant to make, which were handed out against his express wishes, are searched and jettisoned. Journalists now have to wake up and start making notes. Mobile phones are switched on and held up by those who can't do shorthand. Now the bankers are nervous, shifting in their seats.

'The truth is that you have simply become ungovernable. In the past ten years we have seen numerous individual traders out of control, the fixing of Libor rates, miss-selling scandals by the score, needing to be bailed out by the taxpayer, and endless billion-dollar fines from US authorities for money laundering. Who pays those fines? Shareholders? Chief Executives? Directors? Of course not. Taxpayers pay them. Ordinary men and women who, because they bailed you out, see their pay stand still while your bonuses are scarcely dented.'

He lets that sink in. The journalists are staring. The cameras are on him. His Underling is standing white-faced at the back of the room.

'I know this is boring and that you've heard it all before, but the trouble is you still don't get it, do you? The odd trader will be sent to jail, but never one of the bosses, never one of you. Yet there is not a single person in this room who wouldn't immediately close down the account of a customer who had a fraction of such a terrible record.'

They look at each other. Do they stay or go?

Jud continues. 'Fines from the US authorities, note. Not the UK. You've argued with UK governments for years that they should cut regulations and yet, if ever a group needed regulating, it's this group of miscreants I see in front of me now.'

He looks round him. They are caught like iron filings and he is the magnet.

'So what do you do in response to all the fines? What do you do when the government meekly requests that you hold reasonable balances? Do you give back your million-pound salaries to save money? No. Do you cut bonuses to save money? Of course not. Do you wear sackcloth and ashes? Only if it's tailored in Saville Row.'

They are on the edge. Now is the time to strike. He has to get them moving soon if only because he was too lazy to write the rest of the speech. He takes the snarl out of his voice, makes himself sound more reasonable.

'To increase balances you have to make cuts. I

understand that. But where you make those cuts tells us all we need to know about you.' He slows right down and starts to point his finger. 'You all do the same thing. You act like a cartel. You each cut a number of branches in small towns. You make low-paid staff redundant. In making these cuts you, the pampered and the wealthy, turn on the ordinary man and woman in the street. You hit the taxpayer, the very person who has bailed you out. You, fat cats of the City, keep all your wealth while you make innocent, ordinary people walk or drive further to do their banking.'

He glares at them. 'I know just what you'll say in response.' Jud mimics them, turns his voice into a whine. He has to be scathing. 'You'll claim it's because of online banking and the way the business is going worldwide. You'll pontificate on the rules of the marketplace. You'll send out your PR wing to brief on difficult trading conditions.' Now he reverts to his normal voice. 'Well, morally it stinks. Ethically it's outrageous. But, from your repeated actions, I don't expect you even know what that means. When did banking have anything to do with morality?'

They are on their feet and going out. He has a last line which he has to shout above the noise of patent leather on a plush carpet. It's his soundbite and it must be endlessly on television news programmes. 'You think as a politician I am the lowest of the low. But I'm answerable to the electorate. You continue to act as if you are answerable to no one.'

Then he looks down at the lectern as if checking what he is going to say next as the cameras record the exodus.

When they've gone he turns to look for his Underling. He isn't there. He's probably run off to report to the Minister. Suddenly Jud feels particularly randy. That, he hopes, was an alpha male performance, but visiting his mistress will have to wait. If he is successful he may even have to abandon her altogether.

And the loveliest thing about the speech he's just given is that from now on the bankers and hedge fund guys will support Stella. That will go down very badly with the public.

12

It's 12 noon in North Yorkshire. PC Keith Loadstone wants to attend the post-mortem. Every cop in a television show gets to stand by the slab and prove their ability not to vomit when the knife slices through the skin, opening the body up as if it is only one of those multi-layered plastic models to be found in every secondary school biology lab.

The sight of the body has never left him. He remembers Marie washing the blood off the young man's face, the way the arms had twisted. Something isn't right about this death. There are so many unanswered questions.

Why was the man there in the first place, in that spot on a deserted moor? He wasn't dressed for walking. He had no rucksack, no guidebook, no map, and no abandoned car waiting in a layby for his return. What was he doing there?

Why was there absolutely nothing to identify him by? He had no mobile phone, no wallet, no bus ticket, no receipt, nor any of those things people thrust into their pockets and forget about. No car keys. Most damningly of all he had no money, not a scrap of loose change.

How did he fall backwards into a sinkhole? He was seemingly a fit, active man, tall enough to vault over the gap. Yet he stumbled into it backwards. How come? On moorland you always look where you are going. You watch your feet. Keith has never seen a hiker walking backwards.

Why was there a long-bladed knife at the site and several rings of blue binder twine that had clearly been cut through? If the twine had been used to bind the hands of the young man and he'd then been pushed into the hole, it would still have been round his wrists. You don't cut someone's wrists free and then push them to their death.

Finally, why has no one been reported missing?

PC Keith Loadstone has made two requests to be present at the post-mortem, one verbal and one in writing. Both have been denied.

He knocks on the Service Delivery Manager's door.

'Come in.'

SDM Angela Matthews greets him. 'Keith, what can I do for you?'

'I'd like to know why I can't attend the post-mortem.'

Angela smiles at him. 'Simple,' she tells him. 'There isn't going to be a post-mortem.'

'But it's a suspicious death. I said so in my report.'

'We don't agree.'

Keith sits down. Angela leans forward. 'I don't remember inviting you to sit.'

'I thought I'd make myself comfortable while you lecture me on resources.'

She smiles and continues.

'We examined the body. He's laid out on a slab now. Go and check. There isn't a mark on him.'

'On his wrists. I thought they might have been ...'

'Tied. I read your report. They weren't.'

Keith thinks hard about what he is about to say,

mainly because he always says it and it never does him any good. Then he says it anyway. 'I've been a cop a long time. You're an administrator. You've got to have an instinct for these things. That instinct comes from working in the field.'

He looks up. She's mouthing the words, laughing at him. He stops talking and she shakes her head.

'Keith, you're a good cop but a lousy detective. Do you want me to remind you of previous examples when you were so certain that your instinct was right?'

Keith shakes his head.

'The tractor thefts after which we raided a Selby warehouse and found sod all.'

Angela is holding up a hand of splayed fingers over which, he notices, no one has yet slipped a ring.

'The dead farmer you were sure had been murdered until we found medical records, financial hardship, a split from his daughter, and finally a misspelt suicide note in the handwriting of the deceased.'

'Alright.' Keith submits. 'No full post-mortem. But can we take DNA samples? Can I commission some posters? At least try to find out who he is? After all, once we know his name we can bury him and that saves money. How many bodies do we have on slabs at the moment?'

'That's true enough,' Angela admits. 'Hospitals talk about bed-blocking. They should see our morgue.'

She sits back in her chair and considers. Then, 'Yes to posters,' Angela says. 'If you must, yes to DNA.'

'I must.' He gets up and smiles at her. 'Do you play the lottery?'

'Of course not. Why do you want to know?'

'Law of averages. Each loss means you are nearer to winning. One day my instinct will prove true.'

'You spent too long in the Met, Keith. We do things differently in Yorkshire.'

He is about to go out when he turns. 'If I can prove this is a suspicious death, will you let me take you to that new place in Market Square for dinner?'

He thinks she'll bawl him out but she doesn't. 'Okay,' she says. 'But you can't build a life on ifs.'

He's surprised. 'I'd better start saving.'

She laughs. He goes out.

She's said he can go to the morgue. She's said he can go and see the corpse. You don't need a scalpel to do a post-mortem. He wonders what Angela looks like out of uniform.

The morgue isn't locked. It's very cold and dark. He finds a switch and lights come on. He should have brought his coat and hat and gloves. Forensics wear thermals to come in here. He should have done the same. He's never been in before. It's like a cold changing room. On one side is a wall of lockers. Each has a name. He scans the labels, comes across one called Black Rigg Beck. That'll be him. He pulls at the handle and the whole length of the container shudders. When he has the body halfway out he realises something's wrong. He shoves the handle upwards to take the weight, feels for the undercarriage and unlocks it. Now the rest of the container slides out easily and settles on its frame.

His hands are already cold. There's no way that on his own he can tip the body onto the slab. He'll have to examine him here, reaching down into the box. He pulls back the covering. When he last saw the corpse it was clothed and muddy. Now the man lies on his back, cleansed and naked and grey. His penis is tied up; presumably even chilled bodies leak.

Keith looks at the man's face. It's no longer close-shaven and he remembers learning somewhere that the hair and the nails continue to grow for a short time after death.

'Who are you?' He says the words out loud because he's unsettled by being where he is. The face is handsome. Marie noticed that. It's somehow okay to see the body of someone who has lived their natural span but this man is in his prime. Not very muscular, Keith notices. He didn't work out. He didn't play sport. Reasonably built though, and trim. He must have been active. Keith reaches down the side of the container and lifts out one of the hands. The fact he can lift it up without any reaction from the face disturbs him. He looks at the fingers first. Not a manual labourer. Not a scar, not a nick nor a cut. These hands are smooth. Keith looks at his own. If you cook you cut yourself. If you garden you get scratched. It's as if these hands haven't lived.

Nor are they the hands of a refugee. Pampered is the word that comes to Keith's mind. The corpse has had it easy.

Now he lets himself look at the wrists. Perhaps his colleagues missed the tie marks but he'll see them because he's looking for them.

He lifts one hand. The light isn't good, so as well as staring at the wrist he runs his fingertips along the skin. Nothing. The other wrist's the same. He wasn't tied up.

Keith's brought a bit of the cut blue twine with him. He slips a ring of it round the wrist. It doesn't fit. It's not big enough. If someone at the scene was tied up it wasn't him, yet he is the one who died.

He puts the hands back, examines the rest of the body. He can't find anything that will convince Angela. He's really cold now. His sense of touch is going. There's nothing else he can do. He covers the body over, takes a last look at the face. Self-satisfied, he thinks, smug.

As he pushes the container part-way back before unclipping the runners and folding them up, he says out loud and loudly, 'Yes, if I were them I'd just bury you and have done. Only I know there's a story. I know you died in suspicious circumstances and I'll prove it.'

He walks away, back to the door.

There are two switches. Both are on. Did he turn them both on when he came in? He can't remember, but he's in a hurry to warm up so he flicks them both off. The lights go out.

Outside in the April light Keith rubs his hands together to warm them. Posters, he thinks, then I need to arrange for a sample of his DNA.

Keith Loadstone is about to leave the police station when the alarm sounds. He stands rooted to the spot, not knowing the procedure. Others come out of the building. Soon the whole building empties like a rabbit warren when you put the ferret down. There are so many of them they stand together chatting, enjoying the sunshine. Keith can see Angela but she doesn't come over.

After five minutes the alarm stops. The caretaker comes out and the crowd goes silent, wanting to know.

'Some stupid sod switched the freezers off in the morgue. Thank God the alarm worked.'

PC Keith Loadstone heads for his car.

13

Jud won't use Wendy, his constituency agent, at this stage. Her job is to manage the chlamydia, to watch his back up north. Anyway, once he invited her to London she'd never leave. Joseph is an obvious choice. Joseph has already talked to his uncle and helped Jud to be nominated. But that's him done. He won't be reliable even in the medium term. He's only on board because he thinks it's for the good of the party. Jud needs his own team round him, people he can give orders to. People he can rely on. Who?

First, he needs an MP, someone who has it in for Stella and is out for vengeance. This person doesn't need to be good in front of the camera, that's Mindsett's job. He needs a sneak, a teller of tales, a behind-the-scenes worker to go round the tea room and the bar. The men who fit the bill all have obvious problems. They are alcoholics or loners. None of them will do. That's a pity as he prefers to rely on men, but he'll need a woman. It might be better anyway. If you really do fight fire with fire, then you need to fight a woman like Stella with a bitch like … Jud's fingers slide down the list. Most women in his party won't give him the time of day. Then he finds her: Annabelle Pitts-Tucker. Annabelle with her taste for £900 handbags and matching leather trousers. Bisexual they say, which might also be an advantage. Stella slapped her down for her extravagance in an age of austerity, and Annabelle responded by turning up the next day in the

House in a pair of £1000 leather trousers. She deliberately came in late and made a great fuss about finding her seat so everyone noticed. At that time Stella wasn't able to sack her because of the Prime Minister. Now the Prime Minister has gone and Annabelle will be feeling vulnerable, may well be willing to take a risk. She's over-confident, ignorant and untrustworthy. He'll offer to make her Foreign Secretary.

Next Jud needs a political mercenary, an outsider, a hard-bitten political pro with an enormous ego and absolutely no convictions. He needs someone who understands polling, dog whistling and briefing, someone who already has journalist friends. He needs a man with his finger on the pulse. But for that he'll have to pay an enormous sum of money which he doesn't have. Nearer the time maybe, but the odds are still enormously stacked against him. Is there someone with a track record meanwhile who might do it on a no win no fee basis?

Jud doubts it.

If not for money, then for influence. Chief of Staff to the new Prime Minister. If Jud flings that offer into the water, who might bite?

Someone clever. A lad he met at university comes to mind, someone he sparred with. Tall with long hair like his own and a formidable brain when he bothered to use it. Probably not doing much right now. Came from a rich family so didn't have to work, and with enough arrogance to think he could run 10 Downing Street even though he has absolutely no experience of politics. Would he be interested? Might he agree to hold the fort meanwhile? A search on Linkedin gives him the contact: James Goulden, Advisor. That's what he needs, advice. He invites him to a meeting tomorrow. Then he phones Annabelle. He has the 24 hour news on silent. His speech and the walkout are still up there. His candidacy is known. Journalists are bound to ask Stella what she thinks. Then he'll turn the sound up.

* * *

Leah's given Martin the room that her dad died in to store his stuff. It was empty. It's on the ground floor. He's promised not to use it for long, just until he can make room at the shop. He's told Leah about Vikki, described her sadness and the way she confided in him, told her about the row and the letters. He left out any suspicion that Vikki might have fancied him.

Leah asked questions, demanded a description of the house and the girl. She'd offered to help him carry the boxes in from the van but he'd told her that most were too heavy, handed her only the two lighter boxes. By now he's already done a preliminary sort and separated out quite a pile of 'more valuable' books. These are out of their boxes and stacked against the wall. The two shiny cardboard boxes are on a low shelf.

Izzy is doing some gardening so Leah has time to herself. She knows she should go back to the Job Centre and look for work, but she can do that when she turns up for the first GCSE English lesson, whenever that is. Martin suggested enrolling on an

Open University course, made it sound attractive, but that can wait.

She's in a good mood. It was nice spending Sunday with Martin, without urgency, without battles to fight. They made love twice and kept a conversation going in between. He didn't quote a single book to her and she managed not to always talk about Izzy. It was okay, really okay.

Outside, April is behaving itself. Leah can hear a blackbird singing. Izzy doesn't need her. She could go for a walk, but instead she steps into the room she's lent to Martin and approaches the two light boxes. She reaches into one and takes out a bundle of letters.

A spark, a small frisson tingles her fingers just for a moment as she picks up the package. A chemical perhaps, a piece of dirt? She ignores the reaction and starts to read. It's a love letter. It seems to be from her to him. Leah looks for a name but the girl who wrote this simply signs herself S.

> *Dearest Howard,*
> *Your letter was on the mat when I got home. I didn't even close the door before picking it up and opening it. I stood there in the doorway and read it slowly, lost in your words. Outside the world walked past and no doubt stared at me. I was so absorbed that an opportunist burglar could probably have squeezed past me and I'd have taken no notice.*

Dearest. Many are called dear in letters but there is

only one dearest. This was written before emails, before the internet, when letters mattered. She remembers the words Izzy sang:

> *It's going to be a long lonely summer,*
> *But darling I promise you this.*
> *I'll send you all my loving*
> *Every day in a letter,*
> *Sealed with a kiss*

Every day. No texts, and handwritten too. Jane Austen's heroines were always strung out waiting for their letters. She reads more.

> *There is, I have to say, a deliciousness in being apart from you, exceeded only by the deliciousness of us being together. Before you I would have walked home, changed, got my meal, seen if there was anything on tele for later and then settled at my desk to read and think. The phone rarely rang; now I know it might, and it might be you. Working, eating, walking home, even breathing have a different significance because of you.*

Overwritten, or is that what real love feels like? Leah has so little experience, has lived such a sheltered life. She moves onto the next letter.

> *Dearest,*
> *I do love you. I know that for a long while I*

felt it but didn't say it. A certain reluctance to trust in the feeling I had for you held me back. I'm not good at putting my feelings into words. I have to learn that from you, and I am learning. So let me say again, I do love you. DH Lawrence said the word was overused and should be banned for a time until it had won back its real meaning and force. But that's so unnecessary with me. I have never used the word to another man and certainly not to any boy when I was younger. So take heart. My use of the word is new minted, unsullied, undiminished by over use. You are clearly more open, more expressive than I am. Your letters show me that in every sentence. You gush. I make carefully crafted statements, but they mean what they say.

Leah is intrigued. She would like to read Howard's letter to S, the letter that prompted this reply, but there are only her letters to him. She senses a girl playing catchup, trying to placate a lover who wants more commitment, more gush, deeper expressions of love. Howard is the more loving one. Are all couples like that, unequal in the commitment they make, unequal in love? Does Martin love me more or less than I love him … if I do love him? She carefully folds the last letter and opens the next.

The beams settle. The house holds its breath.

14

My dearest,

All the time I was at University I thought I would find nobody to love me. I watched my fellow students pairing off and thought, that is for them. Another kind of life awaits me. I think I cried once or twice. I know occasionally I bit my lip to hide tears.

Not now. Not now.

Finding you has been a revelation, an unexpected treat, almost a dream. One moment there I was, thinking that love was overrated, was mostly about sex,. Then the next moment you were part of my life. It was like going from black and white to colour, from a silent world to one full of music.

All the time I was writing my dissertation I would wonder if the research base was sound, if I was certain about my conclusions. I got a first for it, but even then I still didn't know if I was right in the way that I know I am right about you.

I know. And I know you reciprocate.

I love you. There, I've written it. You have it as a statement for all time.

I can't wait to see you again.

Lots of love

S

To tell someone you cried. To tell someone you felt lonely. It's the intimacy of the letter that strikes Leah. It's the way the writer fights to communicate her thoughts. Leah folds that letter and opens the next.

> *Dearest,*
> *Your letter made me gasp. Thank heavens there was no one else in the room when I read it. All that love crammed onto one page. Am I your soulmate? I think that means we are joined together like Siamese twins. I do love you back. I want you to understand that. I love you more than I have loved anyone else and I miss you when we are apart.*

There's a but coming. Leah can sense a struggle to catch up, a lack of ease.

> *But, and is this terribly wrong of me, I do like aspects of my life apart from you.*
> *Yesterday I interviewed a homeless single mother. Her parents threw her out when she got pregnant. The father of her child had already begun to hit her. She was resigned to her half-life etc. Normal, you may say, not about us, you may say. But should it be normal that some people have to live such shitty lives?*
> *It was when she talked to me about the dreams she'd had about her life that I felt*

the pull. There has to be a better way of helping women like her. We may have a female Prime Minister but women still get a raw deal.

I want to do something, not just be something. Can you live with that?

Howard is lost in his love for S. It fills his life. She doesn't feel like that. She wants a compromise. Can he do that? Leah turns over the page.

Can you live with that? I'm not drawn towards life in a kingdom of two.

Meanwhile I long to be in bed with you. These moments apart make that all the sweeter.

Got to go to my meeting.

All my love, S

The blackbird is singing again. The April sun climbs higher and so slides lower down the wall towards where Leah is sitting. All you need is love, but is love the answer to life's questions? For Howard it seems to be. Not for S. *All my love* is a throwaway, Leah thinks. I've never given all my love to anyone, and certainly not to Martin. We all need leftover love for spring days and landscape, for family and a thousand other things.

A sadness is creeping over Leah. She senses this is not a story with a happy ending. She puts the letters down and picks up a journal. It's in another handwriting, more masculine. She looks inside the cover and sees the name Howard. Will this tell her the

Tuesday 24th
You have fixed my life. Until I met you I was consciousness of an emptiness, something lacking from even the most superb views on the most miraculous days. I've stood by the sea and watched the sun sink into the waves, caught the moment it fires the whole surface of the sea. Then I've turned in the gloom to go back and watched a barn owl hunting along the cliffs like a large white moth. A perfect evening you might think, but no. The more beautiful the landscape and the moment, the more I became conscious that this wasn't enough for me. It's not just that I wanted to turn and share it with someone. It was as if I wasn't right. As if I was a tiny blot on the landscape I was admiring. I realised, even before I met you, that I needed to find a way to fix me. And you have done that.

It's not just that you are more beautiful than a sunset or a hunting owl, although you are. It's not even the pull of sex. Did I tell you that a wonderful landscape sometimes gives me an erection? It's not even the simple miracle of your nakedness (which always has that same effect). It's the seeing myself in your eyes. Because I know you love me I can love myself. Because I know you, I at last feel a part of all the beauty in the world.

Leah gasps as she reads, realises she is acting exactly as S had in response to Howard's letter. Leah shakes her head to get rid of the thought. She warms to Howard. He is so like her, so alive to the natural world in the same way she is. Leah thinks of the house she lives in, the iris vase, the windows, the way the oak stairs turn as they move upwards. This is a man writing as she might about the way the beauty of the world hits her right between the eyes. But his sense of love … she's never felt anything like that.

> *When you touch me. When you smile at me. Even when you reach out your hand to hold mine as we walk down the street, it's more than a touch or a smile or hand hold. What you give me is a sense of completeness …*

Leah tears herself away from the page. If this is what real love is, then what she feels for Martin is only a shadow of it and he's not the man for her. To feel complete. To be someone's soul-mate. To feel a fully functioning part of the world. She's never felt she belonged and still doesn't. She has a voice but does she have a sense of herself to go with it?

Perhaps Martin keeps a journal, perhaps he thinks about her in the same way Howard thinks about S. He is her first. How does she know that he's right for her when she doesn't even know who she is any more?

To be fixed. To feel so certain.

Her parents hadn't really loved each other, had they? She remembers the way Izzy cremated her husband and immediately reached out to find the son she'd never told her husband about. Julia didn't stay married. James and Roz are together but she can't imagine that Roz will stay with him.

> I imagine you standing beside me on the cliff top. When the ball of a sun sinks and fires the waves red and orange there will be no need to talk. We'll know what each other thinks. It will be as if we are one person. A touch of the fingers will be enough just to seal the bond between us.

Leah finds she's crying. Her tears are threatening to drip onto the journal. An overwhelming sadness is sinking her. She feels for Howard when S rejects him as she thinks S will. But more that that, Leah knows she is crying for herself, for what she doesn't have, for what her relationship with Martin lacks. She closes the journal and puts it back in the box. She walks away, out of the room and out of the house. She stands in the driveway, listens to the blackbird singing, and feels partial, unformed and alone.

15

James doesn't tell Roz about the meeting with Mindsett. It seems to him so unlikely that anything will come of it that there's no need to upset her ... yet. Because she will be upset. Jud is everything Roz despises. She shouts at the news when he makes an appearance. There's something visceral about her dislike of him that James doesn't understand.

In spite of all this James makes his way towards the address he's been sent. He remembers Jud from ten years ago, had him down as a prat, but now he's turned into a contender. It might lead to something. What's the harm?

He rings the bell and Jud himself answers the door. 'James,' he says. 'What's with the curls?'

'Jud. Still the same haircut. Only much thinner on top.'

They look at each other like wrestlers, working out where to grab hold, where they might gain an advantage. Then, awkwardly, they shake hands.

'Come and meet Annabelle.'

'Annabelle?'

'Annabelle Pitts-Tucker.'

Jud has turned to go back into the house. James looks round. There are no cameras or reporters. Is it too early, or is Jud so far out of contention that no one has bothered? James follows Jud. Perhaps the meeting is serious. Is Jud going to make him an offer?

Annabelle in the flesh is more impressive than

Annabelle on television. Television shrinks her. She's hefty in build and six feet in her heels but she hurtles out of the settee to greet him. James finds he is looking up into a pair of grey eyes which have enough of a twinkle to attract him.

'Jud says you're clever. I eat clever men,' she tells him.

She sits down and tucks her legs neatly and knowingly underneath her.

Jud waves James to the other chair, urges him to help himself to coffee. 'So what chance do I have, young James?'

'None whatsoever.'

He hears Annabelle laugh. 'That's what I told him.' Her voice is smoky, slightly masculine in tone.

Jud grins. 'Why not?'

'Stella is the one political saint we have right now. She's her own woman, beholden to nobody. She's got every call right for the last twenty years.' James lists them on his fingers. 'She voted against the Iraq war. She called for more bank regulation before the crash. She fought against the UK tax havens, spoke against knighthoods for donors and crooks. She used her position on the Public Accounts Committee to highlight the danger of the richest 1% to the social stability of this country. She consistently voiced the dangers of a minimum wage economy. There has never been a whiff of scandal round her. She hasn't employed members of her family as her assistants. She only claimed the parliamentary allowances she was entitled to. She has never worked for a lobby group. She seems to be married to her job. You haven't a chance, Jud.

She'll beat you.'

Annabelle claps loudly. 'Which means for once in your life you've actually told the truth, Jud. You are on the ballot only to give her a contest and a mandate.'

'Weaknesses, James. What are her weaknesses?' Jud asks.

'She doesn't have any,' Annabelle chips in. 'She has the biggest constituency majority in the country. She's loved and she's trusted. I happen to dislike her intensely but that's because I'm a bitch.'

James smiles. He finds that Jud is unfazed but is looking at him. He clears his throat. 'You do have two advantages over her ...'

Jud nods. Will James confirm his own suspicions? Annabelle looks doubtful.

'She's never sought power. She's not a street fighter. She lives in a moral world and follows its moral rules. If you were to play dirty I just don't know what she'd do. I'm not sure she could cope.'

Jud is staring at him. 'And the other weakness?'

'She's been around a long time. Even though she's fought against the establishment from inside, if you can paint her as one of them that might gain you some traction.'

'Balls,' shouts Annabelle. 'It's a party membership vote, not a general election. It'll be decided by card-carrying loyalists. You don't stand a chance.'

'So you need to change the rules,' James tells them.

'Re-write the party constitution? If only we could.'

James is unfazed. 'If I were you I'd ignore MPs, stand well clear of all that lobbying and appeal over their heads to the country.'

Annabelle spells it out to him. 'John, or whatever your name was, didn't you hear what I said? The public doesn't have a vote in this contest.'

'It's James actually.' He smiles back at her, then continues. 'But if you could set up some public polling, and that public polling showed that Stella isn't as popular as the members think, they might just pause before they vote.'

There's silence.

'Oh, and she has a third weakness. She's the front runner. Any dint in that glossy position might set a panic going. You could exploit that.'

Jud slowly claps. Annabelle is silent, then throws in another idea. 'She's also a truly good person who speaks her mind and in my experience people don't like someone who is truly good. They find them uncomfortable to live with.'

'So shall we give it a go?'

'I've nothing to lose,' Annabelle says. 'Count me in.'

'James?'

'What are you offering me?'

'Political Advisor. Daily rate until the ballot, then Chief of Staff.'

James grins. 'How long do I have to decide?'

Jud hands him a card. 'By 10 tonight.'

James gets up to go. Annabelle follows him out, pinches his bottom. 'Good performance in there. I eat clever fellows,' she reminds him.

* * *

When James gets back to the flat Roz is cooking pasta.

She gives him a quick look and frowns. 'Where have you been?' she asks.

'Talking to an old university friend. He's offered me a job.'

'Great,' Roz says, then peers at him. 'So why are you looking shifty?'

Break it gently or tell her at once? 'I shouldn't really call him a friend. We were sparring partners rather than friends.'

Roz moves the pan of pasta away from the heat. 'Anyone I've heard of?' she asks.

'Jud Mindsett.'

Roz goes very still.

'Look, it's a real chance. We can live better, have influence, be something.'

'But Jud Mindsett is an incompetent shit, with a foul mind and creepy, wandering hands.'

'You've met him?'

She nods.

'Have you accepted this job?' she asks.

James shakes his head.

Roz breathes out sharply.

'I met him at someone's party. He made himself agreeable and I was flattered. Then I made the mistake of leaving the room. I needed to go to the loo. Jud followed me out and grabbed my hand. Then he pressed me up against the wall and started to grope me.'

James is horrified. 'What did you do?'

'I was wearing heels. I stamped my right heel into the soft part of his left foot.'

She pauses. 'James, you are a free agent. We've made

no promises to each other. You can take any job you like. Is this really the way you want to spend the only life you have?'

'Chief of Staff,' James tells her. 'He says he'll make me his Chief of Staff.'

She goes quite still.

There's a long silence.

'Choose,' she says quietly.

He sits down at the kitchen table and she sits opposite him. 'Politics is different,' he tells her. 'Sometimes shits make good leaders. Think John F Kennedy and Lloyd George. Neither of them could keep his trousers on, but Lloyd George kept his word and gave women the vote. John F Kennedy sent men to the moon and started the road to civil rights. Nixon was a crook, but he ended the Vietnam War and made peace with China. On the other hand, Jimmy Carter was a thoroughly decent man and a hopeless one-term president.'

He looks across the table at Roz.

'There's a big difference between being randy and being a sexual predator,' she says.

'I know. You think Jud's like Patrick.'

'Yes.' She tries to keep her voice level but it's laden with sadness.

'James, are you sure you haven't already said yes? I mean, I know where I stand in this relationship. You don't have to ask me.'

'I haven't said yes,' he tells her. 'I said I needed time.'

'But you are tempted?'

The pull of power. His brains and a chance to be someone. Get Jud elected and then make him rule well.

James knows he'll never have another life-chance like this. And even if he fails, he's launched. Because the odds against them are so high it's not a reputational risk. Patrick was one cause. This might be another.

'Yes, I'm tempted,' he tells her.

A rueful smile twitches for a moment on Roz's face, then vanishes. She gets her coat, wraps her scarf slowly round her neck and looks at him for a long time. Without saying goodbye she leaves the flat, quietly closing the door behind her.

The pasta is excellent. There was plenty for both of them. James eats it all.

16

'Good day?' Martin asks when he comes in from work. Should he kiss Leah? Are they now an established couple? Something in her demeanour makes him hesitate.

'Better,' Leah tells him. 'Izzy went out for a drive.'

Leah's sitting in the lounge staring into the fire.

'Where did she drive to?'

'I don't know. Afterwards she went up to her room, hasn't come down yet.'

'So you've had time to yourself, that's good.'

But it doesn't seem that way. She only looked at him briefly when he first came in and she hasn't turned round since.

'It's been a glorious day,' he says. 'Did you get outside, go for a walk?'

Leah's thinking of the journal and the letters, of what love would be like if you felt it properly. She imagines Howard meeting up with S. Surely not like this. Would Howard confine himself to asking if she's had a good day and talking about the weather? Being together again should feel like an ache of separation ending, shouldn't it? She remembers S's phrase *the deliciousness of us being together*. She sighs.

Martin stands there and she knows he's uncertain again, dithering about whether to stay or go. She's caused this reaction and now she resents it. She knows that's ludicrous. She must make herself snap out of it, make a clean break or at least welcome him home.

She gets up.

'What's wrong?' he asks.

'I read the letters you brought home from the house clearance.'

'She told me to burn them.'

'Who did?'

'Vikki. The girl who sold me the stuff. She said her dad had caught her rummaging in those boxes and they'd ended up not speaking to each other.'

'Had she read them?'

'I don't think so. I think he frightened her. She gave them to me as an afterthought. She wanted rid.'

'They're unsettling and so sad.'

He sits down beside her. He wants to comfort her but doesn't know how. Even though they are lovers again he knows he shouldn't put his hand on her knee because it's too intimate for now. But to put a hand on her shoulder could be patronising, so instead he reaches for her hand and holds it.

She squeezes his hand back, then suddenly lurches her head into his shoulder. She's crying now, and it's like when they crashed into the deer. It's heartbroken crying, quite uncontrolled. He reaches down and kisses the top of her head lightly.

'Tell me about the letters,' he suggests.

'No, I need to get tea. Why don't you read them? Then you'll understand.'

She kisses him once and walks away.

Martin does as he's told and collects the two boxes. He does this reluctantly. They were something to do with Vikki's uncle and he committed suicide. Martin is reaching the age where it's an effort to read something that you know will make you unhappy. The boxes had seemed alive when he picked them up, and they have already proved their power by drawing Leah to them in the way a magnet pulls at bits of metal.

Martin remembers Vikki, how nervous she had been of the letters, not wanting to touch them. He remembers her attractiveness and the way she touched the back of his hand.

Vikki's dad must have read the letters because he'd told her, *Knowledge is dangerous. Once you know something it's impossible to forget.* He remembers the sadness in the house, how Vikki had said it gave her the creeps. He brought the boxes here and now Leah is infected with the same sadness. He thinks of the trunk of plague clothes brought to Eyam.

He picks up the letters first and reads them in sequence. They tell the story of a woman who falls in love and then wants a life as well as the loving, finds she needs to extricate herself. He senses in them that necessity of giving pain to someone she loves. One letter in particular shouts at him.

> *Dear Howard,*
> *I told you when we met what I was thinking. Isn't that all we can do in situations like ours: be honest with each other? We want different things from life. You only seem to want me and me and me. You never write about living, only about loving. I want to make a difference. I want to travel. I want power. Yes, I might as well admit it, I want the power to change lives. I feel pulled*

towards politics.

Perhaps all this is my fault. I fell for you in the way you fell for me. I encouraged you as much as you encouraged me. I should not have done so. I'm sorry. I know I must be causing you pain, but I simply don't love you in the way you love me. There, at last I've written it. I'm not the person you think I am. I am more selfish than you. I have tried to let you down gently and you have responded, as I feared you would, with an outpouring of even more love for me. You must stop this. You are stifling me and I won't be stifled. We had a great time. Please don't spoil that.

Everything inside me now tells me that we are not meant to be together. You need someone who shares your idea of love and I need another life altogether, but I gave you my word and I will stick to that.

S

It's the last letter in that bundle. He looks in the box. There are no more.

Martin sits and tries to collect his thoughts. He finds he's sympathetic to S and wonders what that says about him. He fears that Leah will think the opposite. And yes, he finds a sense of sadness creeping over him. Why do we always want love to work out, he asks himself. Meeting and dumping. It's a strange, unnatural selection process at best. At least for Howard and S the process was linear. They met, went out, slept together, wrote letters, then fell in the final furlong before the wedding. Their relationship was conventional. His with Leah is anything but. It began with seduction, with silent fucking. They were each other's wordless release. Then she fled her home to stay in his flat, talked, plotted, shared an adventure, and in all that time he never asked her on a date or leant forward for that first kiss. Now they are some sort of established couple, all without ever talking to each other as Howard and S had. Sex is not the most intimate encounter. Martin thinks he already knew that. The big question he asks himself is what does Leah want from him? Is there always a more and a less loving one in each relationship? In Scotland he thought he was the more loving one. Now he's not so sure. He understands S's wish for a life apart. Does he recognise S as a kindred spirit?

He picks up Howard's journal from the second box and reads. It's like diving into treacle. He comes to the passage, *Because I know you love me I can love myself. Because I know you, I at last feel a part of all the beauty in the world.* And he wants to shout, Whoa, hang on. Life just isn't like that. Now he thinks he understands Leah's crying. It's like a child crying when they first realise the limits of human life, that we will all die. *Margaretta are you grieving over golden groves unleaving?* Did Leah think, when she was an outsider, if only I could belong in this world all my problems will be solved? Was she crying because life wasn't like Howard imagined it to be or was she crying because her life wasn't like that?

What horrifies him is the way Howard has loaded

the burden onto S. He reads on, meets the awful whirlpool Howard experiences as he veers between despair and hope.

> *Perhaps this is only a phase. Perhaps as we get nearer to our union you're having doubts. Is that why I am on this earth, to bring you to love, to teach you that nothing else matters? Whatever I do, I must not give up. I daren't allow that possibility. I'm sure you love me or, if not, everything is lost.*

Martin closes the journal. What was it John Stuart Mill said mattered above all in his great definition of happiness? ... *not to ask more of life than life is capable of bestowing.*

He hears Leah calling. He puts the journal back in the box, wishes he'd never brought the two boxes to the house. What should he do with them now?

Leah looks at him intensely as he walks into the kitchen, but Izzy follows him in and there is no time for anything to be said between them.

'I went to the sinkhole,' Izzy tells them before Leah has time to serve up. 'There's a poster of my son's face in Pickering asking if anyone has any information about who he is. It shocked me. I jumped a red light. How come they have a picture of him if he's still buried in that sinkhole?'

17

All day Danny has wrestled with an idea. Why doesn't he walk out of his old life and vanish with the lottery ticket? That way he can fund a new lifestyle, live wherever he wants and be a different person. The idea is immensely appealing. He can change his name, buy a new passport, purchase a degree, even a doctorate, live in a warm climate or amongst mountains. All he needs to do is claim the money and open a new bank account in another name. Then he can lock his old house, drop the keys through the letterbox and Danny Goulden can disappear for ever. What will his new name be?

As an abstract idea it's wonderful, but whenever he adds detail he knows it won't work. Yes, he can disappear and be someone else, but will he like that person any more than he likes his present self? He pushes the question out into his next gym session when he's on the rowing machine and the answer comes back with each stroke: only if he makes something of himself. These were Dad's continual words to Leah, words she finally acted on and pushed him, Danny, down the family pecking order.

Habit makes him continue with the rowing but his focus has gone. He finds himself saying over and over in his head, to the rhythm of each pulled stroke, the money is the problem, the money is the problem.

He stops before he reaches his target and just sits there, the oars still in his hands. The lottery winnings will only be another form of allowance, and it's the allowance that has meant he has nothing to show for the life he has lived. That generous allowance has guaranteed his indolence. The only pride he has in his life is for his body, and that comes from work, from working harder in the gym than anyone else. If he is to leave his old self behind he needs to abandon the money, both his allowance and his winnings. He needs to start again, build a new life for himself, become a new person. He remembers the rough sleepers under the bridge. They have left home and their old selves. They've made the clean break that he craves. If he's ever going to get away from being Danny Goulden he needs to do it now, before the lottery money traps him for ever. He has to be decisive, leave the lottery ticket on the table and give himself no way back.

For the first time ever he cuts a gym session short.

* * *

Ivor is back in London. The news worries him. If Mindsett is a candidate for Prime Minister, what chance has he, Ivor, of coming face to face with him and blackmailing him into granting citizenship? Mindsett won't hold surgeries anymore. The kompromat Ivor holds on Mindsett will only work if they can sit down together. Ivor can then show him the compromising photographs and they can arrange the deal. The photographs will be handed over one at a time as Ivor's citizenship passes each stage, and the final photo will be retained until he is sworn in as a British citizen.

Because Ivor is restless he walks the streets of London, wonders why the English erect so many statues and monuments to men of war. He crosses Trafalgar Square and glances up at Nelson, shakes his head. Only the English could admire a leader who took such stupid risks that he got himself shot at the moment of victory. What was he doing on the quarterdeck in full uniform? No Russian general would have got so close to the action. Stalin never went near the front, knew he shouldn't put himself in danger. The English are such a warlike people if you judge them by their statues. Ivor passes generals standing and generals on horseback. Each is mounted on a plinth, so you have to crick your neck to examine them. Their pose is the same: ramrod straight backs and eyes gazing out to where their men are screaming and dying, Ivor thinks. What chance does a country have of being civilised when its churches are full of representations of extreme torture and its squares are packed full of generals who never flinched as they watched men die?

The papers and photographs are in his pocket. He carries them with him at all times. In London, public figures still walk the streets. This doesn't happen in Moscow, where police stop the traffic to let their new mafia czars, weary from a long day's money laundering, speed home in smart saloons. In London he might come face to face with the man he stalks.

Ivor heads towards Westminster. He wants to check which protesters are there. It reassures him that the country he has chosen to join allows crazy protests right outside its government buildings. He calls this proof of being civilised. He likes it when the country votes for one thing and everyone who lost the vote immediately starts to protest.

He goes into Westminster Abbey, slips in without paying and makes his way to Poets' Corner. It always amuses him that England has corralled its poets into one tiny space, has kettled them so they can do no further harm. Why be terrified of poets, Ivor thinks. Russia celebrates its writers in public spaces, but then ignores them as if all they ever wrote was fantasy fiction.

He waits on College Green for a while. Today it is empty of camera crews and he knows politicians only come here when there is a camera they can talk to. Ivor gives up, heads back to his digs.

* * *

Danny walks towards his fellow rough sleepers. Most of them look at him suspiciously. Is his sleeping bag too new? Should he have swapped his gym holdall for a Tesco long-life bag? He hasn't a beard. They seem to know each other and he knows no one. Now he's one of them he sees details that he missed before. A pack of syringes, several cans of extra strong, nicotine on the fingers.

'Anaesthetic,' one of them says when he sees Danny looking at him swigging. 'Helps us sleep.'

It isn't as cold as he thought it would be even though the sky is clear. The metal bridge has retained some heat from the day, although you need to lie down square to it to gain the full benefit. He's right on one end. Perhaps it's warmer in the middle.

He sits upright, feet in his bag, trainers still on his feet.

'Better not,' one of them whispers to him as he begins to take his trainers off. 'We often get moved on. It's a fag.'

With his beanie on and his hands thrust into his sleeping bag Danny feels surprisingly warm.

And free. Everything he owns is in his holdall. That's all he has to worry about. He feels reduced to essentials. He needs water and food. That's it, and those are tomorrow's problems. For now he feels full, and he no longer worries about the leak in the roof, the rates bill, the rent increase, the best time to go to the gym, or whether he has put on half a pound. All those concerns have vanished. He's always liked being outside. Summer's coming and he's doing something none of his family has ever done. Maybe he'll walk miles when the weather gets better, live off the land, really get to know England.

'First time?' asks the lad in the next bag.

'Is it that obvious?'

'We can always tell.'

A car goes past.

'Hey, don't I know you?' the face says. 'You walked past the other night. Gave me two quid.'

Danny's seen him in the car headlight.

'My name's …' He nearly says Danny, but it isn't anymore. The point about going missing is not to be found. '… Patrick,' he says. It's the first name that comes into his head.

'Shaun,' the other guy says.

They don't shake hands because that would invite the cold in.

'Tuck the sleeping bag right over your head when you're ready to sleep. You don't have to keep watch,' Shaun whispers.

'Keep watch?'

'Drunks, yobs from the pub, bored teenagers. They won't attack us tonight. There's too many of us here.'

'Right.' Even if he doesn't watch he'll listen carefully. He doesn't expect to sleep much.

He's relieved when Shaun stops talking. He doesn't want to answer questions about himself. He's come here to be anonymous. He's come to disappear.

The others sleep. He keeps watch through the long night. People and cars pass him in waves as cinemas, pubs and nightclubs close down. At 2.30 am the place finally goes still after the last revellers have made their way home. He lies down then and tries to get some sleep but even that doesn't matter. He has nothing to do tomorrow but sleep. The newness of his situation is fascinating. Being here makes him feel alive.

He must have dozed, but at 4am the world starts up again and wakes him. Almost empty buses pass him by. He knows about jobs with early starts where you finish your day by lunchtime. Baking is one. Presumably night watchmen end shifts in the early hours and someone else takes over. He finds he is intrigued. This is a part of London he's never seen. By 5.30am the streets are coming to life but his fellow rough sleepers sleep on. Presumably there's no point waking until cafés and corner shops open.

The sun slides over the waste ground, lights up the

sleeping bags and gilds their ugliness. Someone hands him a half-finished cup of coffee. He says thanks and drinks it.

Someone else's mouth, someone else's saliva. It tastes good. It's a rite of passage.

* * *

The posters have been up for a week. They've featured on Look North and there's been no response. No one has come forward to identify Keith Loadstone's immigrant, as the corpse is affectionately known. Keith's been the butt of jokes about switching off the freezers. *Some cops hide the evidence, Loadstone melts it. Want advice on saving energy, see Loadstone.*

He's from the Met and so he's fair game in the eyes of his North Yorkshire colleagues. He's still the outsider like the corpse. Is that why he's let this case get right under his skin?

Because it has. It niggles him. Everyone else thinks the body is an unregistered immigrant, an illegal who fell into the sinkhole. Angela Matthews has made it absolutely clear that she doesn't have the resources to take it further. She hands him a list of the unidentified bodies lying on slabs in North Yorkshire. There are over thirty. 'Cuts,' she tells him. 'In light of the cuts, what the hell do you expect me to do?'

Then she looks at him kindly. 'I'll give you a day to find me some more evidence or the case is off and your bet is off too.'

He's pleased she remembered, so he smiles at her.

He goes back to the moor but even in a few weeks

everything's changed. The grass is firing itself skywards. The heather has turned green. The path has dried into ridges. Birdsong assails him from skylarks and the grouse have gone to ground, are already nesting. Even the tractor marks are fainter. How does the ground change so much in so short a time? He makes a half-hearted search of the immediate area but finds nothing at all. He's not likely to since by now, with all this good weather, other walkers have been here. He'll have to give up. So he leaves the patch of grass and climbs the hill. He finds a dry bank he can sit on just to absorb this early promise of summer. His world stills. He's aware only of the hum of insects, a thin single piping call from a nearby golden plover. Everything else, like himself, seems to be soaking up the unaccustomed heat.

The sky above him is blue and empty except for vapour trails. He watches the twin sharp lines from an invisible plane widen and join together as people head off on holiday. Is it time to let go?

From his vantage point he can see for the first time the way the land lies. A path wide enough to walk two abreast comes in from each side to meet below him in the sudden patch of grass. The grass attracts him. Its lushness is unusual. Even in this green season it stands out in the way a playing field can against a housing estate. He stretches his eyes to left and right. In this good weather there are walkers about and the car parks are full. To his left he can see his own car glinting, and to the right he notices a small patch of earth that's used as another car park. You can approach the sinkhole from either end.

Then he realises that the green patch is equidistant between the two car parks. It's the perfect place for what the Met call 'a swap'. One party brings the money in from one side, the other party brings the drugs from the other. The green patch is in a slight bowl. A swap can be completed here with no prying eyes. No cameras, no passing police cars, and enough ground to plant lookouts with guns for protection.

In New Mexico maybe. In the outback perhaps. But surely not in North Yorkshire! Nevertheless, Keith readies his phone and takes a panorama that fits in both parking spaces and everything in between.

He looks at the photo and his mind wanders. There are other possibilities. It's also a great place for an execution. The problem with executions is disposing of the body. Here you have a handy site and the likelihood that the body will stay hidden for ever. It's a long way to drag an unwilling victim. How might you get him to come there willingly?

Perhaps you could trick him. There are any number of ways you could do that. He'd come willingly if he thought someone else was the intended victim. Might that be why the cut ties are too small for the corpse's wrist, he wonders. Once the victim is here it's easy. You push him in and he's swallowed by the mud. Even if he resurfaces days later there will be no visible mark on the body. It's perfect. Was this man a danger because he was complaining about modern slavery? Was he trafficked and had to be got rid of?

Nice theories, he thinks, even if a bit far-fetched. Except this body went in backwards. Mind you, with crime, human actions often are far-fetched.

He retakes the photo. When he's sure he's got it right he puts the camera away and stares at the view. A walker in a heavy coat is approaching the grass. He guesses she's a local. She seems to have been this way before and to know about the sinkhole because the moment she reaches the greensward she leaves the path and climbs up to its very edge. There she's hidden by a small thorn tree and the curve of the hillside, so he can't be sure what she's doing. But he can see her head and she seems to be standing there, looking in. She does this for quite some time, then he sees her walking back to the path. There she turns left and goes back the way she came.

PC Keith Loadstone lets her go, stretches and climbs down the hillside. It's time to give up on the case, concede defeat. As a last action, almost by way of apology to the corpse he's letting down, he goes and stands where the woman stood and looks into the hole.

Then he sees it. A bunch of red roses lies amongst the mud and gravel. It wasn't there before he climbed the hill, he's sure of that. The walker must have brought them hidden under her coat. She must have come specially to leave the flowers. Who is she, what does she know? Suddenly Loadstone realises he's been too slow coming down the hill. He needs to talk to her but she'll be nearly back to her car by now. He'll have to run.

* * *

Shaun has appointed himself Danny's mentor. He

shows him the best sites. Some are already taken. He points out good doorways, tells him to ignore taunts, just to say *God Bless* and *Have a good* whatever time of day it is. Unless you have a habit you don't really need money. People will give you food. Keep a bottle for clean water. Fill it in the toilets. Shaun doesn't stay with him. 'You get more if you're on your own.'

So Danny sits there with one arm through his holdall. The sun is warm. He dozes. A special constable prods him awake and tells him to move on. Shaun's warned him about this. He goes and sits on an empty bench for a while before drifting back to the same spot. And all the time he watches people. To most he is invisible. They see him and then they don't. Children stare and get pulled away. He already has stubble, finds that itchy but hopes he'll soon blend in.

Will anyone look for me, he wonders. How long will it be before somebody even notices I'm missing? He tells himself the important thing is to disappear. He tells himself this is a holiday from the old Danny. He needs to hit rock bottom and then he can go upwards, become someone else.

* * *

Keith Loadstone is out of breath. The woman who left the flowers hasn't driven away. She's sitting in her car, slumped over the wheel, crying. He doesn't immediately approach her. Instead he notes the registration, then describes her as accurately as he can. He has her down as a victim, not a murderer. She needs to lead him to others. He waits patiently, notices that she has thin arms. Was she the decoy? Will the cut strings fit round her wrists?

She cries for a long time, then suddenly sits up and starts the car. He lets her go and then follows. He notices that she's not a good driver. She brakes late for tractors, goes so slowly he can't really hang back as he would like to. In Pickering she jumps a red light and he can't follow her. Luckily the lights are short and he soon catches her up.

When she turns into a drive he parks round the corner and walks back. He doesn't know what he expected, but not this house. It looks really posh, a million pounds worth of real estate in Keith Loadstone's book. The drive lets him hide. She's parked but is moving slowly. He's in time to see her go into the house, walk straight in as if she owns it. He wonders whether to knock on the door, catch her off-guard and ask her what she knows, but it's too early in the investigation for that. Instead he makes a phone call and finds the car is registered to the house. It's in the name of Isabel Goulden. He knows of Gouldens, even shops there. How is that grocery chain involved in the death of an illegal immigrant?

Angela Matthews told him he had a day to prove it was a suspicious death. He knows she's bluffing. The Crime Management Unit might eventually wind up the case after checking that all recording standards have been met, but that will take more than a single day. He can bide his time, do some digging. If Gouldens are involved this case could be enormous. If he finds hard evidence, even in a few months' time, the case can always be reopened. Meanwhile he may lose his bet with Angela and she may insist on the body being buried to save space in the morgue. They do that with unknown corpses: number them and bury them in a marked spot so they can always be dug up again. He does make one promise to himself. If the corpse is buried he'll attend the funeral. He owes that to the victim. He'll also keep the knife and the cut string. He knows he should hand them in with the closing of the case but he doesn't want them to suddenly go missing.

His real feeling as he drives home through the brilliant afternoon is that he has a case. Something will happen to break it wide open. Rich widows don't hurl flowers into a grave without good reason. Driving back through Pickering he notices his poster near the lights. Was that why she jumped them? Was that the first time she saw the likeness? If so it's possible she'll contact the police. The more he thinks about it, the more certain he is that she must have seen the poster. In that case it'll be even more significant if she doesn't go to the police.

The posters are due to come down soon, but if he knows North Yorkshire they'll stay up for several months unless the spaces are suddenly needed for a lost dog or cat.

18

Breakfast is the best meal of the day for Stella. She has her routine. She gets up late, showers and dresses. She makes coffee in her thermal-walled cafetière, heats up an almond croissant and takes them both across to the small table in the window that faces south east. Her cat joins her, stretches out in the sun if there is any, curls up in her lap if there isn't. Ensconced there, Stella eats, drinks and scans the papers.

Today is decision day. Will she stand?

Everyone in the party and outside it expects her to. The Prime Minister had phoned her when he had his diagnosis. 'I'm done for,' he told her. 'I need to hand over to you.' He sounded odd, not dutiful or sad at his imminent demise but almost as if he was relieved. 'Hope I haven't buggered things up too badly.'

'I may not stand,' she told him.

'Of course you will, you must. You're the only one I trust.'

'But I fought you on so many issues,' she said.

'That's why I trust you.'

'Is the job doable?' she asked.

'Barely.'

She paused. 'Why do you think it has to be me?'

'Because you don't know if you want it,' he snapped back. 'The only people to be trusted with power are those who don't know if they want it. It's the oxymoron at the heart of politics.'

She thought about that, then said, 'You're right in

one way, Prime Minister, I don't know if I want it.'

He paused. 'Look,' he said, 'this goes way beyond personal wishes. You have a duty. In really old-fashioned terms, your country needs you. Tell me you'll stand.'

She hadn't told him she would. She said she'd think about it and that she knew all about duty. When she put the phone down she realised she hadn't commiserated or said how sad she was for him.

Why hadn't she said the right thing?

She eats the croissant slowly, reaches the lump of marzipan hidden inside like a child's surprise.

But today she must decide and make that decision public.

She pours another coffee, cradles it in both hands. The cat on her lap stirs. 'There already is a cat in Downing Street,' she tells it. 'Do you think you'll get on?'

She rehearses the arguments in her head. I'll become public property from the moment I make my announcement. My clothes, my weight, the lines on my face, every friendship I've ever had, everything I've ever said, every email I've ever sent will be examined. I'll become the hope of half the country and be blamed by the others for everything that's wrong with their lives. Everyone will want interviews and they'll only ever ask me hostile questions. I'll have to pretend I'm in charge of the world at the same time as its forces batter me and push me in directions I promised I would never go.

Worse that all that will be the voices in my own head. I'll tell myself to do something about all the insoluble problems: homelessness, addiction, mental health, prisoner reoffending, too many part-time, low-wage jobs. And if I struggle through the whirlpool (an unfortunate image) of all these things, there lies in wait for me the end that is ordained for everyone who practises my profession: failure. Enoch Powell was right about that. I will be remembered for broken promises and mistakes.

Let this cup pass from me.

Is there a God? She rather doubts it. If she turns this down the country will continue to love her (and she needs love in her life). She could in time be 'the best Prime Minister they never had'. Perhaps she could become another Tony Benn, making money from memoirs and evenings-with, rewriting history in the glowing terms always used by those who have never taken responsibility.

She picks up the papers. Mindsett is everywhere across the front pages.

OUR UNEQUAL SOCIETY

5,117 prosecutions for benefit fraud last year, says Mindsett.

Not a single prosecution for tax avoidance.

Stella winces. She suspects the statistics are true. Her party has not done right by the country's poorest. The Prime Minister pandered to the wealthy. If she becomes Prime Minister she will pander to no one. She reads the article. *As Home Secretary, Stella Stelling must be happy with this unfairness, claims Mindsett. She is known to favour the increase in part-time working*.

Her heart skips. It's a downright lie. She fought the treasury on that one, Mindsett knows she fought the treasury. Who's feeding this stuff to the papers? She knows the answer.

This campaign is too important to be left to the Party. Our poll shows a growing clamour for change.

Clever, Stella thinks, to appeal beyond the party members. Far beyond Mindsett's abilities to think up that one. She wonders who he has working for him. If it is even remotely possible that Mindsett might become Prime Minister she has to stand. There isn't a decision to make. But surely someone else will challenge him if she doesn't. Is it possible, even in these febrile times, for a lying, incompetent, vicious lump of self-love like Mindsett to become Prime Minister? Sadly, she knows the answer to that.

She also knows exactly what she's up against. Truth is constant. It can't grab headlines in the way lies can because it cannot change to feed the media's appetite for novelty. The truth will stymie me, she thinks. So will my loyalty to the current Prime Minister. I never publicly undermined him, so Mindsett can pin each of his policies on me. Can I now turn against a dying man and make him taste the bitterness of hearing me rubbish his achievements? And if I do that because I need to, why should anyone ever be loyal to me?

She knows Mindsett has a mistress. She knows the scandal of the railway contracts. But she also thinks of her own father, a welder working on the Clyde. Each rivet he put into his ships gradually changed the view from the terraced houses she grew up in as the enormous grey structures darkened their streets. Yes, he was exploited; yes, he wanted better for this daughter of his middle-age. But he was also proud of what he did. He belonged to that area, to the clubs and the pubs. He felt part of something in the same way miners felt part of the all that activity and danger. She remembers from her childhood the noise of the hooters and the way the whole street outside the yards filled with men.

She remembers too the days of launches, the rattle of chains, the way the ships lurched sideways into the water creating a wave that stretched across the Clyde. All are empty now, all abandoned, and those men's grandchildren work in call-centres or bars as part of the gig economy. Where's the pride in that?

She hated some of the things her dad said. His casual racism, his homophobia and his misogyny caused terrible rows between them. The world is better now; surely there is such a thing as progress? But she feels for her male cousins still living in Glasgow. One by one all the groups they had once thought beneath them – women, immigrants, gays – have leap-frogged over them. There is fertile ground for the Mindsetts of this world. So many people have a genuine sense of grievance at the way they have been left behind. Mindsett can mine that, blame her for it, and win without having to present any answer that will solve the problem.

It's the world's unstated question: what do we do with the people we no longer need? How do those who would once have been called working class find pride in the way their grandparents did? If she can't find an answer, perhaps she doesn't deserve to be Prime Minister.

* * *

When the day ends Danny returns to the bridge. It's the first day he's ever been a free man, free of his dad's generosity, free of the allowance that was smothering him. He knows he's different from the men either side of him because he has chosen this life rather that fallen into it. Shaun is there, and Danny feels a strange affinity to this rough sleeper who's probably only a little older than he is. Shaun's had a good day begging. He has three cans of extra strong. He offers one to Danny who refuses.

Is it allowed to ask questions? He wants to understand why Shaun is living like this. All day the lad has looked after him, nudged him in the right direction, kept an eye on him. Danny thinks of the personal trainers in the gym. They nurture new clients in similar ways. It's their job. It's what they are paid for. Shaun has done it for free. Danny knows he isn't yet part of the group but no one's challenged him. One or two even nod now it's his second night with them.

They are not as he thought they would be. The ones he's talked to are articulate and friendly. They live a strangely communal life. They give each other tips about the police and share the food that well-wishers give them. They talk about now. Danny finds it odd that they live exclusively in the moment when so much of what makes them who they are must be rooted in their pasts. He's already noticed how they avoid the future tense.

'Sufficient unto the day,' Shaun says as he sips his drink, making it last. 'I'll sleep better tonight.'

Danny feels full. He was there this afternoon when the local Gouldens handed out their past-its-sell-by-date food. He got his share. This irony is one of the things that makes his day. Even the insults have made him feel good.

'Fucking beggar ... lazy cunt ... get a job ... stop sponging.' He looks at the faces as he sits in front of his plastic cup and he knows them, recognises the types, smiles at them and wishes each a good day. They aren't professional men. They aren't family men. They are the ones just above where he is now. They are defending their borders. But more importantly to Danny they are confirming that he is at rock bottom, and that any movement from now on will take him upwards and it will be his own doing.

I'm no longer Danny, he tells himself as he settles down to sleep. I've left Danny far behind. Now who and what can I become?

19

'Are you sure, Mum?' Leah asks. She daren't look at Martin. He'd wanted them to report the death at the time, urged them to go to the police. They'd insisted it was Katherine's responsibility, that the cult could answer the questions the police were bound to ask.

Izzy nods. 'It was Patrick's face, no mistake.'

'Have you told the police?'

Izzy shakes her head.

The sinkhole must have moved again, Leah thinks. How did they get a likeness if they haven't recovered the body?

Izzy is already there in her thinking. 'They must have the body. If there's a body there has to be a funeral. When that happens, in spite of everything, I'd like to go.'

Leah keeps her head down. She waits for Martin to say he never trusted Katherine to report what happened but he doesn't. He's started eating and seems to be avoiding her eyes as much as she is avoiding his. First the sadness of the journal and then this.

'They need to know,' Izzy says.

Leah notices she isn't eating.

'Why did you go to the sinkhole?' Leah asks.

'He's my son, whatever he did. I took flowers.' She says this defiantly.

'Mum, you should have said. I'd have come with you.'

'Would you, after what he did to you?' Izzy has lifted her fork to start eating. Now she puts it back down, leaving her food untouched.

Defiance might mean less dependence, Leah hopes.

'You're right, Mum. I'd have tried to talk you out of it.'

'Exactly.'

'He was your son, Mum. What do you want us to do?'

'I'll go to the police tomorrow.' Izzy picks up her fork again.

'I know it's none of my business, but what will you tell them?' Martin asks.

'What happened, the truth.' Izzy looks at Martin as if he is stupid.

Martin isn't offended.

'Of course, Mrs Goulden, but how much of the truth?'

'What do you mean?'

'Will you tell them who was there?'

'Of course.'

'Will you tell them about the threats Danny made?'

'Yes. He didn't mean them.'

'Will you tell them about Danny's knife?'

Izzy doesn't answer.

'If you do, they might think it was manslaughter, or even murder.'

Izzy says nothing.

'They might think we could have saved him and that we deliberately watched him die.'

Leah joins in. 'Will you tell them why we were all there?' The moment she says this she realises her mistake. Izzy doesn't know about the tape or the smothering. She sees Martin roll his eyes.

'I hate all this,' Martin says. 'We need to find Katherine. We need to make her do her duty. If we can't find her, then perhaps the best thing is to say nothing. They have the body but they have no idea who he is. If we don't tell them, who will?'

'We need a family conference. I'll call the others,' Leah says.

Izzy nods.

* * *

'Danny's not answering,' Leah tells Martin later. Then she adds, 'You were right. We should have gone to the police at once. You must have been dying to say so.'

They are in the bedroom. Leah's sitting on the edge of the bed rolling her tights down her legs. Martin's in his boxers.

'I read the letters and the journal,' he tells her.

'And?' She stops where she is with one tight still on her right foot and the other trailed on the floor. She wants to know what he thinks. It's a high-stakes roll of the dice.

'They upset you, didn't they?'

She nods. He looks at her. She is everything he wants. She is the best thing that has ever happened to him. But it's all been the wrong way round, and standing looking down at her he feels the need to protect her, perhaps from herself.

He's been thinking about the words he will use. He had elaborate sentences ready formed but she's put them out of his mind.

'They made me feel sad too.'

He sees hopefulness flit across her face.

'But mine, I suspect, was a different sadness.'

She's looking at him intensely so he plunges on.

'It was too much,' he says, then in case he hasn't spelled it out he does so. 'Howard's love was too much for any woman.'

'But she led him on. The first letters are full of the same feelings. She waited until he reciprocated and then she snatched his happiness away.' Leah detaches the rest of the tights and stands up. 'I hate her for what she did to him.'

Martin pauses. He knows if he agrees with her they will be as they have been before. They'll strip quickly and rush into the bed. Soon he'll be inside her and that irrational, needy joy will build again. But he doesn't agree, and he suspects they need to have this out.

'Howard took his own life,' he tells her. 'Vikki told me that. He killed himself rather than live without her.'

Facts, especially the unpleasant ones, matter to Martin. He thinks you only have a chance in life if you know the truth. He tells it baldly because it has to be said.

Leah, who a moment ago was standing expectantly in bra and knickers, now wraps her arms round herself as she did in his flat after the rape. She's looking at the floor and he sees how unhappy he's made her.

'Poor Howard,' she says. 'I would never ...' She stops herself in time.

Martin waits for what will come next, but she stands looking at the floor so he goes on.

'I think S tried to love him as much as he loved her,' Martin says, speaking slowly.' I think she gave it a real go.' He stops, then continues. 'You take his side, I take hers. I don't understand it all. There are questions I want to ask but I think she felt smothered. I think she was overwhelmed. She did try to break it to him gently.'

Leah's head jerks upwards and she is clearly horrified. She's looking at him as if she can't believe what he's saying.

He goes on. 'They sound so young. Don't get me wrong; I felt as sad as you did. It's the old story of two people who should never have got together in the first place waking up to the fact that they don't love equally.' He knows he mustn't quote now, but it's part of him. Auden said it best and he wants Leah to understand.

> 'How should we like it were stars to burn
> With a passion for us, we could not return?
> If equal affection cannot be,
> Let the more loving one be me.'

'Howard upset S just as much as she upset him. You can feel that in her letters. She knew she was the less loving one. It was just a horrible situation for both of them.'

'He killed himself. Presumably she's still alive and thriving. How could you?' Leah snatches up her nightie and stalks into the shower room.

Martin reaches down for his pile of clothes and gradually dresses himself. He wonders as he closes the door behind him whether Auden was right and it really is better to be the more loving one.

When Leah emerges from the shower room she sees he's gone. It's both a shock and it isn't. Then she notices that his clothes are gone and she hears the van moving slowly across the gravel. She goes to the window. Why, she asks herself, doesn't she open the window and shout to bring him back? The old van reaches the drive and disappears into the darkness. She hears it turn and sees the lights moving off across the blackness of North Yorkshire.

Tonight she'll have the bed to herself.

And tomorrow she'll try again to contact Danny. It'll be awkward to hold a family meeting without Martin but she'll cope. She can always phone him tomorrow.

20

'I take it nothing has happened, no one has come forward?' SDM Angela Matthews leans forward across her desk, smiles at PC Loadstone and waits.

Keith hesitates. He thinks of the red roses left in the sinkhole, of the woman who lives in the expensive house. It won't be enough. Why is there this obsession with budgets and resources when truth is what really matters?

'Nothing significant,' he tells her.

Then I'll contact the Crime Management Unit. They'll need to check that recording standards have been met. If they have, we'll start winding up the case.

'Then can you also record the fact that I'm not happy with this at all?'

'Okay, Keith, tell me what you think happened.'

'I went there yesterday and climbed up the bank so that I could look down on the scene. It's the perfect site for a swap. There are two car parks, each on different roads. You can't see the sinkhole from either of them. If you had drugs or a kidnap victim to swap for cash it's a perfect setup. No one around, plenty of cover to give protection. I think that's what happened there. I think the man was executed as part of the deal. Perfect for that too. Where else do you find a body disposal site so close to a murder?'

'Evidence?' she asks.

'A knife, two sets of tough plastic string used to bind someone's hands.'

'Nothing else?'

He shakes his head.

'Sorry, Keith. We haven't the resources.'

'SDM Matthews, do you believe that an illegal immigrant just happened to step backwards into a sinkhole when he was entirely on his own in the middle of nowhere?'

She thinks for a moment. He notices again how pretty she is, pretty and clever. Graduate entry to the force. They're becoming more common but they still take some getting used to.

'No,' she says, 'I don't believe that either.'

'Then keep the case open. Give me another month.'

She's not a natural blonde. He can see the darker roots when she shakes her head. She's a soft English rose and she doesn't fancy him. Marie wants everything to do with him and he doesn't fancy her at all.

'Why did you accept my bet to take you out to dinner?' he suddenly asks her.

She laughs and leans back.

'A girl's got to take her chances.'

She looks at him across the table. 'Is the offer still open?' she asks.

Now it's his turn to be stubborn. 'Only when I've proved this is a murder.'

Is she disappointed? She gives a slight shrug of the shoulders. It seems like more than banter.

He adds, in case she hasn't realised, 'You know what happens next, don't you? They give Loadstone's Corpse a number and they bury it in a marked grave so that they can always dig it up again if the need arises.'

He gets up to go.

As he reaches the door she calls him back.

'One last thing, Keith. Don't touch any switches on your way out.'

He deliberately leaves the door open when he exits the room.

* * *

There is no funeral. PC Loadstone attends the body to the grave. Because they don't know which words should be said over an unknown victim, no words are said. A hole has been excavated by a small digger, and the same digger is waiting to fill the hole when the coffin has been lowered in. It's not quite a ceremony, nor is it quite like laying a gas pipe. Before the grave is filled in the men stand in silence for nearly a minute. Then they move off and the digger swings into action.

The other men move away. Keith stays there. He doesn't exactly make a vow, but he goes over in his mind what he knows and what he needs to find out. While he's doing this he sees Marie slink up beside him.

'Am I too late?'

He wonders how she knows, but then the story of Loadstone's Corpse must be all round Ryedale by now.

'Too late for what?'

The remark goes straight over her head. 'For the burial.'

He remembers the way she washed his face as any mother would have done and he relents. She was there when the body came out of the sinkhole. It's right that she's here now.

He turns to look at her and spots another woman standing on the drive at the edge of the lawn. It's not the one who left the flowers; it's someone younger with long black hair, very formally dressed. She has her eyes lowered as if she's praying. She must be a passer-by. How could anyone else know about the burial?

He turns back to Marie. 'Coffee?' he offers.

Her face brightens. She puts her arm through his and he walks her away to the edge of the houses. Then he says, 'Hang on a minute.'

The woman with black hair is still there. The digger has finished filling the hole, leaving a mound that will collapse with time to leave no trace. Job done, the digger has already moved away.

Keith and Marie, in the dark shadows cast by spring sunshine, watch as the woman walks to the edge of the mound and stands there for a long time.

'Go and talk to her, Marie, will you? Tell her you were there when we found him. See what you can learn.'

'That's your job.'

'I'd frighten her away.'

'Will you still be here when I get back?'

'Okay.'

She lets go of him and Keith watches as Marie approaches the stranger. He sees Marie stand to one side, notices the dark-haired stranger is nervous, ready to bolt. Then Marie goes over and stands beside her. The stranger listens when Marie talks to her, but from where he's watching Keith doesn't think the stranger is talking back. They stand together again in silence. They shake hands and then Marie is heading back towards him.

Keith watches the stranger as she walks quickly away. He hopes she has a car parked nearby. He signals Marie to hurry, then they follow, staying back. Marie has hold of his arm again. When the stranger reaches her car Keith reads the number and says it over and over in his head. He finds his notebook and writes it down. Marie is clearly enjoying herself. 'Shall we follow her, see where she goes?' she asks. 'Where's your car?'

Part of him wants to follow but he doesn't want Marie with him if he does. He pats his notebook. 'The number plate will do that. Come on.'

When they've ordered he asks her what she found out.

Marie clears her throat, talks slowly as if she knows he'll bolt as soon as she's told him everything.

'She's about forty, I'd say. Dresses oddly even by North Yorkshire standards. If she was in a fifties costume drama I wouldn't be surprised. She's polite. When I told her about pulling him out and washing his face she listened, but I'd say she's as hard as nails that one. She gave nothing away, didn't even say something like, 'I'm glad you were there,' or 'that was thoughtful of you'... nothing.'

'What was her voice like?'

'I thought you'd ask that so I listened 'specially carefully. She whispered, had a kind of hushed tone to everything she said, which wasn't much. I'd say she's not a woman's woman. I'd say she doesn't make friends easily and she doesn't enjoy gossip.' Marie stopped. 'If this is useful, what I'm telling you, ask me about her hands.'

He'll indulge her. 'Tell me about her hands.'

'Well, they talked as much as or more than she did. It was a struggle, you see. Her voice stayed calm and hushed like, but her hands held her handbag as if she were mixing pastry or kneading dough. Round and round they went, the whole time I was talking.'

She stops again. 'That's about it. Have I done well?'

'Very good, Marie. We'll make a copper of you yet.'

He's finished his coffee. She's making hers last and he knows he has to sit there until she's finished.

'So was she just a passer-by? What do you think?' he asks.

'Oh, didn't I say? She knows who he is alright.'

'Did she say so?'

'She didn't need to say it.'

'Evidence. Give me something I can write down in my notebook and read out in court.'

Marie's face falls. 'I can't do that. I just know it. She was there to say goodbye to someone I would say she knew pretty well.'

Is he too eager when he asks, 'How do you know it? How can you be sure?'

'In the same way I know you're only toying with me, that you won't give me another thought until I happen to bump into you next time.'

She looks at him, straight between the eyes. 'It's alright,' she says. 'I've nearly got used to it. I know you can't help it. As Mam would have said if she were still alive, *it's just one of them things*.'

He stretches his hands out, silently acknowledges the truth of what she's just said. 'You did well,' he tells her. 'I wouldn't have got all that.'

He leaves her finishing her coffee. He can work out how Marie knew the day and time of the burial, but how did this dark-haired stranger know? Two women know who he is, and each of them goes out of their way to mourn him. So who is he, and how did he meet his end?

21

'The game's afoot. Stella is standing. Can't you feel the sighs of relief all round Westminster?' Jud Mindsett is prowling his office. James, who now has his own security pass, is sitting with him. It felt great walking into Portcullis House, showing his badge and being nodded through.

James has dismissed Roz from his thoughts. This new role is all-absorbing. He flings his hair back and stares at Jud. 'Stella will play it the traditional way. She'll set off on the rubber chicken circuit, talking to party members. Those circuits take time to set up, so the first fortnight of the campaign is yours if you grab it. By the time she starts glad-handing you can make sure that all the questions they ask will be the ones you've planted.'

'Populist,' says Jud. 'Isn't it a wonderfully snooty word? They,' he indicates the other occupants of the building, 'love to be popular, but would screw up their elitist noses at the very thought of being populist.'

'Most of what you say doesn't matter,' James tells him, 'provided you grab headlines and cause offence.' He pauses. 'Actually, that's tautological. You'll only grab headlines if you do cause offence. But you have to stand for something that resonates.'

He thinks about what he's just said. 'So who are you going target, Jud? Who do you want to offend?'

Jud pauses, sniffs loudly. 'Immigrants are the obvious target.'

'That's been done,' James tells him. 'It's not new.'

'Elites then, the 1% who own most of everything?'

'Blindingly obvious. A socialist target and you need their funding. Besides, many of them are your party members, and it's the members who have the vote in this election.'

There's a long pause in the room while Jud's limpet thirst for power searches for a rock it can anchor itself onto.

'Why don't I question democracy itself?'

James wasn't listening properly, or was he? 'Say that again, Jud.'

'Democracy. I could question democracy itself.'

The cars in the street outside suddenly seem loud. The peregrine falcon that nests in the faux chimneys takes flight.

James leaps in the air. 'Of course, brilliant. That'll attract notice. And it will force Stella to defend not only democracy, but everything that has been done in its name by either party. Democracy means turmoil. It builds antagonism. To the common people it suppresses their wages and their rights because it's linked to capitalism. It needs funding, so it's a prey to lobbyists. Now that communism has fallen, democracy can be blamed for almost everything, with impunity. And the members of your party have never really believed in democracy, they've just gone along with it because they had to. They think they should rule for ever. You'll offer them a way in which they can.'

'What are we going to suggest as an alternative?' Jud asks. 'You mustn't call it dictatorship. We need another name.'

'Benevolent despotism?' Jud suggests.

'Too 19th century. But the benevolent might work for us.'

The two men sit in silence.

Then, 'Hang on,' says James. 'That isn't how politics works. We don't need to suggest what we replace it with. I'm forgetting my own maxims. We don't have to be positive. All we need is a slogan. It mustn't be more than four words. Three is better.'

'In Stability Is Strength,' suggests Jud.

'Wrong initials.'

Jud has to think about that before he grimaces.

'Ten-Year Terms?' suggests Jud.

James smiles. 'Simple, easy to remember, not in itself anti-democratic but there's no verb. We need a verb, preferably in the imperative case.'

Jud is confused. He doesn't know what that means. He waits for James.

'Build is a good imperative,' James suddenly says. 'Nice positive nuance.'

'Build More Houses.'

James gives Jud a withering look. 'Give is another good word. John Lennon knew a thing or two. Give peace a chance.'

'Give Democracy Time To Build,' suggests Jud.

'Too long.' James suddenly punches the air. 'Give Democracy Time. Three words. It's perfect.'

'But I thought we were anti-democracy. I thought that was the whole idea.'

James sighs. Does he have to spell all this out? Is Jud capable of grasping anything?

'Let's take this slowly, be sure we have this. We

campaign on the need for ten-year terms. That was your slogan, Jud. We attack the speed of democracy, the constant need to pander to the electorate. That will still win you headlines. You can plug the need for long-term engagement with Britain's problems. You can say ten-year governments will be free to do unpopular but necessary things that will make the country stronger. It's perfect. It's brilliant. And the very slogan you use, Give Democracy Time, will make it seem that you are in favour of what you are actually attacking. People hate voting so often. Many of them don't bother. It'll be popular and the opposition party will wither. Ten years is too long for them to wait. Imagine you are forty-five and in opposition for ten years. What's the point?'

'Imagine you are a Junior Minister and you stay with the job for ten years,' says Jud.

James risks it. 'You'd have to read the papers you sign, wouldn't you? You'd have to take much more care. This way you can even turn your own incompetence into an argument in favour of your new stance.'

'Okay, okay. Let's do it. It'll make my name. It'll make me the greatest reformer since 1689.'

'I think you mean 1688, Jud, the Glorious Revolution?'

'Of course, if you say so.'

'You'll have your name and ten years in power. If we win I'll be your Chief of Staff. I want that as a formal promise. I want that in writing.'

'Okay.'

'How about now?' James insists.

Danny and Shaun go back to the bridge later that night. They've spent the day together. They expect the best spaces will be taken but they aren't. When he sees this, Danny runs to get the best spot, the middle space out of the wind. Shaun hangs back. He understands the danger. When Danny has his space he calls Shaun over and in doing so he turns round. Shaun is standing between him and the pavement and there are shadows closing in on him. The shadows have weapons. They look like baseball bats. Shaun's making no attempt to escape. Is he giving Danny time to get away, prepared to take the beating himself to save his friend?

Shit. Danny thinks of the men who've hissed and spat at him all day. Is this another way of asserting social standing, of people who don't have much going for them attacking those who have even less? No one seems in a hurry. Perhaps terrifying the victim before you beat the shit out of him is part of what they enjoy. Now the five vigilantes are surrounding Shaun, shadow weapons raised, taunting him.

And it comes again, the certainty, the glee. This pavement slopes. He has height and shadow on his side but he needs a weapon. He sees the raised bats. It'll be easy enough to grab one. There's no one else about. The cars are passing in their shuttered world. They won't see anything, and if they do they won't stop and help.

Danny removes his trainers. They mustn't hear him coming. He feels his muscles ready, rocks on his toes and charges. He has his target, the one who looks less certain than the others. Is this his first time at a beating? Danny is on him before he realises, grabs the baseball bat and adjusts his grip on it. Its owner never hears the sickening thud, and when the others hear it Danny has already disappeared, taking the bat with him back into the shadows. The group stand round their poleaxed comrade wondering what happened.

Danny waits, chooses again. The tall one on the left. Aim for him. Danny rocks and charges, reaches down for another bat, turns, hits the back of someone's head. The man goes down. Now he has a baseball bat in each hand and there's no need to run away again. The other Danny is with him, that figure who took over at the sinkhole, who held the knife and shouted his contempt. Together they feel invincible. Three against one now, much better odds. But he still can't wait for them to come for him. He has to attack. Legs break easily, he knows that. They think he'll go for their heads as he has done twice already. Instead, he charges straight at the middle one, sidesteps at the last moment and swings long and hard at the outside man. The end of one bat, travelling at maximum speed, snaps his lower leg. Before the noise of the snap has finished echoing under the metal bridge Danny's turning, charging again, taking aim, this time swinging at the legs of the middle figure who's now running away.

'Are you alright?' he shouts at Shaun.

'Untouched.'

They stand together, scan the area for any further danger, see only homeless men now emerging from the shadows with their bundles. Shaun knows them and greets them by name. Bill goes for his usual spot in the middle, but Shaun tells him that's now Patrick's place. Patrick's earned it.

Danny stands apart. A baseball bat dangles from each arm. Now the action's over he sees what he's done. Three men lie on the pavement. Two could be dead, the third is screaming. The police will have to be involved. He walks up to his chosen spot for sleeping, tells Bill he can have it back, puts his trainers on and picks up the rest of his things.

Danny examines the knocked-out men. One is already sitting up. Danny knows all about the dangers of concussion. 'Sit there,' he tells the man. 'Don't try to go anywhere, at least not yet.' He feels for the pulse of the first man he decked. He's alive, and a siren is sounding nearby. Then blue lights are bouncing off the girders all round him.

Danny stands there with his rough sleeping gear and two baseball bats. He waits for what will happen next. In that flashing blue moment he finds he is utterly at peace with himself. An ambulance arrives, attends to the downed men.

'Did you do this?' an officer asks him.

'Yes,' Danny says. 'Shaun will tell you exactly what happened.'

Danny turns round. Shaun is still there but the other rough sleepers have melted away. All the sleeping places are empty again.

'Come on,' the officer says. 'Get in.'

Danny picks up his holdall. He's still carrying the bats.

'I'll take those,' the officer says.

The policeman leaves Danny and Shaun in the car, walks over to the paramedics and talks.

Sitting in the back of the car, Shaun says, 'They wouldn't have killed me, just beaten me up, but you weren't to know that.'

Danny is lost in his own thoughts. He thinks he begins to get a sense of who he really is and what he might become.

'But thanks anyway,' Shaun says. 'I'd rather not be beaten up.'

They sit in silence. 'There's something about you,' Shaun says. 'I noticed it at once. The others spotted it too. It's the way you hold yourself.'

Yes, Danny thinks. All those days in the gym, all that training.

'You don't belong with us,' Shaun pronounces.

'And you do?' Danny is curious. 'What makes you belong?'

'The booze. It's got me. There's no fighting it. Maybe once, but not anymore.'

22

The second blow separates the wood from the Yale lock which is left dangling. The front door of Danny's neat terraced house flies open.

The policeman stoops to move the pile of fast food fliers and other post that has accumulated. He picks something else up from the hall floor, puts it in his pocket, then turns to Leah. 'Wait there, please,' he says. 'Let me go first.'

He expects to find a body, Leah thinks. He wants to protect me. He thinks my little brother Danny may have taken his own life and be lying dead somewhere in the house. She sniffs but there is only the staleness of confined air. She has smelt death before: the stench of sheep putrefying among the heather; the cold saltiness of a seal washed up on the beach, its stomach churning with maggots; the antiseptic, medical smells around her dad at his laying out. This house does not smell of death. With outstretched fingers she gently taps on the inside wall. Leah is an expert on echoes, on the way houses feel.

She taps and listens, then taps again.

He isn't here, she thinks. This house is stuck in neutral. It's waiting for someone else to arrive and take it over. He's not only gone but he's been gone for some time.

The policeman is back, shaking his head. 'He's not here,' he confirms.

Leah walks into the hall, notes the patina of dust on

the skirting boards, the coat pegs with no coats hanging there. Is that normal? She has never been here before. Danny always came to them. They never visited him. Since he disappeared she has realised how little she knows about him.

'Look at this.'

The policeman is in a hurry. She walks through to the kitchen where he's pointing to the table. She sees the passport first. It's square with the corner of the table. She flicks it open. It is Danny's. Next to his passport is a pile of bank statements. Next to those is a birth certificate and a small yellowing card with a National Insurance number. Then there's a pile of exam certificates. Just past the card is a mobile phone and a small rectangle of white paper that turns out to be a lottery ticket.

All are lined up neatly, the gaps exact, as if they have been measured.

The policeman is standing next to her, letting her take her time. 'I'd say he's disappeared.'

At first she thinks the policeman's being stupid, then she understands. 'It's much more common than you think,' he explains. '275,000 people a year vanish in Great Britain. Most of them turn up, but 16,000 each year stay missing.'

Leah says nothing. She's still relieved that Danny might not be dead.

'How old is he, love?'

'Thirty, thirty-one next birthday.'

The policeman holds out his hand to her. It contains a set of house keys. 'I found these just inside the door, hidden under the post.'

She looks at them blankly, doesn't understand.

'He posted them back through the door when he went. I think he did that so that he couldn't just come back in and take over his old life. He must be determined to disappear.'

Leah checks the other documents on the table. Each is a key piece of evidence as to who Danny is, or should that be who Danny was?

'I only did a cursory check before, didn't want to leave you standing on the doorstep. I'd better be thorough.'

He climbs the stairs. Leah hears him rummaging, opening and closing cupboard doors. She looks around the kitchen. There is the same patina of dust but otherwise it's tidy. There's no dirty washing. The bin under the sink has been emptied. The cupboards are orderly. The fridge is not full of stale food. It's been emptied and cleaned out.

The facts sink in. She understands that he meant to go and that he isn't coming back. She remembers the baby who let her make a fuss of him, the little boy singing his alphabet song, the adult standing with a long-bladed knife in front of his half-brother.

'Nothing untoward,' the returning policeman announces. 'Was he always tidy?'

Leah has to admit she doesn't know. What has been sinking in slowly is how little she really knows about him.

'What happens now?' she asks.

'I'll report him missing. I'll add him to the list.'

Leah longs to be left alone in the house but the policeman doesn't immediately go.

'You're going to need a locksmith. We have one we use for occasions like this. Shall I phone him?'

Leah nods, then wonders if she should ask about prices, decides it doesn't matter. She needs to get back to Yorkshire tonight for Izzy's sake, perhaps to contact Martin. Even if she stays over she'll need to lock the door.

'Yes please,' she says.

While he phones she flicks through the bank statements. There are no recent large withdrawals. She'll need to go through them thoroughly, but the only sum over £150 is council tax. The healthy balance hasn't significantly changed in the last six months. He took nothing with him. What prompted him to go?

Is it a need to check that sends her back to the pile of post? She flicks through but there's no handwritten envelope. The only date-stamp she can find on the envelopes is May 14th, only a few weeks after she last saw him.

She needs time. She wants to understand.

The policeman is back. '2.30 alright?'

'Fine,' she says, then adds, 'He'll find the door open.'

The policeman smiles, hesitates, holds up the lottery slip. 'I checked this too, wondered if it might be significant.' He stops and smiles. 'I did wonder whether to keep it, but not all London cops are bent. Your brother had just won more than two million pounds on the lottery. That would come in handy when you are setting up a new life. So why didn't he cash it in? Why did he leave it here? Perhaps he didn't know.'

She reaches out for the little slip of paper. The

policeman lets it go with mock reluctance and she holds it in her hand.

'Are you sure?'

'I checked the numbers twice. You've still got time to claim.'

'There's no will, is there? And I thought only the owner could cash it. This isn't mine.'

'Well, it's certainly not mine,' the policeman says. 'I'm just not a lucky man. And there wouldn't be a will, would there? Your brother's not dead.'

23

'I'm too busy for this,' James announces.

Julia looks at him with contempt. 'You, busy! Universities are not busy places. You're a student for Christ's sake.'

'Not just a student. Not these days.' He's bursting to tell them but he doesn't. Now it's really happening for him he no longer feels the need. He looks around. 'Where's Danny? Out jogging?'

'Danny's disappeared.' Leah sighs. She'd better explain. 'I've been to his house. It's as if he cleaned the place, lined up all his papers and just walked out, posting the keys through the letter box.' She doesn't tell them about the lottery ticket. It will only side-track them.

'Where's Martin? Shouldn't he be here?' Julia asks the question.

'Working.' Leah knows the single word answer won't be enough, so she adds, 'We know what he thinks.'

Julia takes over, pushes her younger sister to one side.

'Okay. We know why we are here. Mum has seen posters with Patrick's face on asking for information. I think that means we can be certain about two things. One, that the ground shifted again and his body was found. Two, that they have no idea who he is.'

'Three, that Katherine never went to the police,' James adds. 'Four, that even if a member of the cult now goes to the police, that person can't know how he died.'

Julia glares at James. 'Have you finished?'

'No,' says James. 'The point I'm making is that it's up to us. If we say nothing, if each of us promises to say and do nothing, then the case will be dropped. Mum says the poster looked old. They can't keep an investigation going for ever; they haven't the resources. By far the best course of action is still to say and do precisely nothing.' He's itching to get away. The last thing he needs right now is to be accused of taking part in a murder.

'I was coming to that,' Julia says. 'I happen to agree with James.' He doesn't interrupt, so she can top his case. 'What James hasn't asked is what happens if we do go to the police. We will tell a most unlikely story that Katherine may well dispute. If we tell the whole truth, then we must include Danny and the knife. How will that look, especially now he's disappeared?'

'And if we don't go to the police no one can prove that any of us saw the poster.' Last words matter, James thinks. Jud needs me. He's not safe on his own. He has to have me with him at all times.

'Agreed everyone?' Julia asks.

James shrugs his shoulders. He needs to get going.

'I've reported Danny missing,' Leah tells them. 'If we go to the police they'll ask if there's a connection. Is there a connection? I don't know.'

'You should have asked us first,' Julia snaps.

Leah ignores this, stands her ground. 'He's gone missing. I reported it. Actually, I hadn't a choice because I had to get the police to break his door down.'

'Why on earth?'

'Because he might have been lying dead in the house, Julia.'

The sisters glare at each other.

'Is that it?' James asks, after leaving a sufficient silence.

'No.'

All three of them turn. It's the first time Izzy has spoken. 'My son is lying on a slab. Alright, I know what he did, and I can guess at how he was brought up, but I want him decently buried. I want to go to his funeral. So if one of you doesn't go to the police, I will.'

Game set and match. James looks at his watch.

Izzy reinforces her point. 'We did nothing wrong that day. It will be awkward, yes, but we did nothing wrong. We need to tell them.'

Her certainty chills her two older children. Leah is the only one who nods.

'I think that's best,' she says.

James shows his exasperation and Julia pounces.

'I'll go,' says Julia. 'I'll tell them the whole story, Mum, but I must warn you that they might already have buried him.'

James stares at her. Leah nods.

'I placed flowers where he died,' Izzy tells them all. 'I should never have left my baby with them.'

Julia snorts. 'I hope nobody saw you lay flowers, Mum. The worst possible outcome is that the police somehow trace him to us.'

The family meeting breaks up. On the way out James collars Julia.

'When are you going to do the deed, Sis? This could

be awkward for me.'

'I'm not,' Julia says. 'I'm not going to tell anyone anything.'

Julia drives her brother to the station. 'What's this new job of yours then?'

He doesn't tell her. 'You'll know soon enough.'

* * *

'Okay Mum?' Leah asks when they have waved the others goodbye.

'One son dead, another missing. How do you think I feel?'

Leah watches her mother climb the stairs back to her room. For a while Leah wanders the house. Where is Danny? Why did he disappear? Then she finds herself drawn back to the journal and letters. She's missing Martin. He knows her better than anyone else. Perhaps if she reads them again, perhaps there was something there that she missed.

But when Leah re-reads the letters she again notices the same spreading coldness from S. In Howard's journal she finds the same wonderful love and it doesn't seem excessive. It's like a man holding on to a dream. Is this her loneliness talking? Everything's falling apart. Roz wasn't with James. Danny has vanished. Martin's walked out on her. Izzy is unreachable.

Love. What is it? She thought Martin loved her, but not like Howard loved S, not like these entries. She reads on, delighting in certain phrases. *We are no longer separate ... You are condemning me to being partial again.* She wants someone to think similar things about her. Why shouldn't life be like that, she thinks. If only Howard had loved me.

She's reached the last entries, the ones before Howard took his own life, and she finds something different there, something she missed the first time. Howard has a surname. He's Howard Shenton, and there's a date too. The last entry is September 1986. Thirty years ago.

She goes to the computer, wishes it would fire up faster, types the name and the date, eventually finds the articles. Drowned in the North Sea. Howard Shenton, aged 24. There's a memorial, a monolith of local stone with the date and the name. It isn't far. The Coastliner bus will take her most of the way.

Can Izzy be left? Leah decides she can, tells herself that as her mother was forthright this morning she will cope. When she's ready Leah shouts up the stairs. 'I'm going out. I'll be back tonight.' The days are getting longer. It won't be dark until 8pm. She has time.

North Yorkshire in spring means daffodils. They are still at their best as she crosses the moors. They splash out from verges and form neat ranks along the fronts of gardens. Occasionally they spread across wasteland, claiming it for themselves. Leah spots another poster with an artist's portrait of Patrick staring out at her. It's already curled and faded. Julia will be seeing the police now, she thinks. Then they can take the posters down. I have to visit Howard's memorial today. Tomorrow all hell may break loose.

She gets out at the terminus and walks towards the high cliffs. The first sea-pinks are flowering by the cliff path. The sand is stretched out in front of her, dry and friable. The nearest rock shoals are dull with dryness. She spots primroses on the cliff edge.

It's a small village, only a shop, a pub, houses and holiday cottages. A few people are walking along the beach. Is this where Howard died? She tries to imagine him walking out into the sea, carrying this burden of love with him. It's a calm day, but beyond the rock shoals she can see where tides and currents meet. Is that the spot he headed out to?

Leah pulls her eyes away from the sea and spots what she thinks must be the memorial. It's smaller than the internet photo made it seem. She heads that way. Now she's here she realises she should have brought flowers. Izzy took flowers to Patrick's sinkhole. She should have brought something. It doesn't feel enough to simply pay her respects. She tries to remember sentences from the journal, but the brightness of the day is distracting and something else is claiming her attention. Someone else is standing by the stone. Perhaps she is only a passer-by, someone curious enough to stop and read the name. Leah pauses and watches. She wants the stone to herself. She'll let the woman move on first. But the woman lingers, then stoops and places flowers. She stands up again and pats the stone. Who is she? Whoever she is, she must have come specially.

It must be Vikki, she thinks. Howard was her uncle. Was this his birthday? The woman has finished her commemoration and is walking away from the stone, walking towards her. Leah stands to one side to let her pass, then suddenly asks, 'Are you Vikki by any chance?'

The woman, who's been watching her footing on the path, suddenly raises her face. Leah sees at once that it can't be Vikki. She's too old. The woman is startled. 'No, I'm not Vikki,' she says.

Leah is filled with confusion. 'I'm so sorry,' she says. 'I thought ...'

'I hope you find her.' The woman is hurrying away, head down, but not before Leah has recognised exactly who she is. Leah thinks quickly, fits the pieces together, then spins round. S is moving at a steady speed, not looking back. A car is waiting for her. A chauffeur opens the door. Leah watches her get in and the car drives away.

Leah turns back to the stone. This is what she came for. She reaches forward, feels the warm granite's utter solidity. She glances round. There's no one near. 'She never forgot you, Howard,' she says out loud. 'Even after all these years.'

24

It's 2.30 am. The rush of drunks has subsided. The police station has quietened. The police have let Shaun go but kept Danny. He's in a cell and feels claustrophobic. The place is hot and airless after life on the streets. He's sweating and he hates it.

As soon as Shaun and he were brought into the police station they were separated. Danny knew Shaun was in the next interview room. A police officer walked between the two. Clearly the stories tallied, so they let Shaun go.

'I'm out of here,' Shaun shouted on his way past Danny's room. 'See you soon, brother.'

Well, he has no other brother now. James is closed off in Danny's past, unreachable.

'You have to charge me or let me go,' Danny says calmly to the PCSO who brings him a drink.

They do neither. Instead they ask him for a blood test and he complies. 'You won't find any traces of drugs or alcohol,' he tells the PCSO.' When you've had it tested you have to charge me or let me go.'

The PCSO tells him there's plenty of time for that, so Danny sits in his cell with nothing but his thoughts. His brain surprises him. It didn't used to be like this: asking questions, reflecting, continually harping back to the immediate past. He didn't have to defend Shaun. The others melted away when they smelled trouble. Had they known this was about to happen? Had they warned each other, but not Shaun because he'd spent the day with Danny?

It had been like watching a film you've seen before, not the shocking first time view of the unknown but something familiar. The challenge from five men with baseball bats; the same utter absence of fear; that other voice inside him, this time telling him to take off his shoes; the same certainty that he would win; the same wild glee.

This is also who I am, he tells himself. That voice in my head isn't a stranger any more, it's part of this new me.

The door opens. The PCSO is back. He asks Danny to follow him. Even the drunks are quiet now, sleeping it off. Danny follows the PCSO down the corridor back to the interview room.

'More questions?' Danny asks.

'Don't ask me,' says the PCSO.

In the interview room a stranger is waiting to talk to him. The PCSO leaves them alone. No one else comes in. There's no recording being made that Danny can see. The stranger introduces himself as Harry. Harry is not in uniform. Danny doesn't think he's police. It's the middle of the night, so Danny guesses that whoever this is he's had to be sent for.

They shake hands.

'Your real name is Danny Goulden. You've come up on the missing list. Do you want to be found?'

Harry looks straight into his eyes. Danny knows he mustn't flinch so he returns the stare. Harry is sitting really still in a way that has to be learnt or inculcated. It's intimidating.

'No,' Danny says. 'I don't want to be found.'

'What name are you using?'

'What's that to you?'

'It's just that we might be able to help.'

'Who are we?'

Harry has never dropped his eyes away from their close scrutiny of Danny.

'One against five. You took them on even though you were unarmed. Two of the gang were savagely knocked unconscious. A third suffered a leg that's broken in several places. You don't have a scratch on you.'

Danny shrugs. 'Who are we?' He repeats his question.

'Shall we say 'we' are a potential employer and leave it at that.'

Harry pauses, maintains eye contact. 'What did you think when you downed the first one with his own baseball bat?'

Danny decides he will answer the question. 'I thought nothing. I looked for the nearest darkness and ran into it,' he says.

'Did you hear the noise your blow made?'

'Yes.'

'Was the next blow louder?'

'Softer.' Danny hesitates. 'I was worried I might have killed the first one.'

'But you kept going?'

'Yes. There were four left. Shaun was still in danger.'

'What's Shaun to you?'

'My teacher.'

Harry smiles. 'In what way?'

'On the streets. He's helped me, given me tips.'

'Why did you want to disappear?'

Danny won't answer that.

Harry waits a long time, then says, 'That's okay. We don't mind if you keep secrets from us. All we need to know is that it was nothing illegal.'

Danny stares at him.

'So, was it anything illegal?'

Danny shakes his head.

'I didn't like being Danny Goulden,' he admits.

This time Harry stays silent.

'I need another identity with another YS number. I'm not going back.'

'I gather the going rate for a false driver's licence is £20 in north Glasgow,' Harry tells him.

'Except I'm not Chinese and there's a missing letter in the ones they sell.'

Harry looks at him, wonders how he knows this.

'There are plenty of places to buy false documents,' Harry tells him. 'Your lottery winnings should cover the cost.'

Danny leans forward. He's both tired and hungry now. 'Danny Goulden won the lottery. I'm penniless.'

Harry scans the man sitting opposite him to check his decision. He looks right. He'd be invisible on the street. He can handle himself. Money doesn't tempt him. He seems ready to move on from rough sleeping, and no one will be concerned if he dies because Danny Goulden is already missing. His blood test shows no sign of dependency.

'We need a new kind of bodyguard,' he tells Danny. 'Are you interested?'

'What kind of bodyguard?'

'The traditional ones are no longer sufficient. It's not enough to have a few overweight bouncer-types close by, protecting a celebrity. We need back-watchers, guys who can merge into the street, guys no one will notice who can handle themselves. You're perfect. People look away from beggars. You become invisible to them. Beggars can occupy a site and stay there. Amongst the shoppers and tourists, beggars always notice the ones not walking to or from somewhere. They are used to making quick assessments. They know who might give money and who never will.'

'Shaun's better than I am at that. I'm new to the game.'

'Shaun has an alcohol problem.'

Danny nods. He's interested. Might this job give him a purpose, a new identity, and a chance to check out his new self?

'Who are you?' he asks. 'Who will be paying me?'

'Think it out, Danny. You already know the answer.'

I'm in a police cell, Danny thinks. Whoever this is, the police sent for him and let him in to meet me. So he must be legit. Something about what I did must have fitted a profile the police have been asked to match. They kept me waiting, so it has taken some time for whoever this is to get here. In that time he's had access to lots of information about me. Someone must have already reported me missing. Someone must have gone into my house, found the lottery ticket and checked it. He knows about Shaun too. That's extraordinary. Who's he spoken to? Which CCTV has he watched? Why do they need background bodyguards? It must be about terrorism.

'You're the anti-terrorist squad,' Danny tells him.

Harry looks disappointed. 'You're not ethnic. You're not a Muslim. Don't do that, Danny. Don't ever leap to a conclusion that can't be supported by evidence.'

'MI something then.'

Harry smiles.

'Work for us for a month. We'll give you assignments, check you out. Meanwhile we'll rustle up some documents for you. Agreed?'

Danny nods.

Harry gives him a mobile and a number to phone.

'Right, you're free to go. But don't go back to the railway bridge. The guy whose leg you splintered has a brother with a gun and he'll be out looking for you.'

They don't shake hands. Danny walks out of the interview room and no one stops him. His belongings are waiting for him and handed over with no formality.

'Don't you want me to sign for them?' he asks the man on the desk.

'That would properly mess up our documentation,' he's told. 'The inspectors would be bound to ask why we handed back belongings we never collected to a man who was never here.'

* * *

'You can lie, but not in a random way,' James tells Mindsett. 'You have to tap into something, and any lies you tell must be about the present or the future, not the past.'

James knows Mindsett is at a low point. They are nowhere in the polls. They want Stella to take them on, but she's staying above the fray, keeping away from controversy. At this rate she'll win by a landslide.

'So I can't re-work my CV.' Mindsett grimaces. 'I rather fancied having played for Tranmere Rovers. I thought I might award myself a PhD.'

'Both those things can be checked.'

'So why is it alright to lie about the present?'

'The old press answer,' James tells him. 'A front page scoop boosts circulation. If you are forced to apologise for inaccuracies, you do so as long as possible after the event and in a small column on page 43. Lying used to send you to hell. Now it just earns a rap on the knuckles. At one time there was such a thing as morality; now there's only legality.'

Mindsett says nothing. James goes on.

'If you tell lies, let's say about the impact of immigrants on the incidence of rape in a Swedish town, you'll hit headlines. Fact checkers will take time to check, then they will produce complicated graphs to prove you were wrong. The only people who study their conclusions are those who never believed you in the first place. You have to remember there are always more thick people than intelligent people. The bright ones, who know truth is complex, are never going to vote for you anyway. It's the stupid ones you're after, the ones who don't understand the fact checkers' graphs. You need to tell them as many lies as possible about current affairs. You need to make them afraid.' James pauses. 'Big lies are better than small lies, especially as you are losing.'

'But this is a members' election. Are our members stupid?'

'No, but they are totally unprincipled. If they weren't, they wouldn't be members of your party. They'll vote for you if they think you have a better chance of winning an election than Stella does.'

'So what do we do next?'

'I've prepared a list.'

Jud examines it, reads what James expects of him, grimaces.

'I know, I know,' James tells Jud. 'But you have to tap into some real grievances. You need to be seen with those who have been left behind. You need to unite them and bring them onside.'

'I call them chlamydia,' Mindsett admits.

'Well now you have to love them.'

Jud grimaces again.

'Are you sure this will work?'

'Of course not. But it's your best chance.'

* * *

The next day Jud stares into a dozen television cameras. He's standing in front of two shops. One is a betting shop, the other a charity shop. The street has been swept that morning, but James has brought litter with him and strewn it round the pavement. The wall was clear of graffiti yesterday, but now it boasts a single slogan: *Where is our PRIDE*. It needs to look genuine, so there's no question mark.

Jud clears his throat and nods.

'I'm here to apologise, to say I'm sorry. All politicians have to apologise for scenes like this. Our failure is huge when you come to places like this.

Where there were once communities, now there are only charity and betting shops. But you know that, don't you? You aren't part of the London elite. You live in places like this, don't you?'

'So why has this happened? Why is Britain in decline?'

Emphasise this, James told him. Really make it go home.

'You are good democrats. You have always voted for things to get better, but things have always got worse. We are meant to be a democracy, but who really rules this country?'

'Not the people.' The cameras should be close up on his face by now. 'Not you. You vote and are instantly forgotten. Global business funds political parties. Global business lobbies so that out-of-town shopping makes deserts of your high streets. Global business cuts your wages, reduces your hours, encourages you to go on temporary contracts. Global business makes you poor while you make them rich. And global business hires lawyers and accountants to make sure the rich never pay the tax they owe.'

Now he turns, swivels, and points at the wall behind him.

'I do not condone graffiti, but I am adopting that anonymous piece of street art as my slogan. If we are to be a stable, prosperous country, then everyone must be able to feel pride in where they live.'

A small crowd has gathered as he has been speaking. There is scattered applause. He's always been able to do that, to engage and carry a crowd.

'Tell it as it is,' someone shouts, dead on cue.

Jud has more to say, but instead he walks towards the small crowd, shakes hands and listens to them, nodding as he does so. James notes with satisfaction that the cameras are still filming.

25

PC Keith Loadstone hasn't given up. He's at home but he's on the hunt. Her number plate gave him the address. It also gave him the owner's name: Isabel Goulden. Her house impressed him. He'd already suspected a connection to the Goulden chain, but now he checks it and whistles to himself. No wonder she owns such a house. But what on earth was she doing laying flowers in a sinkhole? What possible connection can she have with Loadstone's Corpse?

Was he her gigolo, her toy boy? Did the family object and have him killed?

Or is there something rotten at the heart of the Goulden chain?

Out of habit he creates a timeline, writing it on a single sheet of A4 paper. In the middle of the page he places the date when he was called to deal with the corpse. At the top of the page he begins with the date of Gary Goulden's death and funeral. December to April is a blank he needs to fill.

Keith wants a cigarette but he's in the office and he just can't have one. He smothers the craving and works on.

The date of his finding the corpse isn't enough. How long had the body lain there? There was no post-mortem so he doesn't know. He makes a guess: no more than a week. The other date entries are in biro. This one he puts in pencil. Then he sits back and looks at the page. There's a long way to go.

Searching the internet gives him another date. Rumours that the Goulden chain was put up for sale began to circulate in early April, suspiciously close to the day of the murder. He needs to check if the rumours are true. There's a lot about Gouldens on the internet, far too much in fact, but the company didn't seem to be in any trouble. He reads an account of Gary's funeral. It was well attended. The collection was for cancer research. There's a Goulden Road in Didsbury. Goulden and Wind sell pianos. Charles Bernard Goulden was a bookseller in Cambridge and a small-time publisher. He died in 1953.

Keith leaves the internet, then goes onto the police computer. Bingo. One piece of information leaps out at him. Daniel Goulden is on the disappeared list. The date he went missing is uncertain, but he was last seen by his family on a Friday morning, the same day the Prime Minister resigned. It was before Keith discovered the body, but after the likely date the unknown man died.

Were there two deaths that day? Is there another body in the sinkhole?

Keith reads every word of the entry. He knows the house door had to be forced. Leah Goulden, the missing man's sister, reported him missing. Her address is the same as her mother's.

That can't be a coincidence, can it? He now has two pieces of information for Angela Matthews, one about the roses left in the sinkhole by Isabel Goulden, and the second about the disappearance of her son.

He leaves a gap on his timeline, adds two dates. The first is the date Isabel leaves the flowers at the sinkhole. The second is the date Daniel Goulden is reported missing. They are only four days apart! And the roses might not have been for the corpse. They might have been for Danny. What if there were two corpses in the sinkhole, one that sank and one that resurfaced?

He feels he's getting closer. This must be a suspicious death, perhaps two deaths, but he won't go to Angela yet. He remembers the way the mother reacted to the poster in Pickering. He's sure she saw it. Before he goes to Angela he wants to know if this is about Gouldens the company or if it's a domestic. He wants to know as much as he can about the link between the corpse and the family. There is only one test he can think of. He has a DNA sample from the corpse; he now needs one from the family. Was this a swap, or a family squabble over the proceeds of the company sale? He needs to know, and to find out he may have to break the law. He can't arrest Isabel, but perhaps he can get a sample some other way.

He knows what he is thinking is against the law. It might get him a promotion and a girl, or it might land him in serious trouble.

* * *

It's Saturday morning. Leah wakes and wonders what she has to look forward to. Patrick is dead. Danny has disappeared. Izzy, who blames herself for Patrick, now feels guilty about Danny. Martin hasn't come back.

But he won't, she tells herself, not unless I go and see him first.

Then there is the secret she carries. She knows who S is and that knowledge spooks her. The thought that a well-known, much respected woman could have pushed her boyfriend to suicide appals her.

Leah can do nothing about Izzy's hurt. It was not her fault that she was raped by her mother's long lost son. She can't find Danny if Danny doesn't want to be found. She's left a message for him and posted his photograph on all the websites. There's really nothing else she can do.

Her secret, the identity of S, discovered at Howard's memorial stone, is too big and too recent to act on.

There is only one of her problems she might solve, and that's Martin. She could go and see him, encourage him back into her life. She wants to tell him that Danny has disappeared. She doesn't like being so alone anymore. But is Martin as good as it gets? She is confident that, if she goes to see him, she can bring him back with her. But then she might never get rid of him. To go and fetch him risks making her into another kind of Howard. In one way she envies Howard. She envies him his certainty. There was one woman for him and one woman only.

Leah needs to make a decision about Martin.

She dives into the shower. Under its warm caress she asks herself the only question that matters. Do I love him? When the answer doesn't come she alters the question, down-plays it into, do I love him enough?

Drying herself, feeling the life inside her, knowing how alive she is and how young, she determines to go and see him. She can go into town, happen to go into his shop. In view of their previous habits she'll only go in if there is another customer already there. Then she'll listen to her body, see what it is telling her.

One glance at her mother tells her she needs to leave the house. Izzy looks grey and empty.

'Julia must have told them by now. Why has no one been round? I dread them coming but I'd like to get it over with.'

'I'm going into town,' Leah announces. 'Do you want anything, Mum?'

Izzy shakes her head.

'I just wish the police would come,' she says.

* * *

Keith approaches the house on foot. It's the weekend and he's in civvies. He has his badge in his pocket. He can produce it if necessary, but he doesn't want to use it unless he has to. He'll ask about Daniel. He'll say he's from the Missing Persons' Bureau, come to build up a profile.

He's been here for two hours already. He's waited for Leah to leave the house. He's as certain as he can be that Isabel Goulden is on her own when he goes to the front door. It has two bells. One is a real bell with a leather thong attached to a clanger. It looks original. The other is a modern push-button bell. Unable to decide which one to use, he rings them both and waits.

He recognises her at once. She's not dressed as she was, but it is the same woman who left the roses. It's the woman he followed into Pickering and all the way here.

Keith introduces himself. 'Mrs Goulden, my name is

Keith Loadstone. I'm from the Missing Persons' Bureau. It's about Daniel.'

He sees her face go white, notices how she grips the door. 'We've no news, if that's what's worrying you. Daniel's still missing, but we just wanted to ask you some questions.'

She doesn't react, neither shuts the door in his face nor invites him in. He puts his hand in his pocket. 'Would you like to see my identification?'

'No,' she says. 'That won't be necessary.'

'Is your daughter, Leah, at home? I know about her because she reported Daniel missing. It would be helpful if I could talk to both of you.'

'Leah's out, I'm afraid. You've just missed her. You'd better come in.'

He needs to ingratiate himself. He needs to have time alone with her. He needs to be offered a drink. He'll steal her cup if that is the only way. A part-eaten biscuit would be better still but she might miss that. Best of all would be a used tissue rescued from the bin. He has several polythene bags ready.

She leads him into the kitchen, invites him to sit down. The remains of breakfast are still there. He spots the crusts from a piece of toast but he doesn't know who ate it. The daughter's DNA might be enough, but he would prefer to get the mother's. He notices as she makes his coffee that she has small wrists. Could she be the one who was tied up that day, tied with the blue plastic twine?

He dismisses the thought. To make sure he stays in role he takes out a notebook.

'First let me reassure you, Mrs Goulden. Most people

who go missing turn up again. If you look at the figures year on year, only a tiny percentage don't turn up within twelve months. Daniel may be back with you tomorrow or next week.'

She smiles at him but asks, 'How many is a tiny percentage?'

He has to tell her the truth. '16,000,' he admits.

'That's a lot of Dannys.'

'Do you have any theory about why he might have chosen to disappear, Mrs Goulden?'

He watches her. His sixth sense tells him that she knows something. But he recognises how wary she is. He needs to prompt her some more, get her talking.

'Leah says she last saw Daniel on that Friday morning. Is that when you last saw him?'

She nods.

'Did he seem normal?'

'He was quiet, but then Danny's not a great one for talking.'

'Tell us about him, will you? It'll help us to draw up a picture.'

Keith is relieved when Mrs Goulden starts talking about her son.

* * *

Leah, still not certain what she wants from this meeting, arrives at the bookshop. Martin is there and he has a customer.

She pushes the door open. The bell tinkles and she walks in. The shop feels the same. The new books section is empty. A tall man with a shock of pure white hair is looking at the paperbacks. One side of his face is more lined than the other. He stands very upright, is wearing wellingtons and seems to be searching for a novel.

The shop is messier than when Leah cleaned it all those weeks ago, but trade seems okay. She guesses that from the large pile of books waiting to be priced before they go onto the shelves, and from the number of gaps on the shelves themselves. She wanders over to the pile. Did these come from the same house clearance as the letters and the journal? Might any of these be Howard's books?

At first Leah doesn't see Martin but then she does. He's standing talking to a girl who must be about her own age. Another customer? Two customers in the shop at the same time! Things must be looking up. Leah is about to go back to the pile of books when she looks more closely. The girl isn't a customer. She seems to be a friend. Does Martin have friends? And she's leaning in towards Martin as if she fancies him. There's a smile on her face. She has twinkly eyes and a good figure.

Leah wants to laugh. The unfancied Martin, her Martin, has another admirer. How he must hate that, she thinks. She may need to rescue him. He hasn't seen her so she watches the pair together. The girl is definitely leaning into Martin. Her arm movements are open. Her face is full on towards him. Then the girl says something and laughs. Martin laughs too and the girl uses that moment to touch him. She stretches out and touches Martin lightly on the back of his hand.

Enough, Leah thinks. He'll hate that. I need to … but

she doesn't need to rescue him. He seems absolutely okay with the touch, perfectly happy to have the girl so close. And suddenly, greatly to her surprise, she finds she is shot through with jealousy. The feeling winds her. It's so surprising that it fixes her to the spot and she stands still, doing nothing, staring at this transformation in the man she came to make up with. Neither Martin nor the girl has seen her yet. They are engrossed in each other. Leah knows she can't stand here much longer. She should either walk quietly out of the shop or walk towards Martin. But she does neither. She was always a watcher, so she watches. The girl is pretty. In spite of her laughing there's something sad about her. When she talks her face occasionally reverts to what Leah suspects is a default frown. But Martin is oblivious to all this. He seems caught in the headlights of the girl's intensity. Leah looks at the way he is standing and thinks of him the other night in his boxer shorts. He's completely relaxed, enjoying himself, enjoying the girl's attention.

Another stab of jealousy tells Leah it's time to go, but as she hesitates again Martin turns away from the girl and catches sight of her. He smiles. Leah wants to see an action replay of the smile to make sure, but it seems to be one of pleasure and a complete absence of guilt. The girl turns towards Leah and her face is both worried and curious. As if she doesn't know who I am, Leah thinks. But then, who am I? What is there for her to know?

Martin is walking towards her. Has he missed her? He seems pleased to see her. Then it's alright, Leah thinks. If he's pleased to see me, it's alright. I have nothing to be jealous of. But the jealous feeling persists. She was so certain that Martin was not desirable, and so absolutely her property, that he was to be taken up or discarded only by her.

Martin comes over and kisses her on the cheek. That surprises her too. Why has he done that in front of the girl?

'Hello Leah,' he says. 'This is Vikki.'

Vikki has come over with Martin and is standing beside him. She shakes Leah's hand, but there's something wrong about her doing that.

Then Martin turns round and says simply, 'Leah is a friend of mine,' as if Vikki is the one who needs the explanation and Leah is the one who needs explaining.

'I have to go now.' Vikki says. 'I'll see you later, Martin.'

To stick with Martin or twist. That was meant to be her choice. Instead, he seems to have abandoned her and moved on to another relationship.

She was wrong about Patrick. It seems she is also wrong about Martin.

She watches as Vikki pecks Martin on the cheek, then goes.

The other man has gone too. They have the shop to themselves.

* * *

Mrs Goulden has made Keith Loadstone a coffee but she hasn't made one for herself.

'Are you sure Danny's disappeared?' she asks. 'I mean, could it be something worse?'

Keith shakes his head. 'We don't think so. He tidied the house before he went. He posted the keys back through the door.' Keith knows all this from the report. 'Didn't Leah tell you?'

'I think she did.' Mrs Goulden reaches for the tissues box and Keith is suddenly hopeful, but she doesn't take a tissue, just moves the box to the other side of her out of the way. 'Why do so many people disappear?' she asks.

'We don't really know. With girls it can be abuse or a complete family breakdown.' Keith wishes he'd listened more carefully to that lecture, but it was so long ago. He's finding it difficult to keep up his deception. He's dying to ask other questions, but he has to remind himself that's not why he has come. 'With men it's often a sense of failure,' he tells her.

'I can understand that,' Mrs Goulden says. 'I can understand the feeling of being so ashamed you want to disappear.' She says this with surprising force.

'Did Daniel, Danny, have anything to feel ashamed of?'

Mrs Goulden gives him a mother hen look. 'No. All my children, in their own ways, are very successful. Julia is a force. James is too clever for his own good. Leah has hidden depths and surprising determination, and Danny's the good looking one. The mix came right in him.' She smiles. 'He caught everyone's eye when he was growing up.'

Gay, thinks Keith. He's found out he's gay and daren't tell them.

'Are you police?' Mrs Goulden suddenly asks.

'No, Missing Persons' Bureau,' he lies.

'Only I thought you might be. I thought that might be why you've come.'

Keith drinks his coffee slowly. Her question makes him nervous. He's running out of things to say. She's playing with the tissues box again. Keith makes some notes and suddenly snaps the book closed. He can't string this out any longer. The visit was a risk and it's got him nowhere. The crusts are still there. He'll have to snaffle one on the way out. 'Well, I suspect he'll turn up.' There are mugs on the draining board. One of those might or might not be hers. If he picked up Leah's mug by mistake, that would be okay but not good enough. He needs a sample from the mother.

'Thanks for the coffee.' Then in desperation he says, 'I hope you don't mind me saying, but there's a mark on the right side of your mouth. I suspect it's only a smudge, but you'd look better without it.'

'Oh,' she says, 'oh, thank you.'

He watches as she reaches for a tissue and extracts it. 'You'll need to lick it to get the mark off,' he tells her. Surely she'll see through this, but she wets the tissue. He watches her dab at her face. He imagines microscopic fragments of her DNA impacting on the tissue.

'Is that alright?'

'Much better,' he says, and gets up. She's rolled the tissue into a ball and is holding it in her hand.

'Stay sitting down, you look tired. I'll throw that tissue away for you.' Taken by surprise, she hands it over. He pinches it by a corner and goes towards the door. 'I hope Daniel turns up soon. I'll see myself out.'

With his left hand he grabs a polythene bag and

opens it. He drops the tissue in, then seals it up.

'Bingo,' he says to himself.

* * *

It had been awkward between them in the bookshop after Vikki left. Leah wanted to ask about Vikki, to tell Martin she knew who S was, to warn him that Julia was going to the police because Izzy was being difficult. Instead she talked about Danny, told him about going to the house and breaking in, left out the lottery ticket but rattled off what the policeman had said about the number of people who walk out of their lives. He'd listened.

He listened but said nothing so she ploughed on. She found herself repeating details about the orderly way Danny had left the house. She was running out of things to say when another customer saved her. He collected books about the Second World War and asked whether Martin had got Antony Beaver's book about Stalingrad. The two men walked off together to the back of the shop and Leah shouted after them, 'I've got to go now.' She added, 'I'll see you later,' as she fled.

Back outside, walking home, she feels stupid and rude. She kicks at a branch on the bridle path. Because she's embarrassed, she says out loud, 'Vikki's welcome to him.'

To hide the pain she makes herself think about S. S's choice was so clear-cut and so wrong. Howard wouldn't have let S walk out of the shop. Howard wouldn't have put a customer first. But S might have done exactly what Leah has now done: grabbed at the opportunity to walk away.

26

Stella Stelling and Jud Mindsett shake hands in the wings. 'Good luck,' Stella tells him.

Jud knows he'll need all the luck he can get.

'And you,' he says, but it already feels limp, as if she has somehow gained an advantage even before they go on stage. Remember everything James told you, he whispers under his breath. Use every weapon you have. This is a cage fight. There are no rules.

Then they walk together into the spotlights and the audience claps. Jud lost the toss so Stella will speak last. She will have the final word.

Leah watches with Izzy, sitting together on the settee. Martin listens on the radio in his flat. When the camera comes in close on Stella's face Leah smiles. I know who you are, she thinks. I know what you did. There's no way on earth that I'm going to support you.

The adjudicator explains the format and invites Jud to make an opening statement. He walks forward and looks at the audience. He has two minutes.

'Help me out,' he suddenly shouts at the audience. 'Help me out. The bankers caused the crash. You know that. Caused it by gross negligence. You had to bail them out. How many of the bosses went to prison? None. Not a single one. How many of the bosses were personally fined? None. How many of them lost their pensions or their retirement packages? None. None. None. Instead the banks were fined. What a farce, because who paid those fines? You did. You did, because by then you owned the banks. You, the struggling taxpayer, had to bail them out. That is how Britain actually works today. A small group of elite people can do what the hell they like, can act with a thorough disregard for the country they live in and walk away from the car crash they make of your lives, smiling the smile of the winner. You know that's true. Take another example. This is meant to be a democracy. One person one vote. You are meant to call the shots, you are meant to make the changes. But you don't, do you? Those who fund the parties call the shots. Party donors control everything about this country. They lobby. They make policy. They run the newspapers. They turn politicians into puppets. Well, I promise you here and now that I will be nobody's puppet.'

'But my rival tonight is a puppet. If you look carefully you can see her strings. Ask her who funds her campaign. Ask her how many times in the last year she has met party donors. Ask her who deregulated the banks which helped cause the crash in the first place.'

'The country is rotten through and through. Its systems no longer work. Its democracy has been bought and paid for. We need real change in Britain.'

Jud stands ramrod straight. 'Because democracy has failed, democracy must change. This is a massive task. We need stability. We need ten-year parliaments. On my first day in power I will set up a committee of experts to write a new constitution for this country. The driving principle behind that committee will be the need to make sure that the rule of law is no longer synonymous with the protection of the elite.'

Leah is cheering. Martin, sitting alone in his flat, is appalled. The audience in the television studio is stunned, but there are some shouts and there is some clapping.

The cameras show Stella with a rueful half smile on her face. The first question comes from a member of the audience. What would either of the candidates do about the Southern Rail strike? Stella is first to answer.

'I'd sack the Junior Minister. At the heart of every question tonight will be the issue of competence. Who is the more competent to run this country? The contract my government signed actually promises to pay the company for days when its workers go on strike. So what possible motive does the company have to settle the strike? Jud Mindsett signed that contract. I suspect that Jud Mindsett didn't even read that contract before he signed it. Then there was the issue of the other rail contract which Jud Mindsett awarded to a company that was known to be in financial trouble and promptly went bust. It's easy to spout idiocies about the big issues but it's the details that matter most, and the only two practical issues that Jud Mindsett has ever been asked to manage have both turned into disasters.'

Jud Mindsett pauses before he answers. 'Being fair to Stella, there was one bit of truth in that outrageous statement you just heard. My government signed. You heard that, didn't you? My government signed. And the most interesting word is 'my'. Stella Stelling's government. Not the Prime Minister's government, hers. She has been pulling the strings behind the scenes all this time. So let me put this on record now. I read that contract, of course I did. I could see the problem and I argued that it needed to be rewritten. But the train company is a party donor, and they insisted that the contract must stand unchanged. I, as a Junior Minister, signed it because I was told to. It was exactly the same with the construction contract. Ladies and gentlemen, I leave you to draw your own conclusions about exactly who it was who told me to sign.'

James watches from the backroom, sitting by one of the monitors. At this answer he punches the air, and he does so again when the camera does a close-up of Stella's face. Her mouth is hanging open as if she can't believe what she has just heard.

Stella turns to the adjudicator. 'Can I just ...'

'You've given your answer, Stella. It's one answer to each question, no follow-ups.'

Stella stands silent. The adjudicator moves on to the next question and the next and the next.

Then it is Stella's turn to have the last word.

'Politics has always been the art of the possible. All politicians face difficult questions. I have answered every question as truthfully as I can; I am only sorry that my opponent has not. I have taken my share of responsibility when we have made the wrong decisions. He has taken responsibility for nothing. That is how you know liars. They never accept responsibility. Liars can be dazzling, as can the easy answers they offer. But lying erodes trust. Partners know that. Parents know that. You know that, so ask yourself, do you really trust this man with ten years in office? Would you even trust him to run a sub post office for ten minutes? I don't think I'd trust him to run one of those miniature railways that go round in a circle. I know he can't be trusted with a whole network.'

'She's right,' Izzy says. 'You can't trust him. Look at his eyes.'

Leah squirms on the settee and thinks, but I know the truth about Stella. I know she isn't to be trusted either. Then Stella turns to the camera.

'Enough about my opponent. I went into politics because of a conversation with a homeless single mother. Her parents threw her out when she got pregnant. The father of her child had already begun to hit her. She was resigned to her half life but determined to do the best for her child. Some people in this country lead shitty lives. I'm not going to apologise for that word. No other word will do. I have dedicated my life to trying, in small but important ways, to make life better for our most disadvantaged. Each person we help strengthens society. Each person we throw into the gutter weakens us all. I don't expect to get everything right, but I do promise to try as hard as I can to make this society stronger and fairer.'

* * *

In his flat Martin sits up. The interview with a single mother whose partner hits her. He's read that somewhere. Leading such shitty lives. Now he remembers. S must be Stella. Stella was the young woman who rejected Howard. Stella wrote the letters that he picked up from Vikki. Stella was the cause of the row he had with Leah.

* * *

In the Arts and Crafts house the programme ends. Credits roll and suddenly Leah sees a man with a mass of hair hugging and congratulating Jud Mindsett. She'd know that hair anywhere. 'Look Mum, it's James.'

'Where?'

'There.' But by the time Izzy looks the camera has moved on.

* * *

Danny never saw any of the hustings. He's two streets back, crouched down by a wall with a plastic cup in front of him. He hasn't shaved. His hair is a few days more dishevelled than last time. He looks rough but he no longer sleeps rough. Harry has found him a flat. It's scruffy and next to a bail hostel. Now he's employed he has to live his cover. To his neighbours he's taking his first steps back from living on the streets. To passers-by he's a beggar and a scrounger. A comparison between a CCTV image of him taken before the incident with the baseball bat and one taken now would show only minor differences. To all intents and purposes he is the same.

He has a new name and a new NI number. He hasn't used either. In his pocket is a special camera that fits inside his hand. He still pockets any coins placed in his cup. He still goes through the motions, but all the time he watches. They've taught him to watch without seeming to. They've trained him in what they call incidental observation. He's using the technique now. A car is parked across the road from where he sits. It's Stella Stelling's car. He's not here to watch over Stella. He's been told to focus on Mindsett. So far he's seen nothing suspicious during his long vigil. No one's loitered. No one's opened high windows or gathered in small groups to demonstrate. Now he sees Stella herself come out with her minder and get into the car. He scans rooftops again. Nothing. The car moves off, joins the traffic, slips out of sight. As the car moves he looks around him. Is that all the protection she gets, one minder? As far as he can see, no one else is looking out for her.

Everyone else spills out of the front of the building. The street is swamped with people. That means his vigil is over. He picks up the plastic cup, empties the coins into his pocket and squashes the cup. Now he can go back to his new flat and get something to eat. But then he notices a door open at the back of the building and spots a man slipping out, closing the door behind him, pulling a hood over his head and moving quickly away.

Curious, Danny stays where he is. The man is heading his way and there's something furtive about him, not only in the way he left the building, but in how he walks. His head is down and he's walking fast, but he's also glancing round him as if he's uncertain about where he's going or whether he might be being followed. Danny is standing at a junction. The man looks up as he comes towards it, searching for the street sign. Then he ducks his head down, but not before Danny has recognised him. It's Jud Mindsett wearing a different coat. Jud is his responsibility. He needs to follow.

The lights change. Jud Mindsett sets off. He's a big man and so it's easy to keep track of him. Danny finds he can stay back. London is busy, so the pavements give plenty of cover. As he follows, Danny learns more about his quarry. Jud is going somewhere he doesn't know because he keeps checking road signs. When he's sure of the street he keeps his head down. He's maintaining a good pace, but Danny knows it's forced, as if he's late for something. When he gets close Danny can hear Jud's laboured breathing. He also walks with a kind of rolling gait which he keeps trying to correct but soon goes back to. Why is he walking, Danny wonders. Surely he could take a taxi if he finds walking so uncomfortable. Immediately he has the answer: because he's going somewhere he shouldn't. A taxi driver would recognise him and remember where he put this fare down. Jud clearly can't risk that.

Jud is also nervous. Danny can sense it. Those weeks on the streets have helped him to read other people. The fear isn't only about being recognised, it's about what may happen when he gets to where he's going.

It's dark now. Daylight London has segued into night-time London. Street lights, shop fronts, neon signs and curtained windows all spill their lights across the road. Jud may be walking fast but Danny can more than match him. At one point Danny crosses the road to observe Jud from the other side, and also to check if he is the only person trailing him. Danny doesn't know if he's a lone backstop or part of a team. If Jud has a team looking after him Danny ought to be able to spot them. But if Jud has a team he seems to have given them the slip. Danny's instructions are to keep back, observe and report. He's only to intervene if he sees a direct threat to his quarry.

Once across the road Danny can more easily observe the whole street. He sees Jud battling the crowd, occasionally ducking out of view but always moving. Then he appears to bump into a tall, painfully thin man in a gilet that's too short for him. The thin man is annoyed. He shouts something at Jud which makes Jud look up. What happens next is extraordinary. The thin man does a perfect double-take as if he recognises Jud and is surprised. But it doesn't end there. The thin man stands still and immediately reaches into his pocket to check something. Has he a gun? To his relief Danny sees him pull papers out, look swiftly through them and thrust them back into his pocket. Then the thin man turns and begins to walk quickly in the direction he came from, as if he is determined to catch up with Jud who has been swallowed by the crowd.

Danny keeps moving. It's easier to follow Jud now because the tall thin man is also following him. This allows Danny to hang back and be less conspicuous. Across the next road the crowd disperses. Jud is now on his phone and is slowing down. The thin man makes a spurt but Jud has reached his destination. A door suddenly opens as if he is expected. The door lets him in and immediately closes. The thin man shouts but he is too late. Jud has disappeared. Danny fixes the colour of the door in his memory and then slows down. He needs to get the number of the house that has swallowed Jud. He needs to keep watch. Harry's orders were to provide deep cover for the campaign, to watch for any strange behaviour round both candidates. Harry will want to know about this.

As he approaches, Danny sees that the thin man hasn't moved away. He's standing outside the black door and looks as if he is about to kick it in. Danny slips across the road. He's seen a dark doorway on the opposite side. He disappears into it and waits. He's warm now from the walking, but he knows that he'll soon cool down. If Jud has gone into the house he has to come out.

Danny settles into the doorway and reforms his cup.

The thin man has stopped interrogating the door. He takes photographs of the door, of the house and of the street. Then he heads across the road, walking straight to where Danny is sitting.

When he reaches the doorway he sees Danny and looks him over.

'Beggars sit in crowded areas, is rule, no? Beggars sit where they can be seen, not in the darkness. Rough sleepers have bags or cardboard, something for their possessions, something to keep them warm. You are either a stupid beggar or a member of MIs.'

'MIs?'

'MI5, MI6, MI so secret it doesn't even have a number, one of the MIs.'

The man holds out his hand. 'Ivor,' he says.

'Patrick,' says Danny. He shakes the hand and then in a quick movement Ivor is sitting beside him, very close.

'I think we have a long wait for Bastard Jud. No?'

Danny nods. What else can he do?

'And we need to keep warm?'

Danny nods again.

'So none of this English reserve. We sit close.'

Ivor shuffles up and leans against Danny. 'That's better. I'm Russian. We also have sets of initials: KGB, SVR, FSB and FSO. The initials change, the bastards stay the same. I work for the KIB. This stands for *Komitet Ivor bezopasnosti*. The Committee for Ivor's Security. Who do you work for?'

Danny says nothing.

Ivor shrugs. 'Makes no difference. I find out in three days max.'

Danny is watching the door. He can feel the warmth of the tall man and is glad of it. 'Why are you following Jud Mindsett?' he asks.

'I have things on him. Lots of kompromat. I mean to blackmail him into granting me citizenship. What about you?'

'He slipped his security team, but he didn't slip me,' Danny says.

'Is bastard, total bastard,' Ivor pronounces. 'I want citizenship. I have enough stuff on him to fill three front pages, but it is no use unless I can meet him. I wait in his surgery. He avoids me. I seek him in London. He will not let me get near. You can't blackmail a man you can't meet.'

Danny says nothing so Ivor continues. 'Maybe you can get me citizenship. You work for one of the MIs. I hand you my stuff. You make your name. You reward me with citizenship. Yes?'

'It doesn't work like that here,' Danny tells him.

'Is in the world, this England? This works most places. At home it takes three days max before I am either citizen or dead.'

Time passes. They sit together. Then the door opposite opens. Two men come out, look up and down the road and see that it's empty. They stand in the light of the doorway for a moment and shake hands. One is Jud. He smiles. He seems pleased. The other looks like a shrunken form of Jud. He has the same girth but is much shorter. In spite of this, he seems the senior figure. Danny has the camera he was given ready. Without moving he takes three photos in rapid succession. The two men don't waste time. It's a quick goodbye before the door closes and Jud is again on his own in the dark street. He shuffles quickly away.

Danny is about to get up and follow when Ivor holds him down and clamps a hand over his mouth. Jud is getting away, but Ivor has a strong grip and Danny senses that he's afraid of something.

They wait like this until a taxi crawls along the road and stops at the house opposite. The short fat man re-emerges and hustles himself into the taxi. They hear the front door being locked, and only when the taxi leaves does Ivor relax.

'Whole new ball game,' he tells Danny. 'This is whole new ball game. Ivor is maybe out of his depth. Suddenly Russia seems safer.'

'Why?' Danny asks. 'What's happened? Why is Russia safer now?'

'Anywhere is safer,' Ivor tells him, 'anywhere where that man isn't.'

'Jud Mindsett?'

'No, the small fat one. I recognise him. I've seen him before. His name is Borstov.'

27

'Are you sure?'

'I know him anywhere. Mindsett is small scale, is kindergarten compared with Borstov.'

Danny takes out his mobile, phones Harry.

Harry picks up at once. 'Borstof,' Danny says. 'I need some information. Jud Mindsett left the hustings on his own by a back door. I followed him.' He decides to leave Ivor out of this. 'I followed him solo. He came to a house in Doughty Street, Number 52. He met a man there who I believe is called Borstof.'

'How did you know this was suspicious?'

'He walked here in spite of being unfit. He slipped out of the back of the building, pulled a hood over his head and walked. I presume he couldn't risk a taxi driver recognising him or he would never have walked so far. He started fast and was soon out of breath. He phoned the house he was going to before he got there and the door was opened for him the moment he arrived.'

The line goes silent. Then, 'Please spell Borstof.'

'B O R S T O F', Danny says. 'I think that's it.'

Ivor shakes his head. Mouths V. 'Try V at the end,' Danny suggests.

There's more silence on the other end of the line.

'Dimitri Yurovich Borstov?' Harry asks.

Danny covers the phone and repeats the name. Ivor nods.

'Correct,' Danny tells Harry.

'Stay there for now. I want to know anyone who goes into or leaves the house. When we take over make yourself scarce.'

'How will I know it's you?'

'You'll know.' Harry rings off. Danny relays what he's just heard to Ivor, warns him to make himself scarce.

'MI's not that quick.'

'Who is Dimitri Yurovich Borstov?'

'Was KGB, now is FSB. As I said, the initials change, the bastards stay the same.'

'Why is Jud Mindsett interested in an FSB officer?'

'He's either being blackmailed or he is playing games. Have you heard of Kompomat?'

'No.'

'I'm cold,' Ivor says. 'There is a bar nearby stays open late.' He gives directions. 'Meet me there when you are free. Buy me some vodkas, okay?'

Danny nods. A car is coming down Doughty Street from the north. Ivor leaves so quietly that Danny hardly notices him go. The car stops a hundred yards away. Three men get out and seem to vanish. Even with his eyes adjusted to the darkness Danny finds it hard to be sure they are there. Then he sees them. They move like shadows. One uses the darkness behind the lights of another car to cross the road. Danny stays where he is.

The agent reaches him impossibly quickly. 'Patrick?'

Danny nods. 'Time to scoot. Harry says well done.'

Danny gets up and notices there is another car already parked down the road. It wasn't there a few moments ago and he never saw it arrive. He has much to learn.

* * *

Leah is thinking about going to bed when she hears the vehicle arrive and then the doorbell. She opens the door. It's Martin.

'Hello Leah,' he says, and waits to be invited in.

'Is Vikki with you?' Leah asks, suddenly feeling spiteful.

'No.'

'Then you'd better come in.'

He comes in and stands in the hall, waiting.

'Oh, Martin,' Leah says. 'For God's sake stop being so like yourself. Go into the lounge. Izzy has gone to bed. Shall I make you a coffee?'

'Yes please.'

She makes the coffee and carries it through. Martin's just sitting on the settee. Leah hands him the coffee and stands with her back to the fire.

'Please sit down, Leah. I need to tell you something.'

That you're seeing Vikki, Leah thinks. I know that already.

'About Vikki?' she asks.

'Partly.'

Leah notices the frown.

'Well, shall we start with that?' Leah asks. The feeling of being jealous has never left her. When she saw him on the doorstep just now she was both pleased and afraid.

'It concerns Vikki because they came from Vikki's dad's house.'

Leah isn't following him. 'What did?'

'Stella Stelling's letters.'

Leah sits down next to him on the settee, next to him but not touching. 'How did you know?'

'I watched the hustings. Stella told the same story, about the single parent.'

'I went to Howard's memorial,' Leah tells him. 'She was there in a chauffeur-driven car. She'd come to lay flowers. I recognised her.'

'When was this?'

Leah tells him.

'That was the day she announced she was standing,' Martin says.

Leah hadn't thought of that.

'Clearly feeling guilty,' Leah says.

'Or remembering the choice she made. She never married. She's famous for having stayed single.'

'Guilt again.'

'Yes, I expect so.'

'Well?'

'Well what?'

'Are you in a relationship with Vikki?'

She sees him squirm. 'I suspect the answer is, not yet.'

'And what are we going to do about the letters and the journal, Martin?'

'That's probably the same question.'

'Why?'

She watches him take a deep breath and stare into the fire.

'I love you,' he says. 'I don't love Vikki. She seems to have taken a fancy to me and of course I'm flattered, but I've always loved you, Leah, since the first days.'

'There's a but coming,' she says.

'Perhaps.' He goes on. 'When you were in trouble, my love deepened but had to remain unspoken. When Patrick died, I knew what I felt but had no idea what your feelings for me were. I suspect you felt grateful but not much more than that.'

He pauses. 'I stayed and then I took charge of those bloody letters. They'd already caused Vikki not to speak to her dad for twenty years. Then they divided us. I love you, but the row about the letters warns me we might not be compatible. I still think you're just wrong about Howard.'

'He died for her. He died because without her his life wasn't worth living. She led him on and then dumped him.'

'Leah, it is possible to love too much.'

Now it is Leah's turn to be silent. Martin waits.

'You say you love me, Martin, but you walked out on me the other night, walked out without saying goodbye. Why did you do that?'

'Because I don't love you as much as Howard loved Stella. I can contemplate life without you. Please don't get me wrong. I don't want life without you. I don't want to be with Vikki, but I think I now know that you and I want different things from life. In the long term that will split us, so it might as well split us now. I haven't got your grand aspirations. Look at my bookshop.'

There is a long silence before Martin asks, 'So what are we going to do with the letters?'

'They are yours,' Leah tells him. 'That's what you

really came for, isn't it? Vikki sent you because she wants them back.' She hears the spite in her own voice and is disgusted with herself.

He shakes his head. 'They can ruin Stella.' Martin looks straight at her. 'You do know that, don't you?'

'I know things you don't know. I know James is now working for Jud Mindsett.'

Martin is horrified. 'How do you know?'

'I saw him on television hugging the candidate.'

'Your brother is a clever and fiendishly amoral man. What does Roz think?'

'I suspect she's left him.'

'You've lit a fire,' Martin says. 'There's still enough of a fire in the grate. Let's burn the letters and the journal now. Then they can never be misused.' He gets up from the settee to fetch them. He's on the way out of the room when she calls him back.

'Martin, they're not there. I've put them in ... a safe place,' Leah tells him.

Martin stands as if transfixed. He looks round at the room, looks long and hard at Leah. 'You're hiding them from me?'

'I'm keeping them safe,' she tells him. 'Vikki can't have them back.'

She watches him, hears the sigh and sees the way he resigns himself. Always the gentleman. He won't fight her.

'Tell me,' he says, 'before I go. Tell me what you felt for me.'

She hears the past tense, knows this is her moment, that if she says the wrong thing he will never come back. She knows he's a man who likes sex. Vikki will do that for him. Martin would never dump anyone who wanted him. But what about her? She begins to know more about herself and who she is. She didn't speak for all those years. She took on the man who raped her then watched him die. In spite of that stab of jealousy she looks into herself and can find nothing soft there. And the truth is that she's never known what she felt for Martin. The only clue she's ever had was her reaction when she saw Vikki kiss him in the bookshop. She'll tell him that. She still owes him.

'I didn't like it when Vikki kissed you.'

Hope suffuses his face. She sees it take hold there. Is this what she wants?

He walks towards her. 'Then burn the letters. You and I are not power-brokers, but we might hold the outcome of this election in our hands. So let's stay neutral. Let them fight it out between themselves. The letters and the journal have to be burnt.'

She shakes her head. 'I can't do that,' she says. 'Did you hear the things Stella said about Jud?' But this is Martin she's talking to, so she mustn't leave it there. She's never lied or hidden things from him and she feels the need to justify herself, so she adds, 'I aim to even out the odds.'

He gets up. There is a terrible hurt look on his face which she cannot bear.

He makes for the door, then turns in the doorway. 'I really thought you would be on Stella's side,' he says. 'After all, you are so like her.'

And he is gone.

What did he mean, that she's so like Stella? Leah sits there for a long time, sits still and silent. The fire dies down and the last red embers fade to grey. Only then does she get up and go to bed.

She wishes she hadn't told James about the letters and the journal, but they are already parcelled up ready to be collected. She wonders what she did or still does feel for Martin. She wonders most of all exactly what she thinks about herself.

* * *

The place, when Danny finds it, is a dive, a late-night drinking spot full of men downing shorts. Ivor is waiting for him. 'Over here MI. Your people came?'

Danny nods, buys Ivor a double vodka and a single for himself. The barman wants to know what kind. Ivor scrutinises the bar and makes a choice, motions Danny over to a corner table.

'Show me the photos, please.'

Danny hands over the camera.

'Mobile phone?'

Amused, the first warmth of the vodka hitting the back of his throat, Danny hands that over too, then watches as Ivor presses buttons, brings up menus, and scrolls the screens. Then he hands them back.

'Good camera that,' he tells Danny. 'I've copied photos onto your mobile.'

'Why?'

'Insurance.'

'Insurance against whom?'

Ivor laughs. 'Only worthwhile insurance is personal. You need to transfer photos again. You need another copy somewhere else.'

'I work for good people,' Danny insists. 'I don't need to do all this.'

Ivor drinks his vodka in one swallow, calls for another.

'You are right. There are some good people,' he says. 'My dad was a good person. My history teacher was a good person. Both losers. There are good people but there are no good organisations.'

The next double vodka arrives. 'Englishman, if you are going to work in this crazy world, you need to understand the world view of a crazy Russian.'

Danny's feeling good about himself. He feels he did well tonight. He feels important. He feels in the thick of things. Following Mindsett was like holding the knife in front of the real Patrick. He's been on the streets, now he's in a dive. He likes the newness, the changeability of his life.

'Go on.'

'At one time war was tanks and bombs and soldiers. Now only Arabs and Africans fight like that. Second Iraq War finished wars between big nations for ever. Oil was oil and in Saudi. Now oil is fracking and solar and wind and these are everywhere, so who needs to invade anywhere? Look at the world you live in, Patrick. It fights covert. You are Putin. Your country is poor again. There are shortages so you distract your voters, give them back Crimea. Not an invasion. You suborn it, plant agents, manipulate news and bang, it's yours. You have Black Sea port again. UN protests no good. You're in Crimea. You stay there. End of Lesson One. Okay, you understand?'

Danny nods.

'Lesson Two: weapons. So many weapons: football hooligans, drug cheating, small scale insurgencies, fake news, cyber, cyber, cyber. Low cost, no mums crying over dead soldier sons.'

'Drug cheating tells you everything you need to know about modern day Russia. So unnecessary but they do it. Why? Because he likes to stack the odds. Elections are now their thing. Why face a good leader when you can face a poor one? Answer simple: interfere in elections, make sure the incompetent candidate is elected. Putin is vain man, so he understands vanity. Wikileaks another vanity project, so Putin gives them materials to leak, always against the West. Look round you. Open your eyes. Is democracy strong?'

'I think so. It outperforms all other systems.'

'They hate it. They hate it so much.'

'Why?' Danny asks.

'Berlin Wall down, reunited Germany. Loss of power, loss of face. Cold War lost, so start another colder war. Read Russian history, is all there.'

Ivor is on his fourth double vodka by now. His language is becoming more truncated and there is an edge to his voice. The joviality is no longer there. He goes silent. His lips seem occasionally to start saying something else but decide not to.

'What is it?' Danny asks. 'I'm ready for the next lesson.'

'Not sure. New thing happening. Is to do with plutocrats and oligarchs.' Ivor relapses into silence. Then, 'Plutocrats also have long memories. They also buy elections. You know that. I sense new alliances.

Russia, China ruled by elites. America no different. Here too is happening. As if men of business get together, make sure government always works for business …' he pauses, '… and for hedge funds.'

'I don't believe you,' Danny says. 'I don't believe you.'

Ivor reaches forward and grips Danny's shoulder.

'Go back to your old life, Patrick. Stay in your little democratic garden. Don't become watcher on the wall like me. Keep your eyes closed. Is only way to be happy.'

Danny feels and hears the despair and the urgency in Ivor's voice.

'What did you see tonight, eh? A British politician meeting a Russian spy master. Did they seem happy together? Of course.'

'That's just Jud Mindsett, isn't it?'

'Then wait, Patrick, wait for what will happen next.'

In all this time Ivor hasn't relaxed his grip on Danny's shoulder.

'Wait and be afraid for yourself. Your name is not Patrick. They employ you because you are expendable. What you have seen tonight is dangerous for Britain, but it is also terribly dangerous for you, my non-Patrick friend. Join the *Komitet Ivor bezopasnosti.* You need insurance. We all need insurance these days.'

'Another vodka?' Danny offers.

Ivor shakes his head. 'Drunkenness has always been the Russian answer to the problem of living. I do not want to be Russian anymore.'

28

Two days later Keith Loadstone collects the results. He had to lie to get the DNA test done, had to invoke the name of Angela Matthews and insist that she'd given her permission.

'Are you sure?' the lab technician had asked. 'Only we keep getting orders to cut down on expenses.'

Keith had held his ground. 'I can go and get a written permission slip if you want,' he'd offered.

The technician had looked him in the eyes, then said, 'That won't be necessary.'

Keith had handed over the tissue and one of the samples from the corpse. The technician had sniffed at the tissue sample in the plastic bag. 'It's not even in a police evidence bag.'

'I know. I was off duty. It was a chance meeting.'

For a moment it had looked as if he might have to go to Angela after all and beg, but the technician had sniffed again and said, 'I'll book it out in your name. It's no skin off my nose.'

Now Keith held the results envelope in his hands. If there was a match Angela would let him re-open the case. If there was a match, then the Goulden family were up to their necks in the shit and he could crack the case wide open.

But if there was no match the Goulden family were in the clear and he was in the shit. Impersonating an officer from the Missing Persons' Bureau, continuing to work on a case that had been closed, lying in order to gain a test result, and then the most serious charge of all as far as SDM Angela Matthews was concerned: wasting police resources.

He takes the envelope and walks outside, walks all the way to his car and climbs in. Even then he doesn't open the envelope at once. There is so much riding on what it says.

Slowly and neatly he prizes the envelope open and slides out the piece of paper. It takes him a while to work out what it is and what it says. The single page consists of three columns. The first is headed **Locus**, the second **Sample From Tissue**, the third **Sample From Deceased**. Under Locus is a long series of capital and number codes, each with a number to two decimal places. The numbers seem low. He wonders what that means and moves his eyes slowly and carefully to the bottom of the page.

And there is a section headed Interpretation. Keith reads it carefully twice.

> *Based on testing results obtained from analyses of the DNA loci listed, the probability of a close familial relationship between these two individuals is under 20%, which for practical purposes means that they are not related.*

He stares at the result. He was so sure. Could the lab have muddled the samples? Is this the correct results sheet? He looks at it again. He now realises that, incriminatingly, the lab technician has kept his promise, and there is his name on the sheet. Anyway, how many other matches would be asked for between a tissue sample and a corpse? It has to be the right match and therefore the right result, so why was Mrs Goulden placing flowers in the sinkhole? He doesn't have long. The same results will soon be on Angela's desk. She'll call for him and that will be that.

He starts the car. He's in so much trouble already that one more incident won't make any difference. He has the address. He has a fingerprints kit. He has the knife. London is only three hours away. He can be there and back in a day.

* * *

'Why didn't you tell me?' Leah asks. It's the same day. Leah and her mother are sitting on the bench outside the front door. It's warm and still. The only sound is the hum of bees rolling in the tulips. England in April. New leaves on the trees. It doesn't get better than this.

Izzy looks at her. 'It didn't seem important.'

'You should have told me, Mum.'

An orange tip butterfly is working the border.

'And you have other things on your mind.'

Leah grimaces.

'One night Martin's here and in your bed. The next he's gone. Then he turns up late and goes away again.'

Leah changes the subject. 'So what happened?'

'He said he was from the Missing Persons' Bureau. He asked a few questions about Danny. I said I didn't know why he had disappeared.'

'Where did this conversation take place?'

'In the kitchen. I thought he'd come because of what

Julia has told them, but he didn't seem to know anything about that.'

'So did you tell him, Mum? I mean, about Patrick, about what happened?'

Izzy shakes her head. 'No. I'm leaving that to Julia.'

Leah stares at the vapour trails above her. She wonders if Julia has been anywhere near the police.

'He was a nice man,' Izzy says. 'He told me there was a mark on my face. He even put the tissue in the bin for me.'

'Tissue?'

'Yes. He suggested I spit on the tissue to wipe the mark. He didn't want me to have to get up. A very considerate man.'

In spite of the heat and the headiness of the day Leah is suddenly alert.

'Was there a mark on your face, Mum?'

'I don't know, do I? I couldn't see anything on the tissue.'

'Did he give you any ID?'

'What do you mean?'

'Like a badge, like an ID card?'

Izzy shakes her head.

'Stay there, Mum. I won't be a minute.'

She goes onto the internet. There are photographs in the police station of the local force. Leah thinks these might also be on the web. She scrolls down, looks at menus. Soon she has them. It's a chance. She calls Izzy in.

Izzy looks at the screen and goes for her glasses. When she comes back she stares at the photographs and picks him out at once. Leah reads the name: PC

Keith Loadstone. With Izzy watching she cross-checks with the Missing Persons' Bureau. There is a similar set of photographs. PC Loadstone isn't there. He doesn't work for the Missing Persons' Bureau. Leah goes back to the local force.

'Take another look, Mum. Are you quite sure?'

Izzy peers. 'Yes. I quite fancied him. He was a good-looking man.'

They drift back outside to sit on the bench. It's just too nice to stay in.

'He might be in both,' Izzy suggests. 'The force and the Bureau.'

Leah closes her eyes, lets the warmth take control of her, enjoys the pink view through the stretch of her own eyelids. What happened when the PC called? Why did he really come? Leah remembers the numbers of those who go missing. They can't visit all their homes or even very many of them. Suddenly she wants Martin's advice, wants to put the problem to him. But she can't return the letters and journal. James already has them. She remembers Martin's moment of hopefulness the other night. She knows how he'll react to a phone call. Life is so difficult now. It was better when I didn't speak, she thinks.

'You miss him, don't you?' Izzy suddenly says. 'I miss Patrick. You miss Martin. You can do something about your unhappiness. I can't.'

It isn't that simple. Can Martin ever forgive her for handing over the letters to James? Is she prepared to try to get them back? Has he slept with Vikki? She knows just how easy it was to seduce Martin. Has he already made promises to Vikki? If so, there is no way he will break them.

Time matters. If she phones him, then she too is making a kind of promise, is committing to a choice about her own future when she isn't ready to do that. And what had he said to her the last time he left? 'I really thought you would be on Stella's side. After all, you are so like her.'

What did he mean?

She doesn't decide, at least not consciously. But she has sat for long enough and her legs take her to the phone. Her hand picks it up. Her finger presses the right buttons. It's ringing before she's worked out what she'll say.

She listens to the rings, imagines a customer in the shop, then imagines Martin in bed with Vikki in the flat above. The ringing goes on. She holds and holds before putting the phone down and going back outside, back to a life with just her Mum for company.

* * *

London was once Keith Loadstone's métier. Driving in it feels like coming home. He knows the red lines and the road systems. He knows the cut-throughs. He recognises the particular energy that London has, its sheer busyness compounded by the proportion of young people drawn to the city. Does he love the North York Moors more than this bustle, he wonders, or is it the sheer contrast between the two that fascinates him? He finds his way straight to Danny's house. If the worst happens to him he can always come back to London and drive a taxi.

Keith didn't find the DNA link he expected. He's still puzzled about that. If the corpse had been in some family way connected to Mrs Goulden, then he would understand her need to put flowers in what had been his grave. If the corpse had been her long-lost son, fighting for his inheritance against acknowledged siblings, the expensive bunch of red roses would make sense.

But the corpse isn't Mrs Goulden's son. There's no familial link between them, so he needs to follow the other lead, the knife he found by the sinkhole. It's a long shot, he knows that. If the fingerprints on the knife are Daniel's, then he can place Daniel at the scene of the death. All he needs is a set of prints from the house. If they match the prints on the knife, then he might be able to turn the interview between himself and the desirable Angela from a rout to a scoring draw.

The front door lock is new. He knows that because the door jamb hasn't been painted since the lock was fitted. He's sure he could break it but it might take too long, and he'd rather no one knew he'd even been here. Round the back of the house a sycamore has been allowed to grow too tall. If he shins up he can reach the back window. Windows are much easier than doors and can more easily be closed when you leave. He's as certain as he can be that this house isn't alarmed.

He tackles the tree as if he's forgotten that he's twenty years older now. Everything that would once have been fluent is a struggle, but he gets up into the fork. Once there he tests the branch. It's strong enough. The window gives with a single prise of his instrument. It has swollen in the few months or years since it was last opened, and he has to force it upwards. He's not as slim as he once was either. But he gets one foot on the edge of the bath and from there it's easy to step down onto the lino floor.

He climbs back onto the rim of the bath to close the window after him. He needs time in here. He doesn't want to be disturbed. If the house has been cleaned he may struggle to find a print.

But he's in luck straightaway. Toilet handles are the one thing everyone touches and no one cleans. A single flick of his make-up brush loaded with powder and he can see the prints there. He photographs them in situ, but then decides to take the handle with him. He lifts the lid off the cistern and loosens the plastic nut with both hands. Then he gently pulls the handle clear and bags it. Now he can produce two sets of fingerprints for Angela, those on the knife and those on the handle. This time he hopes they will match.

In order to be thorough he continues his search, decides to bag the toothbrush to give him another DNA sample. He finds and photographs other fingerprints.

When he has finished what he came to do he listens before he moves. The house is silent. There are only city noises, traffic, a siren some streets away, a radio playing through the wall and a skip being filled. He goes out onto the landing, makes his way down the stairs. There on the kitchen table he finds all Daniel Goulden's effects. He sees the passport first. Next to his passport is a pile of bank statements. Next to those is a birth certificate and a small yellowing card with a National Insurance number. Then there's a pile of exam certificates. Just past the card is a mobile phone. He clearly meant to disappear.

Keith Loadstone stands in the kitchen and looks at the items in front of him. He's been in houses like this before. Every police officer has their missing person story. His is of a fourteen year old girl whose father took an inordinate amount of time to report her missing. Keith remembers standing on a newly carpeted floor listening to the father's grief and his flimsy excuses for not reporting her at once. 'I thought it was a sleep-over ... everyone needs a bit of freedom,' when all the time the girl's assaulted and murdered body was buried under the floorboards. The stench of her decaying was not quite hidden by the chemical smell of the new carpet and the cloying sweet-pea scent of a room freshener. It was the lowest point of his police career. There was something so pathetic and tawdry about the needs of the father that had led to the murder, and his utter inadequacy in thinking he could ever get away with it.

Keith pushes the memory out of his mind, concentrates on the present. He looks round Daniel Goulden's house and wonders what he can learn from it. There's nothing personal about the kitchen, no postcards, holiday souvenirs or fridge magnets. The lounge is the same. Just a settee, a television, a table for eating a meal, and a single cabinet full of sports trophies, the most recent of which is already eight years old.

The bedroom is functional. The only wardrobe is full of tracksuits, sweatshirts and trainers. There are several different holdalls on the top. No sign of a woman's presence or of another man. The dining room has never been used. It reminds him of something.

Keith thinks of Daniel's mother's house, of its sumptuousness. Why is this so different? What did the others say when they visited their brother here? Or have they never visited? There is a sadness about the place which disturbs him more than he expected, and something else too.

Then Keith makes the connection. This house reminds him of himself. His flats and houses have always been bachelor pads with little to show for the years he has lived. They have been lonely places. This house is lonely too, and London exaggerates loneliness. It's probably why Daniel left, why he couldn't wait to get away.

'Hello Daniel,' he says to the empty building. 'You disappeared. I fled north. But I think you were carrying the knife I found. I think it was something you did with that knife that made you disappear.'

* * *

The pelicans surprise Martin. He's heard of them but never seen them. He's crossing St James's Park. There are new leaves on the trees. He spots a sunbather shivering slightly this early in the morning. The daffodils are over and collapsing back into the earth. Tulips and wallflowers perfume the air and dazzle with their colours. Martin looks across the lake to the tumble of the Admiralty roofs with their pattern of domes and slate. He knows he would be impressed and delighted with all this if it wasn't for what he has come to do.

Stella has found ten minutes in a busy schedule. He's to come to the Ministry. He's been warned that there will be security checks, so he needs to be in plenty of time. All the way down he was worried his train would be late but it wasn't. He panicked about the tube, then found it straightforward to take the Piccadilly Line, get off at Green Park and walk down to Westminster.

The setting seems unreal to him. His purpose in coming here is unreal. All the way down a voice in his head has reminded him that perhaps nothing has happened yet. He doesn't know for definite that Leah has handed over the journal and the letters. He could, almost certainly should, have left the matter alone, let the election take its course.

He's passing a café and he's thirsty but there isn't time. Walking is taking him longer than he thought. He mustn't be late.

If he lets the matter lie he might have another chance with Leah, but he knows what he's proposing to do will drive them further apart. To take different sides in an argument is one thing, but to deliberately undermine Leah's intentions and pre-empt the outcome is something else.

He's dressed in a suit which no longer quite fits him. He feels uncomfortable and slightly sweaty after the walk but he had to wear it. He's never met anyone so important.

He finds the Ministry and gives his name, waits while the woman makes a phone call.

'Really,' she says down the phone, as if she is surprised by what she has just been told. 'Okay.'

'If you'd like to wait,' she tells Martin, and indicates a chair.

He hardly has time to sit down before an elegant young man with a sculptured goatee beard arrives to escort him.

The man makes small talk in the lift. He is wearing a badge on a lanyard but Martin has not been badged up. They arrive at the second floor and walk along a corridor. Martin finds the building intimidating. Perhaps it is meant to be so. There are important paintings and high ceilings.

The young man knocks on the door and they go in. There she is.

The young man announces him and stands to one side. Impressions overwhelm Martin. The room is much plainer than he expected. It's just an office but with a big window and a view. Stella Stelling is much smaller than she looks on television. She's coming across, smiling.

'Welcome,' she says, holding out her hand.

Martin takes it gently. It's small and warm.

'Would you like a drink?'

'Coffee,' Martin says. 'Milk, no sugar,' he adds.

'Please sit down.' Her voice is wary. She looks not at him but through him. 'You said you had information about Howard.'

She pronounces the name with great sadness.

Invited to speak, Martin tells her about being given the journal and the letters. He's not in control and he flounders, pausing when the coffee is brought in, waiting on her signal until the door is closed again. He tells this powerful woman that Leah was upset by what she read and that she went to the memorial, saw Stella there and made the connection. He finishes by telling her about their quarrel and about James working for Jud Mindsett. Towards the end his voice falters in the silence, so he adds lamely, 'I hope you don't mind my coming. I thought you ought to be warned. I suspect your opponent might already have this information.'

All this time she has watched him and listened, occasionally nodding, her eyes fixed on him. Now he's stopped talking she stands up and turns away from him. He thinks she might be about to cry but he can't be sure. Martin sips his coffee, remembering that Leah once told him off for slurping, and waits for Stella to say something. He notices she takes a tissue out and quickly dabs at both eyes.

She takes so long to turn round that Martin wonders if he should go. He's done what he came to do. He wants to be out of here. He feels uncomfortable. He feels as if he should never have come.

Then she sits down again but looks out of the window, not at him. He thinks she's going to ask him some questions but she doesn't. Instead she says, as if she is talking to herself, 'You make decisions in life and they have consequences that can haunt you for ever, even the seemingly ordinary matter of falling in love for the first time.'

She pauses, shakes her head. 'When I heard he'd drowned himself I was paralysed. My brain froze over. I blamed myself. I was appalled. They said it was an accident but I never believed that. He often gave me gifts, and I have wondered if his death was another kind of gift. He was utterly unselfish. I wonder if he knew that I could never be free of him if he was still alive. Is that why he removed himself from life itself? You see, he was a strong swimmer. He was the last man I would expect to drown by accident. His clothes were discovered but his body was never found. I've thought about him every day. In a strange way he still spurs me on. He chose me. I chose politics. Doing politics as well as I can is the only way I can make amends.'

She gets up as if she can't bear to stay still. 'I've kept all this to myself. I've never talked about it to a single person until you.'

The door opens. She turns quickly to the young man. 'Find me ten more minutes if you can, Philip. Tell them I'm sorry.'

Martin watches her. He knows he's in the presence of greatness.

'And now for this most intimate of matters to be made public by that man, by my opponent. For this to be smeared across the front pages. We were young and hopeful and innocent. For this to be talked about. I don't know if I can bear it.'

She stops and Martin feels he has to say something. 'I'm sorry to have been a part of this. Vikki, that's Howard's niece, told me to burn them. I should have done what she said.'

Stella is slumped in her chair. He wants to comfort her.

'Look,' Stella suddenly says, 'you've read my letters. You say you've read all of Howard's journal, which I've never seen but can imagine ...' She pauses for a long time, then suddenly asks, 'Tell me, was I right?'

Among the many forms Martin thought this meeting might take, this disturbing question never featured. She is looking at him, pleading, caring about his answer, putting him in judgement over her. It's as if they are in the confessional and he is her priest.

'I'm sorry, Martin, but I have wrestled with that question ever since it happened, and you are the only person I have ever been able to ask.'

Martin nods. 'I think you were right. I told Leah it was possible to love too much.'

A tremor goes through Stella Stelling. She looks out of the window as if she is staring back through time itself.

'Thank you,' she whispers.

Then she gathers herself, for this is a public office and she is a public person. He watches her resume her public persona. Her voice is firm again. 'When I chose to stand, I went to put flowers on Howard's memorial by way of acknowledgment of what I owe him.'

She stands up. 'Thank you for coming to see me. Thank you for warning me. I will be ready. I know you won't say anything about this. I am greatly in your debt.'

She holds out her hand, and this time the handshake is warm and personal. 'I won't ever forget.'

Martin goes out of the room and finds Philip waiting in the corridor to escort him back to the front desk. A minute later he steps into the sunshine. When he reaches the park he sits there for a long time watching the pelicans.

29

Leah has at last got through to the right person. She had to be persistent. First they asked for the complaint in writing, suggested she filled in the forms on the internet. Then they promised to send a PCSO round to see her. It has taken several phone calls and a lot of being strung out on indifferent music, interspersed with suggestions that she should go back to the internet, to finally get through to SDM Angela Matthews.

Now she is sitting across from Angela Matthews and expressing her fury that PC Loadstone should impersonate an officer from the Missing Persons' Bureau and should, in a totally underhand way, obtain a DNA sample from Mrs Goulden without making a formal request.

Angela is sitting tight-lipped and equally furious. One of the pieces of paper that has recently crossed her desk is the copy of a DNA comparison requested against her express command by Keith Loadstone. He was ordered to drop the case but he is clearly still pursuing it.

Angela wants to agree with everything Leah Goulden is saying. She wants to add her own series of complaints about Keith Loadstone. She wants to adjourn this meeting from the formal surroundings of a police station, reconvene it in the nearest café and have a real woman-to-woman bitch about him. Instead, she must smooth and placate, must promise to investigate.

All this pisses her off more than somewhat. She will have to hand the complaint over to the Police Complaints Authority. They will take months, waste money as they consider prosecution, and decide against it in about three years' time. She wants to discipline Keith Loadstone now. She wants to hang him out to dry, give him a whole stack of final warnings, perhaps transfer him out of her patch to somewhere a long way off. Is the Isle of Man short of bobbies?

Angela makes notes and nods in all the right places. Leah Goulden seems to be coming to the end of what she wants to say. It's then that Angela takes the risk.

'Can I ask, Miss Goulden, what you hope will be the outcome of this complaint?'

Leah looks surprised, so SDM Matthews repeats her question. 'What do you want to happen as a result of your complaint? What's the best outcome for you?'

Leah thinks. The question is hard to answer. 'I want him to leave my mother alone. I want to know why he did this. I want to know what he used the DNA sample for.' She can't say anything more, can she? She doesn't want a massive investigation. She doesn't know if Julia has been to the police as she promised.

'Is that all?' The words escape SDM Matthews before she can call them back. Suddenly Angela sees a way the matter can stay in her own hands and be dealt with quickly. She switches mode. 'I can assure you now that PC Loadstone will take no further part in any investigation concerning your family. I will re-assign him. You have my word.'

'Thank you,' Leah says. 'I appreciate that.'

'And I can set your mind at rest on both your other concerns as well. I happen to have seen the result of the DNA comparison. There was no link between the two samples.'

She shouldn't release that information of course, but if it helps Miss Goulden to decide not to pursue her complaint it will be worth the risk.

Leah is looking confused. 'Whose was the other sample, just as a matter of interest?'

Angela makes her play. 'I shouldn't really tell you that, but if you decide not to pursue your complaint I might stretch a point.'

Leah nods. 'I've said what I came to say. You've listened. I've no wish to take the matter further.'

Angela stifles a sigh of relief, searches for the piece of paper on her desk and finds it. 'The comparison, which should never have been made without permission, was between your mother's DNA and a man whose body we discovered in a sinkhole up on the moors.'

Leah is reaching down for her handbag. She's done what she came to do. Then she absorbs what she's just been told. 'I'm sorry, can you say that again?' Leah asks.

Angela repeats the information. 'The DNA comparison between your mother and a body we pulled out of a sinkhole on the moors shows no possible familial link between the two donors.'

'No family link?'

'None at all.'

Leah needs to leave the room quickly. The enormity

of what she has just heard demands silence and thought. She wants to be alone. She wants to talk to Martin. How will she tell Izzy, and how will Izzy react?

'Thank you for your help. You've set my mind at rest.'

Angela Matthews sees Miss Goulden out, then strides back to her room. She longs to summon Keith Loadstone and paste him but something disturbs her. She is as certain as she can be that Leah Goulden knows about the body in the sinkhole. Why else would the information shake her? Not only that, but she thought there was a link. She thought the body belonged to a family member. She was deeply shocked to find that he isn't related.

Keith Loadstone deserves a pasting but he might be right after all. Just when she has him absolutely banged to rights he comes up smelling of roses. But if she re-opens the case she has to have dinner with him.

Leah hurries out of the police station and leans against the wall. Patrick wasn't her half-brother, Patrick never was Izzy's long-lost son. She thinks of the cult, of God's Man, of the old guy who groped her in the chapel. What was it Katherine said? 'The Bible can justify anything.' Even their misrepresentations, even their smiles and every single one of their lies.

But there is another thought too. Izzy's son may still be out there. She'll need to go back to the cult, meet Katherine, force her to tell the truth about what happened to the baby Izzy handed over. Caught between anger and elation, she leans against the wall a little longer before walking more slowly to the bus stop.

Danny wakes in his new flat. For a moment he doesn't know where he is. Just recently he's woken in too many different places: under the bridge, in a police cell, in a strange flat. Last night he was drinking with Ivor. Ivor was warning him. He grabs for his phone. The photos are still there. He looks again at the clear picture of Jud Mindsett and the man Ivor called Borstov. They are shaking hands, smiling, like men who have made an agreement, men who are on the same side.

Danny has the morning off. He takes it into his head to go back to the front door in Doughty Street and just look around. He worries about what Ivor told him. Was this man really Borstov? If so, surely he was guarded. If Danny's employers have bought in background bodyguards, then the Russians will have them too.

There's milk and bread in the fridge. He has breakfast, switches on the news.

The picture is of Jud Mindsett standing in front of the Russian Embassy making a statement.

'This government has been far too complacent about the Russian threat. The Russian bear is awake again and growling. How long before it attacks?'

Danny is confused. The political correspondent, Louisa Drakutt, also seems to not quite understand what Jud Mindsett is saying. Her face on the television carries a mixture of intelligence and incredulity. The intelligence stares from her eyes. The incredulity slips from one side of her mouth. 'Are you saying that

Russia is about to attack the United Kingdom? Do you have a shred of evidence to support that assertion?' she asks.

The word 'evidence' clearly makes Jud nervous. It needs to be buried under a waste heap of clichés. 'The people of this great country have the right to be warned of the danger of a resurgent Russia. Putin is flexing his muscles, stretching his claws. Look at Crimea, look at Ukraine. I hear things. I see things. We are no longer as safe as we were. If you don't believe me, watch this space.'

The problem with Louisa's job is that interviewing only gives her one question and no follow-up. Television channels allow political answers to stand unchallenged. Too often she's left listening to utter bilge and cannot challenge it.

'My challenger never mentions Russia. Stella is weak on foreign policy. I believe she will hand this country over to anyone who asks her nicely.'

* * *

James, sitting watching from their newly-furnished HQ, thumps the air. He loves 'my challenger' as if Jud is the incumbent. He knows they are still outsiders, but polls show a rising trend and he has the letters and the journal. He's been going through, picking out key phrases and sentences to sink Stella Stelling out of sight, circling them with a red pen. Stella has a reputation for integrity and now, thanks to his surprising little sister, they can shred that whenever they choose. Jud wants to use it immediately. James has urged him to wait.

* * *

Danny wonders what Jud is playing at. He tries thinking it out. If you are about to attack Russian intentions in a televised statement, why meet with a top Russian official the night before? What is Jud up to? Ivor would know, but Danny has no way of contacting the crazy Russian. Harry might know, but Harry ordered him away.

Danny's on his way out when he remembers Ivor warned him to back up the photos. He was too tired last night. Now he feels as if he needs to be outside. He'll do it as soon as he gets back in.

When Danny was homeless he shuffled through the streets. Now he walks with purpose. He wants to know what really happened last night, so he heads back to the venue. Stepping out of the tube station he turns right to reach the building, goes round the back to where Jud Mindsett emerged, then changes his mind. He decides to retrace Jud's steps so he goes in. He still looks the bedraggled rough sleeper. People glance at him but do nothing to stop him. Is he too unsavoury or too purposeful to tackle, or are they too PC to challenge someone like him? He's looking for the route Jud took last night. As soon as he's far enough into the building he takes a door on the left and finds himself backstage. Here there are curtains and a narrow corridor. The back of the stage is virtually the back wall of the theatre. He sees the fire door. A notice tells him it's alarmed, but this must be the one Jud used. He pushes it open and the alarm sounds at once. But last night, he remembers, it didn't sound. He would have responded immediately if it had.

Instead of going through the door he stands where he is with the door wide open and the alarm sounding. Last night there were famous people here. Last night the next Prime Minister was in the building but Danny never heard an alarm. The terrorist threat is severe and yet the alarm was switched off. It doesn't make any sense. Why are they employing people like him if they then switch off the very means they have of protecting everyone in that building? Who switched it off? When was it switched off?

Danny's been standing here for two minutes and no one has reacted. No one has come. He steps through the door and closes it from outside. Now he is on the route Jud Mindsett took. He wants a second look at the house.

Until he reaches Doughty Street he is aware of nothing unusual. He wants to reassure himself that what he saw really happened.

He sees people differently now he's in the business. There are so many reasons why people stand still in a street, some innocent, some not. Smokers time their breaks together, stand close and look round. Mobile phone users tend to keep their heads down when talking, but when listening they lean backwards and gaze skywards. Then there are those who don't know where they are going. He sees them stop and consult a map, stand still and look all round them, look at the map again and move away. There's scaffolding that Danny doesn't remember from last night; perhaps he missed it in the darkness. A plasterer is standing up there finishing his cigarette. He cleans his palette by scraping his trowel carefully along its surface, holding it up against the light to check for imperfections. He's wearing a high-vis top and grey tracksuit bottoms with white trainers. None of these items is new. He looks the part. His tracksuit bottoms are speckled with different coloured paint and plaster splashes. Even perfectly costumed he could still be in the watching business.

A Chinese student and his girlfriend walk hand in hand to the front of Number 52. They take ages preparing for a selfie, and when Danny looks again the plasterer has gone back inside. Was that pre-planned?

It's a street, Danny tells himself. These people are just people, not watchers. I'm looking at it with Ivor's eyes, not my own. Nothing is happening here. Nevertheless, he walks straight past the house with his head down. He's reached a set of shops when he sees Shaun, stops and crouches down beside him.

Rough sleepers don't ask you where you've been or what you've been up to. There are too many unpalatable answers. Danny takes out a twenty pound note, rolls it up and hands it over.

'Eight cans,' he says, 'but not yet.'

'What for?'

Something about the tone makes Danny guess that Shaun has been paid by strangers before, paid for doing God knows what. Danny tries not to think about it and keeps his eyes in front of him.

'Friendship,' Danny says. 'Why not?'

'No one does that for one of us. Did anyone ever do

that for you?'

'I want you to beg in Doughty Street. I want you to watch Number 52. Remember faces, clothing. If anyone comes in or out I need photographs.' He hands over the tiny camera. 'Use this.'

Shaun palms the camera neatly. 'If I ask why, Patrick, will you tell me?'

There's a sadness in Shaun's voice. Danny shakes his head.

'I owe you,' Shaun says. 'They'd have messed me up otherwise, those lads you thumped. Where do I see you?'

'I'll be back here in about four hours. If you get photos there'll be a bonus.'

It's then Shaun breaks the rules, turns round and looks straight at Danny. 'I helped you because I thought you were genuine. Don't disappoint me. I need to believe that out here somewhere, someone is genuine.'

'I'm working my way back,' Danny tells him, still looking in front of him. 'If I ever get there I'll come and find you.'

He stands up, then turns. 'Look after that camera, won't you?'

'Why? How many cans will it buy me?'

'More than enough to send you on the mother of all benders, more than enough to kill you.'

'My way out,' Shaun says. 'We're all of us looking for a way out.'

'Don't even think it.'

* * *

'Before I answer that question,' Stella says, 'I want to make a statement.'

It's evening. Martin is back home in his flat eating a takeaway. Someone phoned the shop but he doesn't know who. He has no answerphone so no one can leave a message. As far as he knows Leah hasn't got in touch. Nor has Vikki. He's on his own again.

Martin's listening to the next hustings. He hears the voice of the woman who cried in his presence that afternoon. She sounds composed. He wonders what the hell she is about to say.

'Democracy itself is under real threat these days. It has always depended on two things: telling the truth and focussing on the issues. Democracy is demeaned by lies and personal attacks. I pledge myself to always tell the truth, however goaded I may be, and never stoop to personal attacks, however tempted. In making this pledge I make it for myself and for my team. I urge my opponent to give a similar undertaking.'

Martin, listening, understands her tactics. James recognises the trap Stella has set, prays that Jud doesn't land in it with both incompetent feet.

'Jud? Do you wish to respond to what Stella has just said?'

'Ladies and gentlemen, I wonder what she can have to hide.' Jud waits for laughter, wins none. In the silence Martin can almost hear him changing tack. 'In the name of supporting democracy, hasn't the honourable lady just demeaned it? Her presumption must be that unless I make such a pledge I am bound to lie, and unless I pledge not to stoop to personal attacks I am bound to do so. I find that deeply insulting of myself, of my team and of my party. That party, which we both serve, has promoted me in good faith, has nominated me in good faith. Her insult to me extends therefore to the party itself and to our great Prime Minister who hand-picked me. Her interjection is both unnecessary and deeply damaging. But I can promise you something. I can promise that I will act as I have always acted, speak as I have always spoken, and fight for the right leader for this party and for this great country.'

Jud waits for the applause and there is some. He waits until it is about to diminish before adding, 'I suggest the lady answer your questions and stop wasting all our time.'

But Stella is not finished. 'Ladies and gentlemen, fellow party members, please note that Jud Mindsett has not promised to tell the truth or to stay out of the gutter of politics. I hope you listened to his words carefully. Football is not the only contest that can benefit from replays. And I could tell you exactly what the Prime Minister thinks of my opponent, but I will not break my promise, nor will I speak for anyone else.'

'Now for your question. Is Russia a threat to the United Kingdom? My answer is not directly, but indirectly, yes. GCHQ has evidence of cyber-attacks that carry the Russian fingerprint. Too much Russian gangster money has been laundered in the UK. The annexing of Crimea and the incursion into Ukraine, which involved the shooting down of a civilian plane, show how dangerous Russia can be to the peace of the region. But Mr Putin has his own problems. Russia is still in recession. Most of Mr Putin's actions seem to be motivated by his need to bolster support inside Russia. In my judgement they do not yet amount to serious attempts to expand his borders.'

'Jud?'

'Too weak, far too weak. This country is not safe in the lady's hands. Russia is a country intent on expansion. Its ships and its planes are on the move. It went into Syria in order to be a powerbroker. It is utterly without a moral compass. If you don't believe what a threat it poses I suggest you watch this space. If you vote for me I will strengthen NATO. I will increase defence spending. With ten-year parliaments we will be able to develop enough experience to counter this Russian aggression. Please remember, I did not vote against British intervention in Syria as the lady did.'

That last point is true, but only because he had wandered into the wrong lobby by mistake.

* * *

Danny is on watch outside the studio. The weather has turned cold again. He has the camera he recovered from Shaun. There are fresh photos, but he hasn't had time to look at them or to show them to Ivor. He's still puzzled by what he knows. Will Jud make a similar escape after this broadcast? He hopes he has all exits covered. The clocks went forward some time ago and it's still light. Danny is leaning back against the wall. He wears a beanie hat and his legs are inside a sleeping bag. He has a white cup in front of him with some coins in. If he has to move he'll leave the cup and the bag, come back for them later. He wonders what is being said in the hustings. Such hustings are always a headache for watchers. It's easier to guard a small-scale event like the tour of a factory or a region than to watch a mass audience move in and out and swirl round you.

Then he sees someone he recognises. It's Borstov. The low sun catches him full in the face as he waits to cross the road. A huddle of men move round him. Others follow farther back, so that Borstov travels like a spider in the centre of its web. And outside the circle, someway back, is a single point like an anchor. Danny recognises him too, his long hair, his tall, rangy figure, the blue gilet. It's Ivor.

Danny scans the margins and sees no other watchers. Harry doesn't seem to have this covered. Danny reaches for his phone, finds favourites.

'Yes?'

'Harry, Borstov is on the move. He's mob-handed. Are you aware?'

'Where is he now?'

'Junction of Coney Street and Spurrier Street.'

'Where's he heading?'

'I don't know. Do you want me to follow?'

For a moment there's no answer. Danny waits and watches. By now Borstov is across the road with his thugs and someone is waiting to meet him, has come out specially. He's an overweight man with a shock of permed black hair. Even from the back Danny recognises his brother.

'Can you still see the target?' Harry asks

'Yes.'

'What's he doing?'

'He's being handed something.'

'What kind of something?'

'A large envelope, papers.'

'Follow, but be discrete. I'll send you a signal when we've taken over.'

'Okay.'

James was there but now he isn't. He handed an envelope to Borstov, then went back into the venue.

What was in the package? How is his brother involved?

Borstov is still moving. Danny extracts himself from his sleeping bag and gets ready to follow. To think what you do is important is to know that you matter. Danny is conscious of how much he enjoys his new role here in the thick of things. The Russian contingent is heading towards the West End, and Danny finds he can track them simply by following Ivor.

They cross several streets. Each crossing with lights and traffic is its own challenge. You mustn't line up together. You have to calculate the last possible moment to get over. Ivor has seen Danny and signals to him. One of them will stay in front of the Russians, the other will follow. That way, the crossings will be less of a problem. That's when Danny moves closer to the back-watchers of the Russian party, only he notices they're not watching. They move as a phalanx but without any sense of danger.

Then his phone goes. It's Harry. 'Okay, we're onto them.' Even two days ago that would have been enough. Danny would have demurred and moved away. Instead, he stops for a few moments. He's seen no one join the cavalcade. The traffic has kept moving. No car has stopped nearby and dropped passengers. He asks himself how this is possible and he moves forward. He passes Borstov and allows Ivor to move back. He wants at least to be able to spot Harry's men. He's as certain as he can be that they aren't there.

What he's taking part in feels like a charade. Is Borstov's entourage a vanity project? Does he walk because he fears recognition and the close confines of a taxi? Does Harry know about this, already knew about it before Danny's phone call? The plasterer? The Chinese couple?

They come to a stop. Borstov and two of his group walk into a restaurant whilst the others disperse. There's no way Danny can follow them inside. It's the kind of place that has staff on the door. He finds a doorway opposite and sits there, wishing he had his sleeping bag and a plastic cup. He does have the camera. He takes a photo of the front of the restaurant. Then he spots a potential customer. It's the hat and the coat and something about the walk. He's the kind of passer-by who gives you either nothing or nothing less than twenty pounds. He too is accompanied. He seems worried, alert to danger, less used to this sort of caper. Danny snaps him, then finds Ivor is by his side.

'We need to go.'

Danny gets up at once. 'No, not with me. Same bar, twenty, maybe thirty minutes.'

He's gone and he's frightened, Danny thinks. He settles down into the role of the rough sleeper. 'Spare any change. Spare any change.'

One of Borstov's thugs leans over him. Danny keeps his head steady and doesn't look up. The thug has a ten pound note in his hand.

'Bless you, Sir,' Danny says. 'God bless you.'

It's as he stretches out his hand and part lifts his head that he hears the camera shutter, that faint unmistakable noise that means he's been spotted.

* * *

Leah hasn't told Izzy her news. She doesn't know what to do with her bombshell. She decides to keep it to herself. She reasons that Izzy has accepted her son is dead. To tell her now that he was always an imposter without having the real son for her to meet seems a cruel thing to do. She wants advice, but from whom? Julia has not been to the police and explained what happened at the sinkhole. Leah's interview with Angela Matthews told her as much. James is working for Mindsett. He's so busy that when he collected the letters and journal he wouldn't stay and talk. She regrets giving them to him. Everything that has happened since then tells her that the world is more complicated than she ever thought.

There is Martin. She could phone Martin. But what if he's with Vikki? How humiliating to be thought of as the ex, desperately trying to hang on to what you've lost.

He is the nearest thing that she has to a rock. Unable to decide, she switches on the debate. Izzy's been watching something earlier and the television is on mute. The remote is too far to reach without getting up. She doesn't want to hear anyway. She wants to think out her problem. She wants to work out if it's worth phoning Martin. She won't go round. It would be awful to find Vikki there.

The camera picks out their faces and Leah watches without the words. Stella interests her. She seems calm, in control. Cold, Leah thinks, too cold to value what Howard was offering her. She remembers the voice when Stella spoke to her. It sounded genuine. Clearly Stella has never forgotten Howard, hence the flowers.

When the camera switches to Jud Mindsett he seems shifty, aggressive, less rooted. Intrigued, she turns the sound on. Jud is speaking.

'On the lady's watch there have been too many migrants, far too many. In some parts of this country indigenous English people don't see another white face as they walk to the shops. They wonder what they fought the war for if we are to be swamped with foreigners.'

Leah hears the loud applause. The camera switches to Stella.

'They fought for freedom, Jud. You know that as well as I do. I suspect you also know that even in the Battle of Britain they fought alongside Polish pilots and Israeli pilots and Commonwealth pilots. They fought against the very nationalism that the Nazis promulgated.'

'Of course, it feels uncomfortable if your neighbourhood changes. I do understand that. But we have always been a mongrel nation: Celt, Anglo Saxon, Norman, Huguenot, Polish, Italian, West Indian. All these waves were assimilated and made us stronger. You know this as much as I do, Jud. Your own family history is part migrant. Time has passed since your grandfather arrived here and was accepted. In time individuals are always accepted and judged for who they are and not what they are.'

Leah hears a change in Stella's voice. 'You know that, Jud, and yet you play the fear card, the anti-Russian card, and the race card. And if you win, which policy will you follow? If you win, which migrants will you send home? The nurses in the NHS, the fruit pickers in East Anglia, the waitress from your favourite restaurant? Please stop pretending that the world is a simple place where simple questions have simple answers. You know that isn't true.'

There is applause. It's sporadic but sustained. The camera pans the audience to see individuals on their feet and clapping. But even Leah can see there aren't enough of them.

She turns off the television, phones Martin's number and immediately puts the phone down. I liked the cult, she thinks. I knew it was evil, but it was clearly evil, a straightforward fight. She thinks about what Stella said. Life is complicated. There are no simple answers to Leah's questions either.

30

Ivor is already there and this time he's buying.

'Sit down Not Patrick.'

'My real name's Danny.'

'Sit down Maybe Danny. Were you followed?'

'They took my photo as I sat on the pavement, gave me a ten pound note so I would look up.'

'Did you look up?'

'It was instinct.'

Ivor grimaces. 'Contact whoever you work for at once, Maybe Danny. That's serious shit. Shave before you leave the bar. Change your clothes.'

Danny looks at Ivor. He's sipping his vodka, not knocking it back like last time.

'Why are you afraid?' Danny asks.

'Not for me,' Ivor says, 'for the whole world.'

'Who was the man? The man Borstov met in the restaurant?'

'I need to check,' Ivor says. 'Show me your camera.'

Ivor manipulates the image, enlarging the face. Then he stares at it.

'American,' he says. 'A US billionaire called Chuck, or to give him his full title, 'Charles Augustus Leventrip 2nd.'

'How do you know of him?'

'I work in the same field. He owns a company called Furlong. This company has developed super sensitive software. It analyses all internet transactions by individuals: social media, what you buy, what sites you visit. At one time in a country like yours you had to put a leaflet through every front door if you wanted someone to vote for you. Not any more. His company can tell anyone who pays enough who you are likely to vote for. It picks out waverers.'

Danny tries to follow this. Politics never used to interest him. He's never voted.

'So?' Danny says.

Ivor looks at him with scorn. 'So Chuck becomes a superspy. He doesn't bother with your pathetic Data Protection Act. He doesn't bother to back political parties. He controls who wins because he can get to the floating voters, the only ones who really matter.'

'Why is he meeting Borstov? Surely they are enemies?'

'Borstov is 1%. Chuck Leventrip 2nd is also 1%. They are the elite, the 1% of the world's population that control more than 90% of the world's wealth. Their interests are international. Put simply, Danny Person, they want to stay in control. They fear 1789. They fear 1917. They fear what happened in Hungary and Czechoslovakia. They fear what happened in Romania and most recently in Ukraine. They fear the European Union. They hated Obama because he had them sussed.'

'Why meet now? I still don't get it.'

'Stella is everything they hate too. She's fair minded. She will be good Prime Minister. Jud Mindsett is their sort of leader: not clever, can be manipulated. Give me your mobile phone.'

Ivor performs the same manipulations as last time, then hands both the phone and the camera back. 'I've done transfer. You are backing these up elsewhere, aren't you Maybe Danny Person?'

'Not yet.'

'Do it. Do it the moment you get home. This matters Maybe. These might save your life.'

Danny looks at Ivor. 'I want to understand what you're saying. Tell me again what you think is happening.'

'Is guess, only a guess. When 1% of the population control 90% of the wealth is not sustainable. The rich are frightened. Any good democratic leader would do something to change the figures. So the rich want bad leaders, poor idiots they can manipulate. Why was Cameron your Prime Minister? Why is Trump president? China, Russia, USA are the same. No communists any more. China ruled by a rich elite. Russia ruled by mafia. All the world over, the elite want to stay elite. Once they built castles, age of the war lords. Once they bribed politicians, age of the party donor. Now they manipulate elections. Reasons are the same. It's what the superrich have always done.'

'You're wrong, Ivor. That won't happen here.'

Ivor shakes his head. 'Is happening already. If you want to understand the world, listen to a Russian. We have been lied to more often than any other nation. We know that you trust no one in authority, not ever.'

* * *

It's the morning after the debate. Angela Matthews sits opposite Keith Loadstone.

'I've had two complaints,' she tells him.

Keith reaches down to the holdall he plonked on the floor when he came in. He takes out two plastic bags. One has a loo handle in it, the other a knife. He puts them carefully on the desk.

Angela ignores this, pretends not to have noticed any of it. 'The first complaint is about a policeman who posed as a member of the Missing Persons' Bureau in order to gain admission to a house and then, without permission, collected a DNA sample.' She stops there and looks at him.

'Guilty,' he says. 'Guilty as charged.'

'That complaint was brought by a member of the public. The next complaint is more significant because it was lodged by a senior officer, your senior officer, me. The nub of this complaint is that you, Police Constable Keith Loadstone, acting against the explicit instructions of SDM Angela Matthews, continued to investigate a case that you had been ordered to drop.'

'You can add a third complaint to the list,' Keith volunteers. 'This same PC Keith Loadstone broke into a house in London without a warrant and without authority in another force's area and took an item from the house, viz this loo handle.'

He points to the bag.

'A fourth complaint, if you wish to add to the charge sheet, is that the very same officer held on to a crucial piece of evidence that he had been ordered to hand over, viz this knife.'

He indicates the other bag on the desk in front of him.

'I plead guilty to both these additional charges,' he

adds.

Power isn't the rank you're given, it's the authority you exert. Angela has never felt less in control. There's nothing contrite about the man who is sitting across from her. He seems more cocky than ever.

'Go on,' she relents. 'What's in the bags?'

Keith Loadstone picks up one of the bags. 'This is the knife I found at the scene of the crime near Black Rigg Beck. It has several fingerprints on the handle.' He replaces the bag reverently on the desk. Angela is amused by the performance but she doesn't show it. Keith picks up the other bag. 'This is a loo handle removed illegally from the house of Daniel Goulden. It too has fingerprints and the two sets of prints match. I can prove that Daniel Goulden was at the scene of the crime. I saw Daniel's mother, Isabel Goulden, place a bunch of red roses in the sinkhole near Black Rigg Beck from which we extracted the body of the deceased. I followed Isabel Goulden to her home and saw her stop at the lights in Pickering. I'm certain that she saw one of the posters you so kindly allowed me to print and distribute, yet she reported nothing. A few days after the deceased became the deceased, Daniel Goulden went missing. At the same time Gouldens, the family chain of stores, was put up for sale with an asking price of many tens of millions.'

He stops. 'That is what I know for certain. My hypothesis is that the family is arguing about how to split the proceeds, and in the middle of that altercation a man died.'

Angela's heard enough. 'A man you thought was a member of the family.'

He admits it. 'I did. I was wrong.'

'A significant mistake.'

He isn't abashed. He's sitting opposite her, grinning. 'You have to re-open the case,' he tells her. 'You have to see this as a suspicious death, and you have to make good your promise and let me take you out to dinner. Shall we say Friday?'

Angela tries again. 'If you can be wrong about a family connection you can be wrong about the rest.'

'Friday at 7.30. It'll give you time to change out of uniform.'

She's not ready to give in. 'The person who made the first of my complaints,' Angela tells him, 'was a member of the public, a certain Leah Goulden. She was appalled at the underhand way you had gone about the investigation. She was shocked that a member of my force could seek to trick a woman who is still grieving the death of her husband and has recently had to cope with the disappearance of her son.'

'We could meet at the Wheatsheaf first if you want at 7pm. They probably have a bottle of white wine somewhere.'

Ignoring that last comment, Angela plays her card. 'She was also shocked when I told her of your findings.'

Now he's listening. Now he's taken notice.

'I may only be an SDM who has never worked for the Met, but when I told her that there was no possible familial link between the two DNA samples it was as if her world imploded. She was shocked, deeply shocked. You could almost see her doing the recalculations in her head. She couldn't get out of this room fast enough.'

He's leaning forward. 'So they thought he was family.'

Angela nods and he realises that she's now wanting his praise, wanting his approval. 'Nice work,' he tells her. 'It's a suspicious death, isn't it?'

'I hate to admit it but you're right.'

'Does that mean I'm free to continue my investigations?'

She nods again.

'Do I need to get that in writing?'

'No.' Then she adds, 'You'll need to start with an apology.'

'Okay.'

He takes his two samples and puts them back in his bag.

'7pm at the Wheatsheaf?'

She nods and smiles. 'Now get out of my office.'

He goes, gets into his car, turns on the radio. There's a newsflash that interrupts his music as he heads towards the Goulden home.

'Reports are coming in of a large-scale incursion into British airspace by Russian planes with their transponders switched off. British fighters have been scrambled to intercept them.'

Keith Loadstone listens but doesn't hear. A grouse flies in front of his car. He can hear the curlew crying across the moor. He has permission to interview the Gouldens. All's well.

* * *

Danny hears the same newsflash. Only a few days ago

he would have reacted as Keith Loadstone does, but not any longer. Now he understands. The commentators don't know what to make of it. He does. Its purpose is to embarrass Stella. It's what Jud agreed with Borstov. He can hear Ivor's response.

'It's win, win, win for the Russian Federation. It's flying practice for the pilots. It costs nothing more than them flying anywhere else. It goes down well on Russian radio. It boosts Putin's strong man reputation at home. It downs Stella, promotes that idiot, Mindsett. You need to see things through Russian eyes. Through their eyes what's not to like?'

Danny got back late last night. He hasn't shaved or changed his clothes. He never contacted Harry. He needs to do so at once.

First he'll back up the photographs onto his hard drive. He picks up his phone, flicks through to find them. But the photographs have disappeared, all of them. He has no proof about Borstov, no proof of a meeting with Charles Augustus Leventrip 2nd.

Ivor warned him and he took no notice. Someone has accessed his phone and taken his photos. He sits on his bed in his boxers. Now he has to be clever, now he has to understand and get this right. Is he up to this? He was never the brainy one.

Who are they really? Borstov? Harry? Ivor? Did Ivor wipe them when pretending to copy them over? He'll keep all the possibilities open. Meanwhile he must act as if he's unconcerned.

Alarmed but also excited, Danny phones Harry.

31

'We've got her. We've got her on the run.' Jud Mindsett is ecstatic, so excited he has to move around the office. They've watched the same newsflash, Jud nodding, James open-mouthed.

'Wow,' James comments. 'What a stroke of luck.'

Jud stops moving, stands still, says nothing.

'I mean,' James says, 'the coincidence with what you said last night is perfect for us.'

Jud nods and for James the penny drops.

'You knew it was going to happen?'

Jud nods again.

'The file! The man I handed it to!'

Jud nods again. He's steamed up with his own cleverness. 'His name is Borstov. He's working for us.'

'Why?' James asks.

'It suits the Russians.'

'Why?' James asks again. 'Why does it suit them?'

'I don't know,' Jud admits. 'They contacted me. They made the offer. It's awesome.' Jud starts walking again. 'The commentators are talking about how right I was to say what I did. In three days' time we play our big card and she'll be finished. We're heading for Number 10.'

'Yes,' James says, 'that's yes if it's still we?'

'It is. Of course it is.'

'Then tell me what else I don't know.'

'Borstov set the whole thing up. He wanted dirt on Stella. What you handed over to him was a copy of all we have on Stella. That was the deal.'

James stares at him. 'You handed over the letters and journal to the Russians!'

'It was the deal. Look what it bought us.'

'My sister put those into our hands. They were for our use,' James protests.

'We're going to use them anyway, aren't we? So what harm have we done?'

James can see the logic of this. 'Is there anything else I don't know?'

Jud holds his hands up. 'Nothing else, I promise you.'

James looks at him, doesn't think he's lying. 'Do you know what Kompromat is?'

Jud shakes his head. 'Do I need to?'

'Kompromat is compromising information collected for use in blackmailing, discrediting, or manipulating someone, typically for political purposes.'

Jud looks flummoxed. 'That's very clever, but what's it got to do with me?'

'When you become Prime Minister the Russians can blackmail you, threaten to expose what's just happened, threaten to have you indicted for treason. It is treason to deliberately conspire with an enemy state. I need to spell this out, Jud. When you become Prime Minister the Russians can give you orders and you will have to do as they say.'

'When I become Prime Minister, I like the sound of that,' Jud says. 'You think I can do this?'

'It's possible. You've been clever. It's just the move we needed. But it's a terrible risk.'

Jud basks for a moment in James's praise. 'Okay, what do I have to do today?'

'Remember the strategy,' James tells him. 'If you have a chance of winning you might need to pedal back a bit, seem more like a statesman. Send Annabelle Pitts-Tucker out to be outrageous. It's time we turned the heat up on immigration. Tell Annabelle not to call them migrants. Use the word illegals instead. Mind you, she needs to steer clear of any mention of the Jews. They have a country and a Head Rabbi who'll take you on. Muslims are always an easy target because they have no archbishop, only local councils.'

'Got it.'

'Remember you're still an outsider. The right-wing press is beginning to love you. That's good. The BBC will report their headlines in the name of fairness in the way they always do. That's working for you. But you need more than that. This is a members' election. You need to make some promises that will appeal to them. Promise to consult more. Why don't you introduce the idea of a lottery of members, the lucky winners to be invited to Number 10 for a consultation every two months? Call it your staying-in-touch strategy.'

'Won't that take up too much time?'

'A focus group by any other name …'

'Oh, I get it.'

The phone rings. Jud picks it up. James hears him say, 'I'm sorry, I'm too busy. Can I suggest Annabelle Pitts-Tucker? I'll get her to give you a call.'

They turn back to the news. The threat from Russia is the only item.

'I came along for the ride but we could win this.' James is full of wonder.

'Yes,' Jud says. 'Yes, we could.'

'Are you ready for that?'

'I'm ready to stand at the door of Number 10 and wave. I'm getting used to the cameras everywhere I go. I think I can cope with the Number 10 staff lined up on the stairs to greet me.'

'I don't mean preening, I mean governing, Jud. If you win you will take over all the reins of power. What will you do? What will be your contribution to history?'

Jud thinks for a bit. 'No idea at all,' he says.

* * *

For the first time since he walked out of his home and posted the keys through the door Danny is frightened. The sense of excitement that has been with him ever since he held the knife and walked towards Patrick has finally tipped over into fear. At the heart of his sense of being afraid is the feeling that he no longer understands what's happening round him.

Harry's agreed to meet him in the café in the British Museum. Danny's never been inside before. He wonders if you have to pay to go in. He enters from Great Russell Street. The place is swarming with tourists. Most of the languages being spoken round him are not his. Every kind of skin tone is represented: too-long-spent-inside-white, pink-white, tanned-white, cappuccino, swarthy, americano-with-milk, black-coffee-with-hints-of-chocolate. A hundred skin tones, a hundred styles of dress: heads with caps, heads with scarves, heads with kippahs, heads with big hats, heads with hair that's blonde-real, blonde-dyed, grey, white, absent, jet-black, blue and harsh-red. So many different groupings: mothers and daughters, fathers and sons, a crocodile of school children, family groups, singles, couples of both and either gender, old people.

Danny makes his way through this throng of humanity. No one asks him to pay. To either side he glimpses wonderful things. He might look round, he thinks. He's never done that. He makes his way under the great roof and it stops him. He stands still, staring upwards. He loves its intricacy, all those different shapes.

He passes the shop and sees the café. He scans the tables and spots Harry, picks him out by his stillness. Danny's thirsty but the queue is too long, so he goes straight over. He doesn't shake hands. He sits down and waits.

Harry is sitting in front of a single espresso. He hasn't touched it. Next to it is a cantuccini biscuit. He hasn't touched that either.

'Why do you need to see me, Daniel?' Harry's voice is soft and measured.

'It's the sequence, Sir. I don't understand it.'

Harry waits, watches.

'I trail Mindsett and he meets Borstov. I take photos. I transfer those photos onto my phone.' He hopes Harry doesn't notice the lie. 'Next night I trail Borstov again. I see him handed a package that comes from Mindsett.' He is about to mention the photograph they took of him but decides not to. 'The next day Russian planes stage a huge incursion. Is that a coincidence? The moment I saw that on the news I looked for the photos I'd copied onto my phone and they've gone.'

Harry has watched Danny while he was speaking. Harry's espresso is still untouched. Annoyingly, Harry says nothing in response to what Danny's telling him. It's as if he knows it all already.

'So what do I do now, Sir?' He'd better come clean. 'The Russians have a photograph of me. They know I'm not a rough sleeper.'

'Go on.' The n is dwelt on, emphasised.

'Borstov met with an American. I followed him to the restaurant but you called me off.'

Harry says nothing.

'The first time I tell you about Mr Borstov you send two cars and a group to stake him out. The next time when he meets the American you call me off and send no one.'

'Yes.'

Danny waits. He needs more than a single word.

'Who is Borstov?' he asks.

Harry suddenly moves, leans forward, picks up his cup and downs the espresso in a single gulp. He gets up as if he's ready to go.

Danny panics. 'Sir, I need to know what to do next.'

'Then don't waste my time. You know who Borstov is, Ivor told you.'

If Harry knows that and knows about Ivor, how much else does he know? Harry is staring at him, poised to go.

'Did you remove the photos from my phone?' Danny asks, deliberately raising his voice.

Harry sits down again, ignores the last question. 'Your job is to watch Jud Mindsett. You need to look out for him. I want him kept safe. That's our job, to protect this democracy. I want to know his movements. I want to know who he meets. Use the camera. If the Russians know you work for us, so much the better. Don't follow Borstov whatever happens, stick with Jud Mindsett. Leave us to think about the rest. It isn't your job.'

'Borstov met my brother, James. James handed him the package.'

'I know,' Harry says. 'I know, but why didn't you tell me that at once?'

Harry gets up quickly. 'Keep me in touch,' he says. 'You're doing well enough.'

'Well enough for what?'

'Well enough for us to keep employing you.'

Danny watches Harry go. He orders a coffee, waits for it, then sits back in the same place, staring up at the roof. He's in a modern space but the past is all round him. He can see the ancient carving of a lion, its face weathered, its pose stilled by becoming an exhibit. He's been Danny the fitness freak, then Danny the rough sleeper. Now he's Danny the agent. But he's something more too. He's Danny at the heart of things. Each change has been an arrival and an expulsion. He expelled himself from his family and from normal life. He then left the friendship of Shaun and the teamwork of the streets. Now he's forced to abandon his positive view of the world. Even though he never voted he'd believed in a politics that was honest. He'd thought the best people got to be leaders.

Not anymore. Thinking is still new to Danny, but with nothing else to do he starts to make a list of what he knows. He knows that the Russians have staged an incident to influence the outcome of an election. He knows his brother handed a file over to the Russians. He knows a highly placed Russian agent dined with a right-wing American billionaire. He knows Borstov matters to Harry, but he doesn't know why or how. He knows the Russians know he is a British agent. He had photographic proof of all this but that has disappeared. He also knows he's in danger. There were two proofs that all this really happened: the first was in the photographs; the second is in his memory. Someone has already destroyed the first.

By the sinkhole James had yelled at Patrick, 'You don't exist. You were never registered. We could, we should, finish you off. You don't deserve to live. I don't think we can be charged with the murder of someone who doesn't exist.'

Danny doesn't exist either. He's left his real identity. He's one of the disappeared. He's the easiest target in the world. Was it a threat when Harry said to him, 'Leave us to think about the rest'?

There is, of course, a way to be safe or at least safer. He can reappear. He can break into his own house and go back to being Danny the fitness freak. But he doesn't want to.

He's eaten Harry's abandoned cantuccini. Then he gets up and wanders into the Egyptian section, stares at the pharaohs and the winged lions. It's crowded. He has to pick his way amongst the people. He finds himself watching them, not the artefacts. He realises they have their own slow rhythm. Their walk between the exhibits is almost a dance: step, step, step; stop for four beats; a slow turn; more steps to the next stone item; stop for another count of four; move on again.

Danny is the exception. He's the man standing still, watching people swirl round him. But then he realises he isn't the only one. The room has another watcher. This man is older, not in a uniform. He doesn't look English. He has a thatch of black hair streaked with white. His face is lined at the temples and round the eyes. His hands are thrust into the pockets of his coat. Is Danny in danger? Is he being watched? Only one way to find out.

Abruptly, Danny turns away, walks to the plan of the museum and decides to climb up to the Early English section. He'll go and see the Lewis chess set. He moves quickly without looking behind him. He climbs the steps two at a time. He plays the man in a hurry. Soon he stands in front of the glass case and looks at the squat, carved figures with their bearded faces and swords spread across their knees. Each of them is a man of action. Each belongs to his time.

By changing his focus Danny can use the glass as a mirror. Moving his focus to one corner he can see most of the room reflected. The chessmen are ready for battle. Anxiety is written on their faces. A knight rests his chin on the top of his shield. A king brings his hand to his face. The pawns look like a palisade. Danny sees them and he also sees, reflected in the glass, the ghostly figure of the tousle-haired watcher already in position on the edge of the room. Should he run?

No. Danny turns and looks at the man, stares straight at him. Then he deliberately walks towards him as he did at the sinkhole. He walks slowly. The other man stands still. Danny is ten metres away and he closes in with deliberation, walks forwards until his trainers are nearly touching the other man's shoes, until he's right in the other man's space. Then he speaks. 'I'm here if you have anything to say to me.'

He feels as he felt at the sinkhole. He feels as he felt under the railway arches. The two men stand nose to nose, face to face. But a uniformed museum attendant is walking towards them. 'Is there a problem?' he asks.

Danny hears the fear in the attendant's voice.

'Not at all,' he says. 'I've made my point.'

As he steps back the other man moves away.

'Only that's not the kind of behaviour we can tolerate in this museum, Sir.'

'I'm sorry,' says Danny.

The attendant seems to want an explanation so Danny gives him one. 'He's a Russian agent. He was following me.'

The museum attendant clearly doesn't believe Danny. He's reaching for his radio when Danny walks out of the room and heads for the stairs.

He's realised what he has to do next. It's the only action that makes sense in his circumstances. He doesn't know how he'll achieve this but it has to be done.

* * *

It's lunchtime when Leah hears the knock on the door. She has no reason not to open it.

A policeman in uniform is standing outside holding up a badge.

'PC Keith Loadstone,' he announces.

'Yes,' Leah says.

'If you are Leah Goulden I'd very much like to ask you some questions.'

Izzy has come down the stairs at the sound of the doorbell. Now she pushes her way past. 'It's the man I was telling you about Leah, only he didn't say he was a police officer.'

'I'm sorry about that, Mrs Goulden. You see, I was sitting above the sinkhole when you put the red roses in.'

Izzy starts. Her mouth opens but she says nothing.

'I followed you back here. I saw you jump a set of red lights. It was when you saw the poster. It seemed to confuse you.'

Izzy stares at him.

'So I decided to come and see you. You see, I want to know everything you know about the body in the sinkhole.'

There is a pause. Leah wonders if she ought to intervene, but can't think of what to say so says nothing. Izzy pulls herself up to her full height. 'He was my son.' She says it with pride. She says it with determination. 'Whatever he did to Leah, and whatever he tried to do to me, he remains my son.'

Leah knows what will be said next if she doesn't stop it.

'Come in, come in.' She commandeers the moment and fills it with noise. 'Would you like a coffee? Let's go through to the kitchen.'

She's playing for time. She wants to prepare Izzy for what this PC might say, not have it blurted out. 'Coffee or tea?'

'I'm alright, thanks.'

'I presume you've come to apologise,' Leah says, indicating a chair. 'Lying about being from the Missing Persons' Bureau. You admit that, don't you?'

'Yes,' he says. 'If it makes you feel better, I've been hauled over the coals for that.'

'Then there's the …' no, she can't mention the DNA sample illegally taken, '… failure to identify yourself properly. I mean, who did you say you were? Please can I see your badge?' Leah knows she's wittering, digging herself in deeper and deeper. But with a bit of luck Izzy will be sufficiently distracted.

Keith Loadstone hands the badge over. Leah makes a fuss of checking the photo against the man and then hands it to Izzy.

Izzy takes a brief look and gives it straight back.

PC Loadstone has not forgotten why he's here. 'Mrs Goulden, you were saying the flowers you laid were for your son?'

Izzy glances at Leah. She's thought better of what she said earlier. She clams up, doesn't respond.

PC Loadstone persists. 'How many children do you have, Mrs Goulden?'

'Four,' Izzy says without thinking. 'Four,' she asserts shamelessly. 'Julia, James, Leah and Danny.'

'Now Daniel has gone missing, hasn't he?'

Izzy nods.

'And it wasn't Daniel in the sinkhole, was it?'

Izzy shakes her head.

'And it wasn't James, was it? James is very much alive.'

Izzy nods.

'So why did you say it was your son we pulled out of the sinkhole?'

Izzy caves in. 'I'd better tell you. I had another son. I was very young and I had him adopted. When my husband died I went looking for him and I found him. But he turned nasty and tied me up. He fell into the sinkhole. It opened suddenly and swallowed him. We couldn't do anything to save him.'

Leah decides to let this happen. She doesn't intervene. Julia obviously hasn't told the police and they need to know.

'Who else saw this?'

Izzy seems relieved, seems lighter after her initial statement. She lists everyone who was there, counts them off on her fingers. 'James, Danny, Julia, Leah, Martin (that's Leah's friend) and Katherine.' She stops and frowns, then adds, 'And, of course, Patrick himself.'

'Was it Patrick who fell into the sinkhole?'

'Yes,' Izzy confirms.

'Is this Patrick?'

PC Loadstone unfolds a copy of the poster. Izzy looks at it and nods.

'And was Patrick your son?'

Izzy nods again.

'How do you know?' PC Loadstone asks.

'I went searching for him. I met the people who adopted him. They confirmed he was Patrick. When we met up he even had the same baby photo that I had.'

'Can you give me the name of this agency?'

'The Church of the Living Saints.'

Keith Loadstone writes that down. He's hardly

breathing because he now knows he was right. This was a turf war between the four full members of the Goulden clan and the person they thought was their half-brother. He writes, then glances at his notes.

'Who was Katherine?' he asks. 'Do you have a surname or an address?'

'She was Patrick's fiancée.' Izzy almost spits this out.

'Will she confirm what you've told me?'

'I doubt it,' Izzy says, and her voice is full of contempt. 'She's a devout Christian,' Izzy adds by way of explanation.

PC Loadstone turns to Leah. 'Did you know Katherine? Do you have a surname or an address?'

'Neither,' says Leah, 'but I can show you where to find her.'

'Where's that?'

'The headquarters of the Church of the Living Saints.'

He turns back to Izzy. 'Why do you dislike her? Didn't you think she was good enough for your son?'

Izzy has now reached the point of not caring. At this suggestion she nearly explodes. 'They deserved each other,' she says. 'Katherine tied me up and Patrick helped shove me into the boot of their car. Some son he turned out to be.'

'Do you remember that I got you to wipe a smudge off your face when I came to see you last time?'

'Yes,' Izzy says, wondering.

'That tissue gave me a sample of your DNA. You do know what DNA is, Mrs Goulden?'

'Of course.'

'Well, I checked that DNA sample against the DNA of

the body we pulled out of the sinkhole.'

Now Izzy is fully alert. Leah stretches out her hand to hold her mother's, but Izzy pushes her away. 'And?' she asks.

'There was no match.'

'What do you mean? What are you saying?'

'If he had been your son, half of his DNA key characteristics would have come from you.'

Izzy breathes in deeply, holds her breath.

'They didn't, so he isn't. I mean, so he wasn't your son.'

'He had the photograph.'

'Then it can't have been him in the photo.'

Izzy leans forward as she grabs the table with both hands.

'Are you quite sure?'

Keith Loadstone emphasises each word of his reply. 'There is no scientific possibility that he was related to you.'

A wail escapes Izzy. It expands and seems to spread through the kitchen, bouncing off the walls. 'What a fool I've been. I should have known. I thought blood spoke to blood. I thought I sensed he was mine. What sort of mother am I that I didn't know he wasn't my son?'

She thumps the table. 'The shits, the absolute shits. They let me think. They duped me.' She holds the finger and thumb of her right hand nearly together. 'I came this close to giving them everything.'

The gesture looks like a vicious claw in the air.

Leah has watched her mother's reaction with a mixture of awe and sympathy. She stretches her hand out again and lets it rest on Izzy's shoulder. This time the gesture isn't rejected. Her mother's head is down. She's crying for herself, crying for all the mistakes she's made. Keith Loadstone watches with pity. He itches to ask what happened just before the man who called himself Patrick died, but he doesn't ask anything. He just watches the woman opposite him and keeps silent.

Suddenly her head comes up. Her whole demeanour changes. 'Then where is he?'

'We buried him. I can show you the plot,' Keith Loadstone explains.

'Not him, my real son. I gave birth to a boy and handed him over to the Church of the Living Saints all those years ago. That's true. That happened. Is he still alive? How do I find him?'

32

Now Danny watches his back. Now he is wary of his own shadow. He makes his way across London and heads for the House of Commons. He needs to see Stella Stelling. He needs to warn her. He trusts no one and nothing. The tube would be faster but platforms are death traps. He fears the sudden untraceable push, the tea laced with plutonium, the umbrella spike coated in poison, a little light hint of novichok.

So he walks, heading downhill towards the river. He keeps to the edge of pavements. He darts quickly across roads, taking risks with cars and vans. He allows himself quick glances back so he is fairly sure that no one is following him. He knows he attracts glances. His appearance is against him. Ivor had told him to shave and change his clothes. He's done neither. They must wonder, these people he skips round, why this rough sleeper is in such a hurry. He knows he looks suspicious, but the real danger is if he is the only one who carries this secret. Once he has told Stella, once the secret is known outside the secret services, he thinks he will be safer.

The trouble is that he knows so little and can prove even less. He wishes he had a badge so that he could make his way into Portcullis House, find her room and wait there, but he has no idea how the security works. He must see her but where will she be? And who will be guarding her? Harry's men is the answer, and they will recognise him. Have they already been warned against him? In all those keep-fit years he never watched the news, never read a paper. How can he be this old and know so little?

The thought makes him glance at the headlines on newsstands he passes. *MINDSETT GAINING IN POLLS. IS STELLA'S STAR FADING?* He even accepts a free paper when he's offered one. *RUSSIA ATTACKS ON CUE.* He tucks it under his arm. There may be time to read it later.

The road dips in front of him and he finds himself at the top corner of Trafalgar Square. People are everywhere. He sees fountains, lions and an empty plinth. Then the road dips again and he finds himself in Whitehall, walking down towards the Cenotaph. He's nearly there. He can see Big Ben. But where is Stella, and how the hell can he get to meet her? He remembers what Harry told him to do if a suspicious member of the public suddenly approached Mindsett. If you think they are a danger do everything you can to prevent contact. It doesn't bear thinking about. Opposite the Cenotaph Danny hesitates, turns round and looks back up towards Trafalgar Square. People move round him. People go up and down but no one stops. He's as sure as he can be that he isn't being followed. He's out of breath, so anyone following him would be exhausted too.

He sinks to the ground, leans his back against the wall and breathes deeply. The fear subsides. He needs to go to her house, not meet her here. He needs to use the moment when the day's protection team hands over to the local force. That will be his only chance to see and talk to her. But where does she live?

He makes a list in his head of those who might know: journalists, television crews, her PA, her protection team. He's worked solo so far, but the men who came in the car and staked out Borstov's house might know where Stella lives. Harry would know, but Harry won't tell him. The situation feels hopeless. He's stuck. London is such a big city.

A coin bounces on the pavement in front of him. He leaves it there. His brain hurts with the effort of being racked. It feels like his muscles used to feel during the last three bench presses of a training session. So he stacks the problem as he would the weights, placing the difficulty on the stand and rolling out from underneath it. He watches the street, finds again the almost catatonic stillness of the rough sleeper. He'll let time pass because until he has an answer that is all that time is good for.

No answer comes to him. He wonders if he shouldn't get up, shave and go back to being Daniel Goulden. Could he still cash the lottery ticket? He doesn't wonder this for very long. Even fear is better than boredom. He is on a famous street in the heart of London. He has information that few people know. Even slumped down, stuck and frightened, he feels alive.

Another coin. He places both on the newspaper and drops his head, starts the mantra, 'Spare any loose change. Spare any loose change.' Slowly, more coins are spilled from hands that are never connected to eyes. If Harry asks him what he's doing he'll say he's keeping his hand in, living his cover.

People pass the whole time. Shadows edge along the

pavement and start to climb the wall. A shower of cherry petals settles on him like a benediction. He brushes them away. He's thirsty and hungry, but he can push both those imposters away as easily as the cherry petals. He needs to find Stella, but he can't work out how to do that.

Another sleeper drags himself along the road. He's limping and carrying a rucksack that skews him sideways. Danny looks up. This guy is far into rough sleeping. Danny can see he's an addict. He knows they drink and lose everything, then drink more because they have lost everything, and then move from drink to any kind of anaesthetic that masks the reality of where life has led them. The man's smell radiates out from him, greets Danny before the man himself does. Danny's head dips lower.

'Share that with me,' the man says. His voice is slurred and tobacco-coarsened. 'This is my patch you know.'

Danny looks up. The mouth is drooling. The eyes are focussed halfway between them as if his soul has given up on even the possibility of human contact.

'People will tell you it's my patch,' this wreck of a human being insists.

His smell is like sour milk laced with sweat. The man's skin is grey like river mud. Danny stands up. 'Take the lot.' Something makes him add, 'I was keeping the place warm for you.'

Then he is moving again, getting away from the smell, heading down towards the House of Commons. He buys a coffee and a Snickers from outside a café. Then he notices the crush round a woman, television cameras and journalists shouting questions. The woman stops, puts up her hands. 'One at a time. I'll do my best.'

Members of the public stare and then carry on. Danny drifts to the edge of the group and suddenly Stella Stelling is within touching distance. But it makes no difference; he can't speak to her. He hears Louisa Drakutt unwinding one of her killer questions. 'Minister, nothing matters more than the security of this country. When your opponent was so obviously right about the Russian threat and you were so obviously wrong, why should party members trust your judgement on any other issue?'

Danny doesn't listen to the answer. He turns round, looks for the deep protection personnel.

He scans the crowd on both sides of the road but sees nobody. They must be good, he thinks to himself, if I can't spot them. Even when the circus round Stella moves on, he fails to identify his opposite numbers. He hangs back, follows at a distance. Still he sees no sign of any but her immediate bodyguard. Then she is hailing a taxi and he has his answer and has his chance.

He jumps into the road in front of another London cab, forcing it to swerve before it stops. He wrenches the door open and jumps in.

'Get out,' the driver snarls. 'I don't have your kind in my cab.'

Danny throws three twenty pound notes onto the seat beside him.

'I'm clean,' Danny says. 'I don't smell. If you want all three notes, follow that cab and don't you dare lose it.'

The driver mumbles an apology as he sets off. 'Sorry,

didn't recognise you gov.'

Danny leans forward. Stella's cab is three vehicles in front of them. Whether they can stay in touch will depend on the lights. As they move off, Danny scans the cortège of journalists that had surrounded Stella. They are scattering, going their separate ways. By jumping into the cab he has proved what he suspected: Stella has one bodyguard and one assistant, no one else. There is no back-up vehicle. It makes him add another question to the bothersome list that stretches his mind: why is Mindsett so much better protected than Stella?

* * *

'Here's the list, Jud,' James explains. 'I've chosen the best passages. Those are the extracts that will do most damage.'

Jud scans the printed sheet. 'Why the colours?'

'Red is what she wrote to him. Black is from his journal.'

'Got it.'

Jud bends his head over the task in hand. He has never found reading easy. It's why he never read the railway contracts, but he must master this. He needs to be able to read this stuff in front of cameras.

'OMG,' he snorts as he reads. 'James, did you ever keep a journal of your feelings?'

'It would be blank. I famously don't have any.'

'Nor me. I mean, this stuff Howard writes is weird. It's all about love and nothing about sex. Was there something wrong with him?'

'She hurt him so badly she drove him to suicide, point one.' James pauses there. He's learnt Jud now, knows he is a slow learner. Only when he's sure Jud understands does he move on. 'Point two, she made Howard a promise and she broke it, so all her promises are invalid. Those are the two things you have to get over.'

Jud reads on slowly, reaches the rejection letter, then exclaims, 'Underneath all that caring exterior she's nothing but a cold-hearted bitch.'

James is exasperated. 'Imply that yes, but for God's sake don't say it. If you play this right then they, the great British public, will say it for you.'

'Good point.'

'But you have to play it right. We need to practise this, Jud. We need to rehearse over and over. If you get this right, the keys to Number 10 are in your pocket.'

Jud allows a smile to spread across his features. In view of the polls he is letting himself dream of success. 'It's remarkable isn't it, James? I know my fellow MPs. Most of them are much cleverer than I am. But I'm about to leapfrog the whole pack. I'm going to be the one who makes it. Another week and I'll be Prime Minister.'

James nods but presses on. 'Try reading some sentences out loud, Jud. You've got to get the tone right.'

Jud takes a deep breath. *'I do love you. I know that for a long while I felt it but didn't say it. A certain reluctance to trust in the feeling I had for you held me back. I'm not good at putting my feelings into words. I have to learn that from you and I am learning. So let me say again, I do love you.'* He stops reading. 'Sounds like she's hedging her bets. Reluctant as hell, I'd say.'

James is exasperated. 'We've all said we loved someone and gone back on it. The key phrase is *I do love you.* Try to get the emphasis on both *do* and *love.'*

Jud tries again, but it sounds sarcastic.

'They have to hear it as Howard read it,' James almost shouts at him. 'You must read it straight. Again.'

Jud tries, but it sounds unreal.

'Better.' James knows he needs to be encouraging. He realises Jud can't do serious and can't do love at all. 'Perhaps we should ditch that whole section. It might make people sympathetic. Go for the next sentence straight afterwards.'

Jud reads, *'My use of the word is new minted, unsullied, undiminished by over use.'* 'Shit,' Jud adds. 'I don't know if I can do this. It so isn't me.'

'Again,' James says, ignoring him. 'Again, as if you mean it.'

Jud does it again and it just doesn't work. James throws both hands up in the air. 'This is our one chance and you're going to blow it.'

'It's too flowery,' Jud says. 'Can't I just re-write it, put it into my language? I mean, Stella won't remember what she wrote all those years ago. She certainly won't have kept copies. What's the risk?'

James pushes his hair back with both hands. 'Listen to me, Jud. Remember why we are doing this, Jud. You have the reputation of being a liar. Stella has the reputation of being caring and honest. We are out to boost your reputation and shred hers. We want people to think she is shifty and you are honest. Therefore we mustn't lie. We may be asked to produce the originals, and if we are they have to chime word for word with what you read out. Geddit?'

Jud nods.

'And remember, the Russians have a copy. It was the payment they demanded for that show of strength.'

'Kompromat,' Jud says. 'I remember what you said. They're going to use it against me, aren't they?'

'Perhaps.'

'So we may have to do what the Russians want?'

Jud looks crestfallen. James needs to cheer him up. 'It's not so bad, is it? I mean, you don't have a foreign policy of your own. And the Russians lie about everything: doping, being involved in Ukraine, Assad doesn't have chemical weapons, there were no Russian agents in Crimea. The list is endless. No one believes them. They don't even believe themselves.'

'Okay,' Jud says. 'Back to work. I have to win or I'm toast.'

'Try the next bit,' James advises. 'It's stronger.'

Jud clears his throat. *'Finding you has been a revelation, an unexpected treat, almost a dream. One moment there I was, thinking that love was overrated, was mostly about sex, then the next moment you were part of my life. It was like going from black and white to colour, from a silent world to one full of music.'*

'It's better, Jud, definitely better. Read it again as if you were saying it to your wife.'

Jud snorts. 'Don't be stupid. She'd faint if I ever said anything like that to her.'

'Your mistress then.'

'Do you know about her?'

'Everyone knows about her.'

'I thought I'd been so discreet.'

James ignores that. 'Read it as if you are speaking to your mistress, explaining why she has no need to worry that you turned up three days late. That should do the trick.'

Jud smiles, reads, and suddenly the piece has a life of its own.

'That's it,' James shouts. 'Stay with that voice. Do it over and over again.'

* * *

Stella's taxi stops in a street of semis. A line of plane trees runs down each side of the road and the small front gardens are filled with flowering cherries. There are so many cars that the taxi has to stop in someone's driveway. Three people get out.

Danny too disembarks. He doesn't ask how much the ride cost, simply leaves the three notes on the front seat and says nothing to the driver. It's about 8pm. Twilight is setting in, making the globules of cherry flowers glow like candles. He walks down the street slowly, knowing that Danny the keep-fit man might belong here but Patrick the rough sleeper certainly doesn't. The taxi is still outside Stella's house. Her assistant comes out of the front door and the bodyguard walks off along the street. The taxi leaves.

Danny approaches the door. It has a camera and he lets himself be seen. He rings the bell and the intercom on the right of the door clatters into life.

'Yes?'

He has one chance. A few sentences and then that will be that. She'll let him in or shut him out. All the way through London he's been thinking of what he will say to make sure he gets a hearing. He stands still and looks straight at the camera as he says, 'My name's Danny Goulden. I'm a deep bodyguard for Jud Mindsett. I saw him meet a high-ranking Russian agent the night before the Russian incursion. My brother, James, works for Mindsett. I saw him hand documents to the same agent the night of the last hustings.'

The door clicks. Danny pushes it open. He sees Stella Stelling standing at the top of the stairs cradling an enormous cat. 'Come on up,' she says.

Danny holds up his hands as he climbs towards her. 'I know what I look like,' he says. 'I slept rough until recently. No one notices beggars. It gives me an edge in my new job.'

She's softer in real life than she looks on television, and shorter. Is that, he wonders, because she has kicked off her shoes? But when she speaks her voice is anything but soft.

'First convince me that you are who you say you are.'

She looks tired. She looks worried. Holding the cat is a comfort to her.

'I have no badge and no ID,' Danny tells her, 'so this won't be straightforward. I have various names but my real name is Daniel Goulden. You must have a number for your police bodyguard. If you ask him to look up my real name he will tell you that I disappeared. If someone broke into my house and there is a police report, they will say the keys were posted back through the letterbox and I left an unclaimed winning lottery ticket on the kitchen table. That's the best I can do.'

She stands watching him. He's sure she has her back to an alarm, but he can't see the button and so far she hasn't pressed it. She's stroking the cat as she watches him. Its purr is continuous.

'Who recruited you?' Stella asks.

'A man called Harry. No, I don't have a surname for him, but I do have a phone number. You can ring him to check but I'd rather you didn't. It may be paranoid of me, but I've come to think he might be working against you. So instead, I wonder if you have a high-placed contact in MI6 or a fellow Minister with security contacts. If you have, ask them about Borstov. Dimitri Yurovich Borstov is the man Mindsett met. While you are phoning about Borstov you might also ask about an American called Charles Augustus Leventrip 2nd. My informant tells me he is an expert in manipulating elections. Borstov met him in a swanky restaurant.'

Stella seems to make up her mind. 'I'll make that call. Are you allergic to cats?'

Danny shakes his head. She moves towards him and hands him the cat. 'Sit down and keep stroking her.'

Danny sits. The cat is clearly used to being indulged, doesn't seem to mind being handed round like a parcel and continues purring.

'I won't be long.'

She goes. The cat looks up quizzically at Danny, then closes her eyes and begins to dribble.

Danny listens but can't hear what Stella is saying. He

wants to laugh at his situation. For a moment he stops stroking the cat to look round the room he's in. No photos of people, he notices at once, no souvenirs. Functional and tidy, tasteful but understated. Like my house, he thinks. It's the house of someone who has put their life on hold. The cat begins to thump his hand with the back of her head, so he goes back to stroking.

Stella returns and sits opposite him. Her look is serious, strained.

'You seem to be who you say you are. Please tell me what you know.'

As he talks he notices how she listens. He tells her about Mindsett coming out of the back door from the hustings and slipping away, about his unfitness, about the mobile call he made before he arrived so the door was open when he reached it.

She doesn't interrupt.

He tells her about the call to Harry and the two cars he sent, but the complete lack of response when Borstov met the American.

When he stops talking she asks, 'How much of this can you prove?'

'Nothing. Someone got to my phone and wiped the photographs. It wasn't actually my phone. It's the one Harry gave me.'

Then he tells her about Ivor, how Ivor copied the photographs over, how Ivor was there and saw the first meeting between Mindsett and Borstov. He knows where Ivor will be if she needs to contact him.

Stella looks at the ceiling and says, as if she is speaking to herself, 'A rough sleeper and an asylum-seeker. It's almost certainly true but it isn't enough.'

'Why have you come to see me?' she asks.

'I saw my brother James, who is working for Jud Mindsett, hand something to Borstov. There is clearly a connection between the Russians and your opponent. I thought you could use this.'

He leaves it there but her eyes demand more from him. He's aware that she has a power about her so he tells her the rest.

'I was frightened. I'm expendable. No one will look for a disappeared man.' It's the truth but it sounds pathetic, so he adds more. 'Why are you guarded by so few and your opponent by so many? I've wondered if Harry wants you to lose.' She's looking at him intently now, so he goes on. 'I don't think you knew what I've just told you, so if the secret services know, why haven't you been warned?'

She seems to ignore all his questions. Instead she asks one of her own.

'What did your brother James hand over to Borstov?'

'A file. I don't know what was in it,' he says.

She drifts away. Danny sees her eyes lose focus. Then she startles herself back into consciousness. 'When did you last eat?' she asks him.

'This morning sometime. It doesn't matter.' Danny moves to get up and the cat stirs, gives him a baleful look.

'Stay where you are. I'll get us some food,' she says.

Stella disappears and comes back almost immediately with a beer in a tall, wide-topped glass.

'Thanks,' he says. 'Are you sure this is alright?' It has crossed Danny's mind that she might be keeping him here until someone arrives to take care of him. He knows the gym, the London house and his Yorkshire home, but not much else. Nothing in his new life would surprise him.

'You came to help me. I'm grateful,' she says.

A few minutes later he smells pizza. The smell reminds him how hungry he really is. Then the doorbell rings again. Stella is clearly expecting the ring. She looks at the screen and buzzes the person straight in.

A tall thin man walks into the room. Danny guesses he's around 6ft 6in. He stoops as if he has spent a lifetime around people of lesser stature. He wears glasses which he immediately turns on Danny as if he expects him to be there, as if he's been warned.

'Yes,' he says. 'Yes.'

'Danny, Michael.' Stella does the introductions. 'Danny, will you please tell Michael your story while I get the salad mixed?'

Michael eases himself into a chair and balances his pointed chin on the tall thin cradle of his hands.

Danny picks the cat off his lap and puts it on the floor. It shuffles away to find Stella. Danny tells his story. This time it isn't new. This time it's like repeating a statement he's already made. He tells his story baldly. Michael listens as Danny imagines the grim reaper must listen to his victim's final pleas. Danny wonders how old Michael is. He seems ageless and his eyes are hooded.

Stella comes back in before he finishes and hovers until he stops.

'You see what I mean?' she says to Michael.

He nods.

'Both of you, come through.'

The kitchen is as pristine as the sitting room. A table is laid for two. Stella motions Danny to sit down, urges him to eat. The other two seem to ignore him but he listens as he eats.

'It's happening, isn't it?'

Stella sits at the other laid place and fills her plate with salad.

'I think so.' Michael's voice is extraordinary, deep and sonorous.

'I've tried to keep the balance, but the security services always want more. They demand more access, more freedom to listen to who they want, what they want and whenever they want.'

When Michael speaks it's as if what he says comes straight from the rock at the centre of the earth. 'Their job is difficult. You can't blame them for wanting it to be easier.'

'You warned me when I made that speech. You told me what would happen.'

'I'm so sorry I was right.'

'What do we do now, Michael? What does our friend here do?'

'We have to presume they know he's here,' Michael says. 'His phone will be being tracked.'

Danny looks at Stella. She's gone again, turned in, is talking to herself.

'I refused to give them automatic access. I refused to let Britain become a police state. There has always been an unwritten rule that the intelligence services stay out of elections. Now that rule's being broken but

I can't prove it. Jud Mindsett is no more capable of contacting Borstov than I am of lying. They have the Russian threat and they have another weapon too. Tomorrow, just before the postal ballots are issued, they will seek to destroy me.'

Just as last time she snaps out of her trance. 'Michael, is there anything we can do?'

Michael shakes his head. 'Politics already has a bad name. You are the exception. You have always stayed above the bitching and in-fighting. You can't stoop to his level now. Trust the members. Stick to talking about policy. Stick to what you know is right. You have to be you. Take a leaf out of Obama's playbook: when they go low, we go high.'

She nods. 'And Danny?'

'Add him to your team. Let him be seen with you in public. He'll have to shave, dress differently. The best way we can protect him is to keep him in the public view.'

'Okay Danny?' Stella asks.

Danny considers, shakes his head. 'It's a good offer, but I'm not trained for close protection. Besides, like so many disappeared people I don't want to be found. Thanks, but I'll take my chances.'

Stella nods. 'I understand that.'

'Go for a long walk. The West Highland Way will be beautiful at this time of year,' Michael suggests.

Danny gets up. Stella walks over to him, holds out her hand. 'I am grateful for you coming to see me. If I can ever do anything for you in the future ...' She leaves the question in the air.

'What about my phone?' Danny asks.

Stella nods to Michael.

'Keep the phone. Keep it switched off. Remember it needs a signal if they are to track you, so why not buy a tent and go for a long walk, somewhere without mobile signals, perhaps somewhere north of Glasgow?'

As Danny heads downstairs he hears Stella ask Michael, 'Is there any way we can get the photographs back?'

And he hears Michael's reply. 'I'll see what I can arrange.'

Then Danny's outside under the cherry blossom, unemployed and a wanted man.

33

Izzy parks the car outside the Church of the Living Saints. The moment it comes to a halt Leah opens the door and steps outside.

'Wait there,' she tells her mother.

She's seen the van. He's come. She wasn't sure he would, but he has.

She stands for a moment and looks at the van, then she moves towards it. As soon as she does so Martin gets out and stands waiting for her.

He seems to be on his own. He hasn't brought Vikki with him. What does that mean? She doesn't know.

He looks so much the same. There is something unchangeable in Martin. Since they last met her world has turned upside down. He runs the same shop, drives the same van.

'I wasn't sure you'd come,' she says to him.

'When have I ever let you down?'

It isn't a genuine question. It has no accompanying smile.

'I know that,' she says.

He doesn't walk towards her. He waits for her to come to him. He doesn't say anything else. It's as if he's waiting for her to say something. She wonders what that might be, then she realises.

'I was wrong about Howard and the journal. I was wrong about Stella.'

His face registers what she's said.

'Your views shocked me. I went to see her,' he says.

'Who?'

'Stella Stelling. I went to warn her.'

'What was she like?'

'I liked her.' Martin pauses. 'More than that, I admired her.'

Leah hangs her head. 'I'm so sorry about the letters and journal. I should never have handed them over ...'

'No, you shouldn't. I tried to warn you.'

She hears the new tone in his voice. Perhaps he has changed inside, perhaps he only looks the same.

'You did. I didn't listen. But,' Leah grasps at an excuse, 'no damage has been done. They have not been made public.'

'They will be, Leah. She's dreading that. How I wish I'd burnt them, then ...'

He doesn't finish the sentence. Instead he becomes business-like. 'But we are here on a quite different matter, aren't we?'

She feels crushed. She has never known him so cold.

'Mum's waiting. Let's get this done.'

He walks with her, greets Izzy in a perfectly friendly way. The three of them head back towards the place they each hoped never to see again, the Church of the Living Saints.

Leah takes the lead. 'We're here to see Katherine. She knows we're coming.'

'I'll take you through.'

They walk down the corridor that only Leah knows. The receptionist knocks on the door that Leah once fled through to get away from the pounding steps of the man she now knows wasn't her half-brother.

'Come in.'

Katherine's hair is streaked with white now. Was it always that colour underneath? Is she now God's Woman?

When Leah was last here it was a sick-room and a crime scene. She glances round but there are no remnants, there's no wheeled hospital bed or pile of towels. She looks instinctively to the spot where an old man was smothered, but there is only carpet.

Katherine stands up to greet them. She seems to have forgotten who Martin is, so Leah reminds her.

It's not only her hair that has changed. The woman who faces them is more relaxed than she was before.

'Are you ...?' Leah asks, not knowing whether to use the title God's Man or God's Woman.

'I am the Leader of the Church of the Living Saints, if that is what you mean. Please be seated.'

The title must be new, Leah thinks, noting the pleasure that Katherine couldn't quite suppress as she pronounced it.

Leah and her mother sit. Martin defiantly stands.

'I know why you are here,' Katherine says. 'I have been through the files and I am truly sorry, but I have no information to give you. We believed that Patrick was your son. We do not trust the so-called science of DNA.'

There is a shocked silence in the room. Izzy cries out and Leah turns to comfort her.

'You never went to the police,' Martin says.

Katherine looks up at him, doesn't deign to reply.

'You never reported the death. Why was that?'

She stares at him.

'I thought you were here to discuss Mrs Goulden's

adopted child. Martin, won't you please sit down.' Katherine's tone is sweet and reasonable.

Martin stays standing.

It's then that Leah becomes aware that Martin is furious. Even though he stands away from her Leah can feel his anger.

'The trouble is', Martin explains, speaking slowly and distinctly, 'the last time Mrs Goulden asked her question she was given the wrong answer.' He spells that out. 'She was told Patrick was her son. She was lied to, a lie that had terrible consequences. A deliberate lie and it came from a church.'

'I think the past is better left undisturbed, don't you?' Katherine suggests.

'But I need to know if you are going to tell the truth now,' Martin persists. 'I care for these people. Your church put them through hell. I heard what you shouted at Leah on the day of the murder. 'With a true understanding of God, there is no rape and no murder.' Those were your words, weren't they?'

Katherine smiles. 'Yes, and I stand by them. There have always been two kinds of truth: man's truth and God's truth. St John puts it best. *If you abide in my word, you are truly my disciples, and you will know the truth, and the truth will set you free.* He meant that only God's truth sets you free and you can only know that from inside his church.'

Leah starts. It was the quotation Martin gave her to use against Patrick. Now it's being turned against them.

'Dear God,' Martin says, and takes a deep breath. Then he goes on. 'Look Katherine, I'm not a church leader. I sell books and not many of those. I get by. I'm nothing special, but there are things I've been taught and there are things I've learnt for myself. One of the things I've learnt is that we are only truly human if we can admit somewhere deep inside us that we might be wrong about everything. We are only human if we change our minds as the facts change. I saw very little point in our coming to see you because you have locked your mind so tightly nothing can touch you. I guessed you would not divulge anything to us that might damage the reputation of your church. I was against us even coming here. But we need your help. So here are some facts I think even your warped and twisted God might recognise. 1) Leah's mother gave birth to a boy out of wedlock. 2) She left that child in the care of the Church of the Living Saints. 3) The dead man called Patrick was not that child. 4) You must have records that tell you what happened to the child Isabel left with you. So if you have any touch of humanity about you, will you please tell us what you know so that a mother can learn what happened to her real son.'

'I've told you,' said Katherine. 'We have no records of what happened to her son.'

Izzy gets up to go, shoving her chair back.

Leah stands with her.

Katherine remains seated. As the other two turn to the door, Martin moves forward and leans across the desk, planting both hands on the leather surface. 'That lie won't save you.'

Katherine's head comes up. 'Are you threatening me?'

Martin ignores this. 'I didn't expect you to be honest. That's why I appealed to your humanity. Since that has failed I must use other means. I now demand to see, in full, the records you have of all the children who were in your care between January 1st 1966 and December 31st 1968. Unless you produce those records in the next thirty minutes I will report you to the Charities Commission on the grounds that we suspect serious safeguarding failings by the Church of the Living Saints. They will investigate. They may even dig up your lawns. Church groups have been known to bury unrecorded births. Do you want the kind of scandal that has accrued to Magdalene convents in Ireland and brought down even an institution as powerful as the Christian Brothers?'

Katherine stands her ground, winds her fingers resolutely round a keyring. 'There was a fire,' she says. 'We think it was caused by an electrical fault. All such records were destroyed. Now I order you to leave my room.'

Martin sits down at last. 'Make me,' he says. 'Just make me.'

Leah leaves her mother and sits beside Martin. 'If you want to call the police, can I suggest you ask for PC Keith Loadstone? Ask for him by name. He wants to interview you anyway.'

Katherine reacts to this show of intransigence by getting up herself and moving towards Izzy who is standing by the door. 'I'm sorry about all this, Mrs Goulden. I know you are upset, but can you please ask your daughter and her friend to leave my room?'

Izzy shakes her head. Katherine pushes her out of

the way, so Izzy slaps her hard and the sound reverberates.

'You need to know, Katherine,' Izzy says, 'that I fully intend to press charges for kidnapping and false imprisonment. It was my sense of shame that stopped me at the time, but anger trumps shame.'

'You have twenty-eight minutes left,' Martin informs her.

Izzy stands resolutely by the door. For a moment it's stalemate.

Then Leah gets up and goes to stand by her mother. 'If all your records have been destroyed,' she asks, 'how did Patrick happen to have that photograph?'

'Which photograph?' Katherine asks.

'Show her, Mum.' From her handbag Izzy takes out the only black and white photograph she has of her real baby. She hands it to Leah.

'This one. Patrick the imposter had the exact same photograph. It's what convinced us that he must be genuine. So someone in this organisation knew that it was the photograph of my real half-brother. That means you must have records and archives and carefully kept files. There was no electrical fault, no fire.'

Martin joins in. 'Sadly, it means that when Mrs Goulden came to you to try to trace her son you couldn't produce the real Patrick. He'd left or he'd been cast out or perhaps he'd died. Which was it?'

Katherine unwinds the keyring from her fingers and unlocks the drawer of her desk. She takes out a file and hands it over to Izzy. 'This is all we have,' she says.

* * *

For the press conference Jud has dressed in a dark suit and a sombre blue-black tie. He looks like a man about to attend a funeral, which in a way he is. His appearance and the way he walks to the lectern disarm the journalists. One or two wonder if he has called this press conference to announce his resignation. There is no swagger, no sense of the bombshell to come. They look around and exchange glances.

There is also no sign of the brash voice. Some politicians mumble and you have to strain to listen to them. Jud is reliably loud, but not today.

'When information reaches me that is injurious to an opponent, I usually disregard it,' he begins. 'Politicians have a bad enough reputation with the public without us trashing each other in personal, spiteful ways. That is why, when a member of the public thought it was her moral duty to trust me with important information about my opponent, I hesitated to share it. We are each of us entitled to private lives. We each of us have things in our pasts that do not always reflect well on us. I hesitated even though I was convinced that what had been brought to me was true. Part of it is in my opponent's handwriting, so I could make the match and verify it.' He stops there, pauses as if he might not go on.

Leah watches calmly. This is what she brought about. This is her fifteen minutes of notoriety.

'Even now,' Jud continues, 'as you can all sense, I am doubtful about what I am about to do. I do not like any part of what I am about to say, and I would wish this information had never come my way. But I have been persuaded that we all have a duty to tell the truth.'

Stella is at home watching, holding her cat.

Jud knows his audience is riveted. He has them. 'And when that truth concerns a death ...'

There is an audible gasp amongst the hard-bitten hacks.

'... then the truth must be told, mustn't it? You cannot want as your leader someone who ...' Jud pauses again. In his head are James's last words to him, *Remember to tell it more in sorrow that in anger.*

'... someone who abandoned every one of her promises and pushed a young man to take his own life.' He lets that sink in.

Stella cringes. She knew what was coming but it is worse that she imagined.

'This is about trust,' Jud continues. 'Stella made promises to Howard.' He holds up her letters, makes sure the cameras get their pictures. 'Stella made cast-iron promises in these letters to a young man called Howard, the same kind of promises she is now making to you.'

He brings the letters down as he manages to produce a croak in his voice, a little hiccup of strong emotion. 'But she betrayed Howard and he died. I feel it is my duty to bring this to your attention. I do not want you to become her victims and her dupes in the way Howard was.'

He stops and stands there for a moment as if he is about to say more, as if there is more to be said, then he suddenly turns and walks off the stage.

* * *

Izzy and Leah pore over the file Katherine finally gave them. Izzy's real son walked out of the Church of the Living Saints a few months short of his sixteenth birthday. Because he was so close to that crucial birthday they never reported him missing. That was their policy.

Katherine gave them information only reluctantly and only in response to direct questions. Martin asked most of them. Martin insisted on knowing. In response to his insistent questions they gradually learnt that the church felt no responsibility. The boy had rejected them. They had done their best for him, but sainthood isn't for everyone. They had the records. They had his birth certificate. The name on the birth certificate was Patrick. They knew they were at fault for not reporting his disappearance to the police, but this was a long time ago. He had been a healthy boy, curious and questioning. He was in the choir and had a good singing voice. They had a photograph of him as a choir member taken only months before he disappeared. When he left he had nothing but the clothes he stood up in.

'Why then?' Martin had asked. 'Why did he leave at that precise moment?'

'There had been a beating for a misdemeanour. He'd been caught drinking. Perhaps it might have been a little too fierce.'

34

When Leah, Izzy and Martin left the Church of the Living Saints they went straight to the police. This time it was Leah who insisted they do things properly. The police listened and made notes. Izzy's real son was under sixteen when he vanished. His disappearance should have been reported. It follows that the Church of the Living Saints has serious safeguarding issues which need investigating.

'A church?' the policeman interrupts. 'You can't expect us to investigate a church.'

'We were lied to twice,' Martin points out, 'once when Izzy was palmed off with the wrong son and once, just now, when they claimed to have no records and then produced them.'

'Do churches lie?'

'This one does.'

The policeman looks doubtful but takes details. 'I'll see what I can do,' he tells them.

Izzy pipes up then. 'There's also the little matter of a body. Katherine, the leader of their so-called church, watched the victim in the sinkhole die and never reported his death. You really have no option. You have to investigate what we've told you.' She pauses. 'But that's not the important point.'

The policeman is shocked. 'Is there more?'

'We need your help to find my real son. How do we go about it?' Izzy asks.

The policeman shakes his head. 'The trail will have

gone cold a long time ago. He must be in his forties, living his own life, perhaps under another name. I'm sorry, but we can't help you there.'

'Can't or won't?'

'16,000 people who are reported missing stay missing. 16,000 each and every year. It's thirty years since he vanished. I'm sorry, but do the maths. Your only chance is if he wants to find you.'

'How can he do that? I bet he doesn't even know we exist.'

'I'll put his photo on the website,' Leah tells Izzy.

Leah has already put a photo of Danny on the Missing Persons website. Now she scans the photograph they have been given of the real Patrick as a chorister. She blanks out the other boys until there is only a photograph of her half-brother. When they've sharpened the image as much as possible she puts it on the Missing Persons site alongside Danny's photo and adds as many details as she knows. The message is the same as for Danny. She begs him to get in touch. When she has done this and shown Izzy, Leah checks that it has gone live.

Then there's nothing more she can do. 'It's a long shot, and even if we do find him he may be a real mess,' she warns Izzy. 'He walked out with nothing. He didn't go to the police. He just ran away. He has no qualifications. How on earth has he lived?'

'Then we need to find him and help him,' Izzy says.

* * *

Keith Loadstone is in the Wheatsheaf. He has a pint of

Landlord in front of him. He wonders if Angela will come. She said she would. He's fairly confident that she is a woman of her word. If he had not found that fingerprint match she would have pasted him and given him a final warning. He's sure of that. But as he waits he can't help thinking that was only her professional self speaking. Is her personal self as reliable, and what is her personal self like anyway? Her uniform has allowed him to guess at her figure, but he's never seen her in civvies. The moment she walks in he'll look at her, read her face. Then he'll know if this is a duty evening to keep her word or if he stands a chance with her.

He was going to save the first sip for her, but he's early and she could be here on time or late or not at all. He raises the glass to his lips and drinks. Hops, yeast, barley and a sweet bitterness pamper his tongue. He swallows.

What does he want? Is he ready to try again after so many failures? Does he think for a moment that a younger woman might be attracted to him? He must be twelve years older than she is. That's problem number one. Then she is his boss. Why should she slum it with a lower ranking officer? He was promoted before she joined the force and unfairly demoted for independent thinking, as he likes to call it. Nowadays it's called whistleblowing. Men, he thinks, don't exactly have a sell-by date, but he knows about the categories women apply to them. If he was ever a hunk he isn't one now. He's not a sweetie either. Long ago he was a piece of rough, good for a few wild nights but not for steadiness. He's never been good at going steady. He likes to jump at life. Is Angela a jump or a landing?

The moment she walks into the bar he knows she's up for this: pressed jeans, fluffed hair, lipstick and a top showing cleavage. He sees to his relief that she has a bit of a tum so she probably likes eating and perhaps drinking. Better still, he won't have to make sure he holds himself in all night. He lifts a hand and waves her over. He won't kiss her yet. He won't presume anything. He'll offer her a drink. She's in good time. They might get two drinks in and then share a bottle at the restaurant.

* * *

Jud and James have been joined by Annabelle Pits-Tucker. The phone rings constantly. They take it in turns to pick it up. If it's a journalist they say they have nothing to add to what was said at the press conference. Mostly it isn't journalists. The callers are MPs building bridges, former supporters of Stella wondering if there is any way they can be useful to the Mindsett campaign. With each of these callers James, Jud and Annabelle play hard to get and gain satisfaction from sensing the desperation in the way many of their former detractors attempt to scramble on board. Only members have votes, but if so many MPs are making calls they must be in touch with their constituents.

There is champagne in the house but the team hasn't opened it. To do so would be to tempt fate. Nor has anyone yet said, 'Winning is the easy part. Governing will be much harder'. They will wait until the votes are counted.

* * *

Stella is on her own that evening, if you ever can be on your own with a cat like hers. There have been requests for interviews but she has nothing to say. Her phone is ominously silent. No one commiserates. Staunch supporters have not complained to her about the tactics used against her. She wonders what the headlines will be in the morning papers. She knows it is all over. She has inherited the curse of the front-runner. Even Michael has not been in touch with her.

It feels like mourning, grieving for an easier, more polite age. She knows she could mount a counter-attack. Borstov, Mindsett's mistress, Mindsett's incompetence could all be exploited, but the party would be the loser. It would make it almost impossible for whoever won to govern effectively. She's tempted, but she won't go down that road. She already feels that she belongs to the past. In five years' time she might become a commentator, a venerated elder statesperson, but only if she behaves with dignity now.

* * *

Soft cool air surrounds Danny. He is standing on the shore of Loch Lomond. He risks turning his mobile phone on. There is no signal. The water laps quietly against the stones. Across on the western side cars pass on the main road heading to Crianlarich and Fort William. Above them the hills are held in cloud. Better weather is coming from the north. There is enough breeze to keep the midges at bay. He stands there for a long time drinking in the freedom provided by a wide sky. This exists, he thinks. It existed when I was born. It existed when I was in the gym. It existed when I was under the railway arch. It has always been here.

Nearby is a small group of geese, four adults with nine young. Danny sees the crow waiting. The adult geese stretch their necks and hiss at it but it never flinches. It bides its time, watchful and alert. When they turn away it hops forward quickly, snatches a goose chick by the neck and flies off, the yellow ball of down fluttering under the black shadow of the crow flying across the water.

Even here, Danny thinks.

He waits for the other geese to react but they don't. This is their world. They know what happens. They are already turned away with heads down, feeding.

Walking hasn't stilled his thoughts. The trudge of the miles slipping away under his feet hasn't dulled the questions that are always in his mind. Who am I? Who do I want to be?

He has made some progress. He is not who he was, he knows that. Offered the safety of resuming his previous identity he surprised himself with the completeness of his refusal. He knows that today he walked further than is usual on the first day of the West Highland Way. For some reason this matters to him, even though he shares the information with no one. He is beginning to divide his life into two: the time he exists and the time he feels alive. The knife in his hand is still his talisman. Following Mindsett, being photographed by Borstov's thugs, meeting Harry in the British Museum, coming face to face with Stella: these are the highlights. But today was something else. He felt glorious, loving the sense of putting Glasgow behind him and walking away from suburbia. Each successive hill rose a little higher and a little wilder. No one followed him, he's certain of that. Tomorrow he must face a long tramp along the edge of Loch Lomond. He finds himself looking forward to it as if he senses that somewhere along this path he may make the discovery he craves. He's looked at the map. He could climb Ben Lomond on the way. There's a good track up from the Rowardennan Hotel. He is sure he can find another way down as he heads north.

The low cloud is tinged with pink and the mountain in front of him is rising out of it. If he goes to his tent now he can be away early. He is used to the euphoria induced by exercise, but this is something else. It will soon be dark. It will soon be tomorrow.

* * *

Leah hears the doorbell and wonders who it can be. Danny? It's possible. Is it a very late delivery from an underpaid foreign delivery man? Have the journalists already found her and named her as the source of the letters and the journal? She hopes not. There is another possibility but she discounts it.

It's still light, but only just. She pulls the door open.

He's standing with his back to her. He turns as he hears the door open. They are silent, but they look at each other.

'I thought you might need company,' Martin says. 'I can easily go away again.' He looks steadily at her.

She nods and he follows her inside.

'Coffee?'

'Please.'

Single words will do for the moment. In their best days they managed without words altogether, but that was in another life.

She makes him a coffee and he watches her, watches the way she checks the weight of the kettle to see if there is enough water before switching it on, notes as she reaches up for the coffee jar how her heels lift off the floor and the front of her foot splays out to take the weight. He observes the careful way she checks the spoon level before turning her wrist over to drop the granules into two of the white mugs she has pulled forward from under the cupboard.

She sniffs the milk, passes it as fit, splashes white into the deep brown and hands him a mug.

'Thanks.'

'Izzy's in the front room,' Leah says. 'Shall we stay here?'

They sit at the breakfast table and just drink.

There are so many different kinds of silence. This silence is unthreatening. It feels like the last tired act of a busy day. It is not without a sense of relaxed pleasure.

They sit and sip. Leah eventually breaks the silence. 'Say it, Martin. Please just say it.'

'What?'

'That you were right and I was wrong.'

'That's not what I was thinking.'

She gives him a half smile. 'What were you thinking?'

'Not much, really. Just something about how nice it is to be here like this.'

She reaches out a hand and touches him on the arm. It isn't like Vikki's touch, he thinks. It doesn't demand he takes notice. He looks round the kitchen. Can life be a sink, a dishwasher, a set of cupboards, a bin, a table in the middle of the room, and an odd pile of stuff ready to be recycled? Something to look back on, much to look forward to?

* * *

The last daylight has already disappeared in Malton when Angela and Keith leave the restaurant. They've talked Met and County, talked promotion and disappointments. He's paid the bill and she never demurred. The square is empty of all cars except for their taxi, waiting.

'Who lives nearest?' she whispers.

'You do,' he tells her.

She gives the instruction. She reaches out and holds his hand in the darkness.

* * *

Ivor is depressed. He watches the news and weighs his options. If Mindsett becomes Prime Minister there will be no one-to-one blackmail opportunity, and he will have to join the long queue of asylum-seekers going through official channels. Except the queue is diminishing. Britain isn't the place it once was. Germany and France now seem better bets. Britain, once the bastion of democracy, the country that thanked Churchill for leading them to victory by voting him out of office, seems to Ivor as vulnerable to corruption and electoral interference as any other country in the world. He looks round him and asks the question every tourist asks in Athens and Rome: how did this run-down country ever dominate the world? The things he loves about Britain, he now realises, belong too much in its past. It isn't any longer his fabled land. It certainly isn't the country that in 1914 welcomed Belgian refugees in their tens of thousands and looked after them for the duration of the First World War.

If he wants to stay here he'll have to find another way. Might Danny help? He doesn't think so. Danny is such an innocent.

* * *

In a Franciscan friary perched on the cliffs above Alnmouth a friar in his late fifties dreams and smiles at what he is dreaming. He went to bed early as he always does because his day begins at 4am, well before the dawn. The chapel faces east like every other, but there is no stained-glass window here. When he processes into the church to begin morning service a wall of blackness will greet him. He knows the rhythm of the service intricately. He has lived with it for nearly thirty years. He will pray and he will raise his head and see a streak of dawn. He will pray again, and when he looks up the light will have spread outwards. Sometimes it is pink-tinged, sometimes an eggshell blue. No stained-glass could match the intensity of that changing view. As the service reaches its crescendo the light always comes into the church and begins its walk along the ceiling, moving lower and lower until it touches him and fills his soul.

35

Angela wakes first and looks at the man she slept with last night. It's six thirty. They need to be on duty in a couple of hours. He's fast asleep. She surprised herself last night and he was even more surprising. She knows she shouldn't wake him. She knows if she lets him sleep she can say it was the wine talking and she can leave it at that. He is older than she is. His face is already lined round the eyes. Last night might be the biggest mistake she's ever made, but then her grandmother once told her that making mistakes was what life was for. If you don't make mistakes you haven't been alive. This older policeman makes her feel alive. She swings her feet out of the bed and goes to make coffee.

* * *

Louisa Drakutt is enjoying herself. Today there will be no need to strain for a story. Today there is only one story and it's summed up in all the newspaper headlines. *HEART BREAKER. ISSUE OF TRUST. STELLA FALL. KILLER PROMISE.* Today Louisa can use some of those once-every-two-year phrases: *decisive shift, historic moment, knock-out blow.* She will, of course, give Jud Mindsett a hard time when he becomes Prime Minister. And if she ever gets hold of the journal and the letters, she will look for the feminist angle to this *girl dumps man* story. But all that can wait. The ballot papers are already distributed. The votes are being cast. It's a lovely morning in Central London. Pink cherries are everywhere. Spring is late this year but is racing to catch up.

She takes the phone call. She always takes phone calls. She's an avid collector of political snippets, but this time she snaps her name out as she answers to show her sense of urgency. The best places on Sanctuary Green are filling up and she needs to get there. She keeps walking as she listens, urging her crew to hurry up. But then she stops, gives the phone call her full attention and stands quite still.

The world carries on in its hurried mode. Her crew shrug and keep going. They are used to her ways. She'll catch them up as soon as she can.

Readers of her face would see she is energised. Her eyes are wide, her mouth pursed and level. 'Are you sure?' she suddenly asks, and listens intently to the answer. Normally she'd be scanning what's going on round her. Every hour of every day she has to live up to her own image of herself. That means being in the thick of things, being ahead of the game, but the game has moved on and she might need to be somewhere else as quickly as possible.

Her camera crew have gone ahead of her to find a good spot.

She stands, glances at her watch, listens, nods several times.

'And you're certain he is who he says he is?'

She listens again. The pavement is already full of people who move round her. Some have noticed her stillness and are focussing on her. What has she got that they haven't?

'Wow.' She says this under her breath as if it is only for herself. This might finally be her moment, her definition day.

'And he wants to speak to me?'

Another urgent nod. This mustn't escape her. The BBC's Political Correspondent knows the BBC is short of funds. 'Helicopter?' she asks. She dreads the taxi, train, hire-car routine that would fill the whole day and mean she wouldn't be able to front up or even follow up her own lead. 'It's the quickest way,' she insists. 'It guarantees the scoop.'

Through a thinning in the crowd she sees that her crew have grabbed a good spot and are setting up. They are close to the Burghers of Calais bronze which she wanted to work into her piece, but now all that can wait. When they look her way she gestures them back to her. They stare, check what her furious hand gestures mean, then shrug and start to pack their gear. Another team soon moves into the spot. Annabelle Pitts-Tucker has made her appearance and the hacks have another focus.

* * *

England in May is beautiful from the air. They fly over green fields edged with pink and white blobs of blossom. The rape fields are warming up like old-fashioned electric fires but in yellow. It's the shapes that enthral Louisa, the way the fields tessellate, the interplay between ancient villages and modern housing. Her camera crew look and point. They shoot footage that may come in useful one day. Louisa keeps her eyes on the horizon. The noise is tremendous, but she must concentrate on the job. This will be an interview like no other. She must ask questions, but the important thing will be to let him talk and make sure he does that well. She's never met a friar. She will call him Father. She thinks that's the right way to address him.

They don't know how long they can hold the secret amongst them. Their producer is a pro. He'll give no hint to anyone. He'll follow the result of the vote story, the expected Mindsett upset. A local outside broadcast unit will meet them in Northumberland. This unit has not been briefed, so they cannot spill a secret they don't know. For this story they need several camera angles. The producer wants the piece edited and ready for the one o'clock news. There is time but it will be tight.

They don't spot a broadcast unit as they approach. That's a bonus. Has the friar been told he must speak to no one but them? This is the big worry. The air is calm. Their pilot has found a landing spot and there are two brown figures waiting to greet them. They touch down, wait for the rotors to stop, and then Louisa is walking across fresh grass to shake the friar's hand. She notices his rope belt is tied with three knots and he's wearing sandals. Her shoes sink into the earth. She wonders if she should kick them off. Her shoes don't matter. She is Louisa Drakutt. They concentrate on her face. No one ever films her shoes.

The unit van comes straight across the grass from the road. There is a quick discussion. If the light breeze won't mess up the microphones they'll do the interview outside with the abbey in the background. The local crew haven't met Louisa. She greets each of them and they settle to work, check the light and sound. Louisa shakes her head, pushes away the usual strand of hair and raises her chin.

* * *

Leah woke early. She has dreaded today. She fears that Mindsett will win, and if he does it will be her fault. Even now journalists will be asking who leaked the letters and the journal. They will trace the family and find Vikki. Vikki will tell them about the house clearance. What will Martin say? Even now journalists and cameras may be tracking her down. Then half the country will blame her for releasing such personal information. And she was wrong. She knows that now. She was utterly wrong to do what she did. What will she say when they find her? Martin went home last night. She wanted him to stay but knew he wouldn't. She thinks he's no longer with Vikki but she's not sure. He's promised to be back later today. She now knows she needs him and not just for this.

Then there is another problem. Patrick, the real Patrick, is somewhere out there. Izzy will want to find him. Where do they start?

Without a clear sense of what she should do, Leah switches on the 24 hour news and sees Louisa Drakutt, hair out of place, standing in the middle of a field with an abbey in the background. She is actually smiling.

'When I got the phone call this morning I thought it

was a wind-up. Sensational is such an overused word, but what I learnt in that phone call was, and is, truly sensational. So I'm away from the world of politics, miles away from Westminster. I'm in Northumberland and I'm here to meet a ghost.'

The camera shot pulls back and reveals a smiling, bemused Franciscan friar standing at her side. A gull swoops towards them and rises again.

'Why do you want to talk to me, Father?'

'Because a lie has been told about me. That lie is everywhere, and so I thought I should put the record straight.'

'So who are you?'

'These days I'm known as Father Brian, but my birth name was Howard. Once, long before I took my vows, I had a wonderful girlfriend called Stella Stelling.'

He stops. Louisa prompts him. 'What happened between you? I do need to ask you that.'

A look of pain spreads across the friar's face. 'That's simple,' he says. 'It's a very human story really. I came to realise that I loved Stella much more than she loved me. Looking back, I think the way I loved her frightened her. She wanted to serve others. She took up causes. She believed in people and so she wanted to go into politics to make a difference. I think in those days I was a very selfish young man. I wanted her to be wholly wrapped up in me, as I was in her. I now know it was most unreasonable of me. I saw how torn she was between her promise to me and her yearning to help others. I couldn't bear that. I knew it would end badly and I wanted her to be free, so I went for a swim.'

'In other words, you faked your own death. Do you regret that?'

He smiles broadly. 'I wouldn't put it like that. I think what I did that night was to make a bet with God. I swam into dangerous waters in total darkness and let God decide. He saved me, I came ashore and made my way up here. I've been here ever since.'

He pauses. 'I stayed here because I came to realise that I have a special gift for loving, but that I just have too much love in me for one human being to cope with. That kind of love swamps people. It stifles them. That kind of love belongs to an ideal or to a country. In my case it belongs to God. He saved me, so here I am.'

Louisa Drakutt, the journalist who always has a killer question formed in her head, says nothing.

The friar pauses. 'Perhaps Stella has the same kind of love as I have, but it's for her country and for ordinary people.'

'Have you seen this morning's headlines?' Louisa Drakutt asks, and holds up a paper. 'They must have been a shock to you. How do you react to what's been said about the woman you once loved?'

'So unfair. So hurtful. Stella is a good woman. I have nothing whatever to reproach her for. We weren't meant to be together. She stuck to her calling. I have cheered her on from the sidelines for thirty years. She's honest and truthful and she never fights dirty. I hope she can still win.'

'Is there a part of you that still loves her?'

'That is a question too far, young Louisa.' Father Brian lifts his cincture. 'Look,' he says, pointing at the three knots. 'I made my vows and I've largely kept to them. The thing about being a friar is that you don't have a personal life.'

'Have you anything you would like to say to Jud Mindsett?'

'Only that I'll be happy, at any time, to hear his confession.'

'You know Stella has never married?'

'Yes,' he says. 'I have often wondered at that.'

The focus shifts back to the studio. News never stops. It continues somewhere else as it always does. Leah knows what she's just seen, understands what she's just heard, but she needs to hear it again. So she keeps watching until it comes round a second time.

* * *

Jud, James and Annabelle are plotting together. At 1pm they take a break and turn on the news. They expect more excitement, more coverage, more defections from Stella's team to theirs. Stella has not been seen in public since yesterday. More MPs have switched to Mindsett. His team feel they are on the verge. They want to bask in their moment before the enormity of what they've achieved begins to weigh on them. There will be so much work to do. They need to fill ministries. They need to set up their teams. There is no transition time. Next week, as soon as the votes are counted, they will be in Number 10. They know most members fill in their ballot papers the moment they arrive. They have got their timing absolutely right. It really is all over for Stella.

First they are surprised. They've never seen Louisa

Drakutt so far away from the sources of power. Then their jaws slacken to the point where mouths fall open. Language spirals downwards. 'It can't be.' 'OMG.' 'Shit.' 'WTF.' 'Oh fuck.' The interview with Howard is over. Louisa stands on the edge of a field of rape to give her comments. She screws her face up in an effort to disguise her delight. 'I would say this is unprecedented, Hugh. To say this changes everything is an understatement. When a devastating attack by one candidate on the other turns out to be absolutely untrue we are in unchartered territory. Not least there will be the question of members who have already voted wanting to raid post boxes to get back their ballot papers ...'

Jud recovers first. 'The BBC should have asked for our comments before that went out. They're bang out of order.'

James shakes his head. 'In the same way you alerted Stella and the BBC to your bombshell, I suppose. That friar has stuffed us.'

'Your family, James. The letters came from your sister I believe.' The blame game has begun.

A phone starts ringing, then another. Annabelle picks one up. Jud and James decline, but listen as Annabelle goes on the offensive.

'We are the victims of a dirty tricks campaign. When we received the letters and journal we did our best to check. As Jud Mindsett said, we took our time, made a decision and placed them in the public domain. If ever anything was in the public interest those documents were. How could we possibly have known that this individual faked his own death?' She slams the phone down.

The other two silently applaud her. Jud picks up the next phone. 'We acted in good faith. We took our time and came to a decision. You need to imagine the outcry if we had suppressed information that was pertinent to the great choice our party members are facing. Anyway, is this new witness wholly reliable? He did fake his own death.'

Another phone rings. This time it's James who picks up. There are more calls. After an hour has gone by they reckon they are still in with a chance because so many members have already voted.

* * *

Martin hears the news on the van radio. When he reaches her, Leah is sobbing. At first the tears worry Martin, then they don't. He has never seen her like this. She cries and smiles and cries some more. She almost seems to laugh at the way she has lost control of her face. He reaches out to hold her hand and she clasps his. 'Look what I made happen,' she says, as soon as she can speak. 'Has Stella seen this?'

* * *

Stella wasn't watching. A phone call alerts her and she is in time to see her lover from thirty years ago. She takes in his habit with its cinctures and imagines the small cell he sleeps in, but above all she sees the contentedness that suffuses his features. All too soon the interview is over, so she switches onto 24 hour news and he's there again. She watches the whole thing twice. Eventually she understands what she is seeing and a weight she has carried for years lifts inside her. It's a long time before she can put anything into words, and when she does the words are not commensurate with the enormity of all she feels. 'You bugger,' she says to the cat, the television and the balding friar. 'You absolute bugger.'

* * *

It was wet when Danny woke up. The loch was shrouded. He breakfasted, packed the tent and got on his way. His boots are soaked after the first hour but the cloud is already lifting. At Rowardennan he turns off the West Highland Way and heads up to Ben Lomond. The path is steep to begin with, then the gradient eases. The top is still in cloud, but already he has a sense of the wilderness around him. When he pauses he can pick out the peaks of the Arrochar Alps to the west. They are splendid dark shapes against the lit banks of cloud. Ben Narnain is even wearing a cap of fresh snow. He can make out nearly the whole length of the loch. When he's drunk some water he sets off again. The sun is out. The landscape glistens. He moves across it with ease. In front of him Ben Lomond emerges from the cloud and it's a real peak. The mass of the mountain blocks the sight of anything further north. The view from the top should be quite something. He bounds towards it.

He's on the final part of the climb when his phone pings. He's surprised but there must be a signal up here. He locates the phone and pulls it out of his pocket ready to turn it off. There's part of a message from Michael. *Enjoy the walk. I thought you might be glad ...* He quickly switches it off. He doesn't want to be traced.

From the top he can see the whole of the Highlands stretched out in front of him. The view is spanking clear after the rain. He spots the ridge he must take and checks the map to find the path down to the Cailness Burn.

Before he sets off he quickly checks his phone again and opens the message. His own photos stare back at him. He sees the door. There is Borsov shaking hands with Jud Mindsett. There is the American and there again is Borstov. His proof is back and there's nowhere he can save them to. Then he notices the other part of the message. *I thought you might be glad to see these again. After all, they are yours. Use only if necessary. Michael.*

He switches the phone off at once. Michael already has the photos, so he needn't do anything to save them. The rucksack feels heavier as he heads down towards Cruinn à Bheinn, but he's making good time and he feels a sense of completeness wash over him. As Scotland slips slowly south under his feet his fitness makes sense. It thrills him that Michael should bother to send him the photos. He feels he's doing alright. When he gets back from Fort William they might even employ him.

36

Three days pass. Danny has reached Bridge of Orchy and is having breakfast. He watches the news and sees that Jud Mindsett has won, but by the narrowest of margins, fewer than 300 votes.

The sound is switched off so he follows the subtitles. Some members are crying foul. They'd cast their votes before the resurrection bombshell. The dying Prime Minister has not yet been to the palace. No time has been set for the new Prime Minister to kiss hands. James is everywhere. James is being mentioned as the next Chief of Staff. James is being credited with the great victory. James, the brother who always scorned him, has won again.

Stella is in the political wilderness. Jud Mindsett has won and the Russian leader has already sent his congratulations.

Danny's phone pings even though it wasn't switched on. How does anyone do that? There's an email from Stella's advisor, Michael, marked urgent.

You know what to do. M. The deleted photos are there again, this time as attachments.

Danny looks back up at the screen. James's face fills it. He's talking about governing for all the people, about the need to make Britain great again. Danny stares at his smirking older brother. Yes, he thinks, yes I know exactly what to do.

Danny abandons the West Highland Way. He promises he'll come back and finish it someday, but he needs to act now. There's a bus to Glasgow in twenty-three minutes. He can be in London this afternoon. He replies to Michael with a single word, *Yes*. He checks the photos. They are still there. His bag is packed. The bus stop is right outside the hotel.

* * *

The Guardian office is next door to King's Cross, so Danny goes there first. The receptionist doubts his story, doesn't think there'll be a journalist who can see him. They are all so busy. Even as little as a month ago Danny might have let himself be put off, but not now. He insists that he has their frontpage story for tomorrow. Eventually she picks up the phone and a few moments later an intern comes down to meet him.

From there things pick up speed. The intern looks at the photos and speaks into her mobile. Two other journalists come down, examine the evidence and invite him upstairs. He's interviewed. He meets the editor. He insists they do not use his name. He'll be a high placed source in the security services. Only when this is agreed does he give them dates, places and times. They ask him to do this twice. They have to be certain the meeting happened before the Russian incursion. Once they are satisfied, the photos are carefully downloaded from his phone onto their computer. When he leaves the office he texts Michael with a single word, *Done*.

Then he is back outside in London, nameless, unemployed and in danger. He can't continue to work for Harry now that Harry is the danger. He walks south, down the ironically named Jud Street, and wonders if they might need to change the name later today. He could go home. But both his homes may be being watched. He's safer on the street. He has a day's stubble and his walking gear stands out in London. He's wearing trainers but his boots and tent are in his rucksack. Part of him wants to go back to Scotland, but the journey south has taken most of his spare cash. He reaches the house where Borstov met Mindsett. As far as he can see it isn't being watched. Its windows stare blankly back at him. Have the Russians left, job done?

For days he's walked with purpose, heading north. Now he's come back to London because he had to. Before that it was all action: guarding Jud, trailing Jud, meeting Harry, making his way to Stella's house, doing his job. Now he stands still. He feels like someone who has reached his own full stop. Now he waits to see what kind of ripples spread out from the stone he's thrown into the pond. He hopes for a tsunami. He liked Stella, and to beat his brother at his own game ...

But what does he do while he waits for whatever comes next? The question roots him to the pavement. He takes off his rucksack and stands looking at the roofs with their assorted antennae and the plane trails scraped like chalk marks on a translucent blue slate. He knows he won't go back to sleeping rough or to being his gym-haunting previous self. Somewhere, as his boots scuffed the turf in the long trek across Scotland, a new, more confident Danny was baptised and confirmed. Perhaps one day when he has fully established his other self he will go and see his family, but not now or any time soon. There are two people he does want to talk to. They will be somewhere nearby. One he can always find in the drinking den. The other will be sleeping rough. Perhaps, if he simply sits down here on the warm pavement, one or both of them will come by.

* * *

Jud, James and Annabelle are closeted together with their advisors in Jud's ministerial office. Jud Mindsett is busy choosing his Cabinet. Annabelle Pitts-Tucker is in complex negotiations with the Palace to arrange the resignation of the previous Prime Minister and the kissing of hands ceremony for Jud Mindsett. James is fielding a whole range of enquiries. Everything is going their way. Removal vans are already at Number 10. Senior figures warn of the damage Jud's accession will do to the party but the Chairman is standing firm. The party will accept a Mindsett premiership.

At one time a story like the one Danny has taken to The Guardian would be kept secret until it appeared in newspaper headlines the next morning, but that doesn't happen anymore. The Guardian puts it on their live edition where other journalists immediately pick it up. The phrase *The Guardian is reporting* begins to ring through every news bulletin.

Blissfully unaware of Danny's bombshell, it is no longer Jud, James and Annabelle coping with everything. The three of them are now encumbered with help and the phones never stop ringing. They no longer pick up calls. That is done for them. Answering phones will soon be a thing of the past.

And so it happens that the Underling is the person in the room who hears the news first. He listens and a smile spreads across his trained civil service features. It quivers for a moment, then is quickly extinguished.

'Please hold. I'll hand you over to the Chief of Staff.'

'Mr Goulden.'

James looks up. 'Is it urgent?'

The Underling nods.

For the first time in his life James is pleased with himself. He's read Alastair Campbell's memoirs. He knows what his new job entails. As he walks over to take the call he is thinking that until today there were lots of men called James, but from this moment onwards he will be the one they think of, in the same way that years ago, out of the thousands of Margarets, there was only one Maggie.

As he crosses the room he tosses back his mane of hair which he knows will be such a gift to the cartoonists. Not for the first time he wishes his father was still alive to see this moment, to watch when later today he'll walk into Number 10 and start to give orders. It is important he gets back to the meeting as soon as possible. He doesn't trust Jud to pick the right Cabinet. They have to include Stella for the sake of party unity.

He takes the offered phone. 'James Goulden here.'

In the few moments he listens to what is being said his vanity shrivels and his intelligence kicks in. He's bright enough to know that it's all over, that Roz was dead right, that he always knew Jud was a tosser who could screw anything up. He kicks himself for not leaving the team as soon as he spotted the danger. The one time Jud escaped James's leash this happened, and these are the consequences. And he knows the other unfortunate thing. He gave the file to Borstov. He will sink with his captain. There is no way he can claim innocence.

He does his best. 'We completely deny this. Stella is simply a bad loser. This is yet another dirty trick, another item of fake news. And I have to add that it's desperate stuff, released just before we go into Number 10. The campaign was over days ago. The members have spoken.'

He puts the phone down and breathes deeply. He might get a job in PR if he can go down spitting and yelling. He might become a spokesman for bankers, for hedge funds, for makers of diesel cars, even for oligarchs. There are lots of high-profile well-paid jobs where the only two items on the person specification are the ability to ignore reality, even when it thumps you in the face, and the ability to lie with real conviction.

He walks into the room where Jud is meeting with civil servants. Jud ignores him, doesn't even look up, so James walks round to the television and switches it on.

At first there's no sound. One person looks up, then another. These people nudge those closest to them. Last of all Jud looks up and sees the photograph of himself shaking Borstov's hand. It's beautifully clear. James, still standing by the set, picks up the remote and unmutes the bulletin.

'... The Guardian's source is absolutely clear that this meeting took place before the Russian incursion.'

The picture suddenly shifts to one of Jud Mindsett

standing in front of the Russian Embassy and making a statement.

'*This government has been far too complacent about the Russian threat. The Russian bear is awake again and growling. How long before it attacks?*'

It's Louisa Drakutt. It would be. 'Perhaps with the benefit of hindsight we should have spotted that the timing was just too convenient,' she says. 'So let's make sure we get the sequence right. According to a senior security service officer, on the night before Jud made that statement he actually met a key aide to the Russian President. On the day after this meeting, just before the last hustings, the Russians staged an incursion. The Mindsett camp may well claim that this is a coincidence or perhaps, even worse, a security service stitch-up, but there is a prima facie case that a candidate for the highest office in this land actually conspired with an enemy agent to influence an election. If that is the case, I cannot imagine a more serious charge.'

'I've denied it,' James says. 'I issued an outright denial.'

Annabelle stares at Jud. 'Is it true?'

Jud slowly nods. 'We were losing. I had to do something.'

'I knew nothing about this until it had happened,' James says. 'Jud made me complicit by asking me to hand over key documents to a man who turned out to be Borstov.'

Jud nods again. 'You were always a cocky sod, James. I had to make sure you were implicated. It's not over. We can deny everything. The Russians certainly will.

We still won.'

The phone rings again. The Underling picks it up, and after listening for a moment he hands it to Jud. 'Minister, it's for you. It's the Party Chairman.'

* * *

PC Keith Loadstone and SDM Angela Matthews pull up outside the Arts and Crafts house. It's time to get to the truth. The body from the sinkhole may have already been re-buried, but they need to know what really happened that day. They need to know who he was and why he was there.

Waiting to meet them are Mrs Goulden, Leah and Martin. Keith recognises Martin, has been into his shop, but they've never been introduced.

'If you are to understand why there was a body in the sinkhole,' Leah tells them, 'we need to begin before the day itself. If you are to believe us we need to begin with the one piece of real evidence that we have.'

Martin cranks up his computer and they begin by watching the film of a smothering. It's silent. They watch a man pick up a pillow and advance towards a much older man lying on the bed. The man with the pillow says something and then presses the pillow down on the old man's face.

'The man doing the smothering is the man in the sinkhole. We called him Patrick, but we don't know his real name,' Leah explains. 'I filmed this sequence. The man being smothered was God's Man, the Leader of the Church of the Living Saints. He was dying and Patrick finished him off.'

In silence they watch the sequence.

'There were words, but the microphone stopped working. The man we knew as Patrick said something about this being in payment for all the beatings. When the old man's legs stopped kicking, Patrick calmly removed the pillow and said, 'Sure, isn't it better for him now.''

'Why?' Angela asks.

Leah answers. 'We don't know, we can only guess. We suspect the man we knew as Patrick had been told he could be the next God's Man, but only if he brought my mother, Izzy, and her fortune back into the cult. The dying God's Man must have nominated the man we knew as Patrick as his successor because he told me he wanted to change his mind. He got me to write a note which he signed. The note said *Not Patrick*. We think Patrick smothered him so that he could succeed to the title. Katherine told him to do it. I heard them talking before it happened.'

'Who's Katherine?'

'Patrick's fiancée. She's still alive. She's the new Leader.'

SDM Matthews says, 'I don't see how this links with the sinkhole.'

'They, Patrick and Katherine, had Izzy locked up in one of their safe houses. They were trying to force her to sign over the family fortune. We offered to swap the film of the smothering for my mother Izzy.'

'So it was an exchange,' PC Loadstone interjects, looking at the woman he now thinks of simply as Ange. 'Two car parks and a place to meet in between them.'

'Yes, our mother for the film. We chose that spot

because they had to bring Izzy with them. It's a childhood picnic site we always used. Mum's famously bad at reading maps. She has to smell her way to places. They had to bring her with them.'

'And what happened?'

Izzy takes up the story. 'I showed them the place to park and the path. Then they tied my hands up and locked me in the boot. They didn't know it had an internal catch, so I let myself out and part crawled, part walked to the spot.'

'Blue plastic twine,' Keith Loadstone said. 'I found the blue twine they used to tie you.'

'It wasn't dignified,' Leah goes on. 'James and Patrick began scrapping. Patrick knocked James over. Danny, the one who's disappeared, still had a knife in his hand, the one he'd used to cut Mum free.' Leah pauses. 'I think Patrick saw the knife and panicked. He stepped backwards and fell when the sinkhole shifted in the same way it had done when I was a child. Patrick fell in. There was nothing we could do.'

PC Loadstone has heard the evasion. He needs to check. 'Are you telling me that Patrick fell backwards into the sinkhole and that no one pushed him?'

Leah nods. 'Actually, Martin was protecting Patrick before he fell. He'd stepped between them, between Danny and Patrick. No one pushed anyone. The ground shuddered and Patrick vanished. There was nothing anyone could have done.'

'How much money did they stand to get for their church?'

Leah answers. 'We sold Dad's business for over £200 million.'

Angela takes over. 'We'll need full statements from all three of you. I doubt if we can build a convincing case against this Katherine, but we'll do what we can.' She turns to Leah. 'That was brave, what you did. Officially I couldn't condone it, but if you walked into their weird church to rescue your mother from their clutches, that was brave.'

As they drive away Angela puts her hand on Keith's knee. 'What am I doing with an old man who was wrong about everything? I mean, there were no drugs, no illegal immigrants. There was no human trafficking, no family feud about the inheritance. Actually, there wasn't even a crime, only an accidental death. You're a lousy cop, PC Loadstone.'

'I was right about the swap. I was right about the connection to Danny. And I helped you to help them.'

'How?'

'The DNA results. Mrs Goulden knows there's a chance her real son's still alive. We've given her hope.'

* * *

As PC Loadstone and SDM Matthews drive away, Stella opens her front door. The world's press is already camped outside her house. The whole street has been cordoned off. She is due at the Palace soon. Then she will arrive in Downing Street.

Everything has hurriedly been made ready. There is an official car and outriders. Her Majesty must not be kept waiting. Stella thinks, what have I done? Is this what I really wanted? But then the answer comes back: better me than Mindsett. She feels excited. She feels apprehensive. She has known for a long time that competence and principles are burdens because they propel you upwards. She knows that honesty isn't only right because it's moral; it's also right because it makes everything you do easier in the long run.

She walks towards the gate. At one time she would have had to push her way through. Now they move back to let her pass. So she stops. She'll break with precedent. She'll make a statement.

'I want you journalists to know how much you are to blame for what is about to happen. It's your fault. Without good journalism from The Guardian and the BBC I could have kept my freedom. It's your fault that I am about to be locked up in the most secure penal institution in the country, Number 10 Downing Street. Please remember your responsibility for these events when you begin to criticise what I do in office.'

They laugh. Stella changes tone.

'The last few days have shown the value of a free, unfettered press. This country needs you to carry on making my life as difficult as possible by honest reporting. This is a democracy and that is your crucial task.'

She climbs into the car and waves at well-wishers. The car and its outriders sweep her away.

Only later will those same journalists begin to sniff the real story of the last two hours: how Mindsett refused to resign, how he threatened to sue The Guardian for printing fake evidence of a meeting which never happened, how any fool could see that the photos had been photoshopped, how Mindsett insulted the Chairman, how he claimed that dirty tricks were the bread and butter of a politician's life and insisted on the vote standing. In eighteen months' time the BBC will produce a docudrama about the events that finally forced Mindsett to resign, the dramatic climax of which will be when his wife and his mistress arrive simultaneously, each of them summoned by the Chief Whip.

* * *

Ivor is in the bar. Five shot glasses are lined up beside him. Two are already empty. 'Hello Danny,' Ivor says.

'So I'm no longer Maybe Danny. Did you decide I was telling the truth about my real name?'

Ivor pushes over a glass. A little of it spills. 'Good vodka that.'

Danny sits and sips. 'I looked you up,' Ivor says.

'Where?'

'Missing Persons site. I found you there.' He flicks his mobile phone, grunts, and then shows Danny a photo of himself.

'Danny Goulden. Your father owned shops. Quite a lot of them. Where've you been?'

Danny tells his story. How the photos disappeared and came back to his phone.

'Then I blame you, Real Danny.'

Ivor takes the papers and photographs out of his pocket and tears them to shreds, dropping them on the floor. 'Is useless. I hear mistress has now met wife, end of kompromat. Ivor is finished in this crazy country ...' He pauses. 'Whereas you ... you are made for life.'

'Come up to Scotland with me, Ivor. We could finish

my walk.'

'I hate open countryside. I love forests. I love cities. I breathe wi-fi speeds and bad air. My visa has run out. If they catch me now, they send me home.'

'Is there anything I can do about that?'

Ivor shrugs. 'It is a simple matter of what life really is. You won. I lost. I like your idioms. If you can't beat them ... I have skills, they either shoot me or use me. Almost certainly use me. We'll see.'

He knocks back two more vodkas.

'Look, I show you something else on the same site, also posted by your sister.'

He punches, flicks, scrolls, and Danny peers at another photograph on Ivor's phone. This one is black and white. A single face of a teenage boy stands clear from the photo. The others have been pixilated.

'Why your family go for so much disappearance?'

'My family?'

'Same phone number, same name. You have sister called Leah?'

'Yes.'

'Then he is your half-brother.'

'He can't be. My half-brother is dead. I saw him fall into a sinkhole.

Danny studies the screen, looks again at the photo. 'My half-brother was called Patrick. That isn't him.'

'Then why your sister post this? Some crazy family yours.'

'She was there. Leah was there when he died. She knows that isn't Patrick.' He hands back the phone. Something about the image on the website disturbs him but he can't say why.

'Are you going back to Russia?'

Ivor shrugs. The vodka shots are empty. Danny orders more.

'Are you going home, Real Danny?' Ivor asks.

'Not yet.'

'Nor me. They have to catch me first.'

* * *

Stella announces her Cabinet. Mindsett has his old job back. He recognises this as an act of political revenge. The Underling seems to have lost all sense of deference. 'There are two issues that demand your urgent attention,' the Underling announces. 'The rail strike and the construction company that went bust just after you had awarded it that enormous contract. Now here's what you are going to do.'

* * *

Two evenings later a Franciscan friar walks past the Cenotaph and arrives at the entrance to Downing Street. Stella offered to send a car but Howard wouldn't hear of it. He approaches the gates anxiously; everything about London is so different from his normal life. He doesn't have to tell them who he is, his friar's habit does that for him. A pass is handed over. He's quickly ushered through the gates and the security checks. He walks along the street slowly with wide eyes as if he can't believe he's here. He glances round. There are no cameras, no press. How has she managed that? As he reaches Number 10 the door opens and Stella herself is waiting to greet him.

He looks at her for a long time. He has watched her age through thirty years of photographs and news interviews. He knows what she looks like now, how she talks, that she is almost certainly no longer the woman he fell in love with. Time changes people, and not just in appearance. He stares at her and, ignoring God for a moment, he asks his heart what it is feeling now.

Stella looks back at Howard. She has only two pictures to call on: the image of the young man from thirty years ago and the much older friar who was interviewed just after the ballot opened. He has lived his life discreetly in Northumberland, on a cliff top with the incessant cry of sea gulls. She has lived hers in the public view on the political stages of the world. Both are nervous.

The flunky is uncurious. He and the door he commands have seen so much. He simply waits for the friar to step inside, then he can close the door and sit back down at his desk. Do friars have mobile phones? If so, it must be handed in. He bows his head and waits as the hostess and her guest stand quite still, and all that could be spoken between them is, for the moment, left unsaid.

In the gap between the two protagonists, between the mat and the floor tiles, between the door and the stairs, time reveals itself and has a presence. The thirty years since they last met are there with them, like a thick polythene sheet that needs to be pulled aside. And time asks each of them the same question, the question it always asks: *Back then, when you were both young, did you make the right choice?*

They hold each other's gaze for a long time. Stella speaks first. 'Father Brian, please come in. Howard, is it alright if I hug you?'

Chris Bridge,
December 2016 to September 2019 York and
Wintringham

If you enjoyed this novel, I'd like to send you a free, unpublished short story as a thank you for buying it. All you need to do is send your email address to candsbridge@btinternet.com I will also keep you up to date with future publications.

You can find me on twitter https://twitter.com/ChrisBridge313 and I occasionally blog about writing https://chrisbridge.blog

So far, I have published three novels and a book of poems.

2014 November *Back Behind Enemy Lines*

http://amzn.to/1zaUqyP

When Anna returns to England in 1944 after serving in Normandy she is sure her spying days are over. But old age feels like being back behind enemy lines. If she is to keep her independence she must bring her intelligence skills back into play, find the gun she never handed in and face up to the ghosts that have haunted her ever since. Amazon ebook or paperback.

2017 May *Walking Through*

A book of poems published by Graft Poetry. Available from the author, please enquire via email.

2018 March ***Girl Without a Voice***

http://amzn.to/2FR2ApT

Childhood trauma robs Leah of the power of speech and forces her to be a watcher on the margins of society. But when her mother goes in search of the child she gave up for adoption, Leah is tempted out of the shadows. At first Patrick is everything she could hope for in a half-brother. Then Leah makes a shocking discovery that leaves her with a moral dilemma and the overwhelming need to do what has always been impossible for her: to take action. Amazon ebook or paperback.

2020 March ***Other Selves***

Acknowledgements

Jamie McGarry for cover design. Paul Bridge for reading an early draft and giving it the thumbs up. Mathew Harrison for softening my mug shot so that I look younger. Everyone who has ever written me a review and made the comments about my novels that keep me going. Above all my wife, Sheila, who proofreads everything twice and is prepared to tell me when my writing isn't good enough.

First published in 2020 by White Frog

Jacket design by Jamie McGarry of Valley Press

Cover photographs by MJ Klaver and Robert Sharp

Printed in Great Britain
by Amazon